“MAKE LOVE TO ME.”

Ja[illegible] g?

“L[illegible] e.”

He crossed the room and stood beside her languid body, his heart beating a mad rhythm of desire. He steadied himself by focusing on her elaborate tattoos. A rose vine curved around her thigh. A band of black twists wound around her ankle. Amy watched him study her markings, then rolled over to reveal an elaborate dragon in the small of her back.

He bit his lower lip and sank to his knees. Her naked skin peeked out from the bold black and green lines as if sheltering behind the beast. His blood crashed through his body so violently, he could hear the torrent. He traced the scrolled dragon with his finger and she tossed him a smile, daring him.

He traced it with his tongue, enjoying her murmurs of delight, holding her hips down firmly, so she couldn’t squirm. The scent of clove and cinnamon swirled around her. He rolled her over and she complied willingly.

“How’d you know I’d come?” His voice was thick with longing.

“I’m a Gypsy, James. We’re psychics. We know everything.”

Please turn this page for rave reviews for Diana Holquist.

PRAISE FOR DIANA HOLQUIST

SEXIEST MAN ALIVE

"A humorous tale with lovable characters enhanced by the paranormal."
—***Midwest Book Review***

"4 Stars! This sequel to *Make Me a Match* is a quite entertaining and enjoyable read. The bit of paranormal . . . adds an intriguing twist to this romantic tale."
—***Romantic Times BOOKreviews Magazine***

"A funny, sweet, and tender contemporary romance."
—**DearAuthor.com**

"A quirky, humorous, yet thoughtful read."
—**RomanceReaderatHeart.com**

"Diana Holquist has another hit on her hands! *Sexiest Man Alive* is tender, amusing, and purely fantastic!"
—**ARomanceReview.com**

more . . .

Also by Diana Holquist

Make Me a Match
Sexiest Man Alive

Hungry for More

Diana Holquist

FOREVER

NEW YORK   BOSTON

Cover photograph by Herman Estevez
Handlettering by Ron Zinn

Forever
Hachette Book Group USA
237 Park Avenue
New York, NY 10017
Visit our Web site at www.HachetteBookGroupUSA.com

Forever is an imprint of Grand Central Publishing. The Forever name and logo is a trademark of Hachette Book Group USA, Inc.

Printed in the United States of America

First Printing: September 2008

10 9 8 7 6 5 4 3 2 1

Natasha, this one's for you.

Acknowledgments

Too many cooks may spoil the broth, but they definitely help the book.

To my restaurant advisors, Shannon Hildenbrand and Hermie Kranzdorf, thank you. Everything right about restaurants and food in this book is thanks to you guys. Everything wrong is on me. To Baily Cypress, who makes the world's best gnocchi. And to all the great restaurants of Philly and New York, whose dishes inspired me.

Thanks to my writing buddies Ellen Hartman, Leslie Daniels, and Carolyn Pouncy. I owe you all lots of toner fluid, my sanity, and a really nice meal at a great French restaurant.

This book could never have happened without everyone at Grand Central Publishing, especially my editor, Michele Bidelspach, who has impeccable taste, every time.

And, finally, thank you to my amazing readers. The support I've gotten from you makes it all worthwhile.

*Cooking, like sex,
is best done right or not at all.*

—James LaChance, Executive Chef and Owner,
Les Fleurs Restaurant, Philadelphia, Pennsylvania

Hungry for More

Prologue

The studio lights were hot and blinding. A bead of sweat slid down Amy's spine and dropped onto the mike pack duct-taped to the small of her back. *Focus on Oprah. Oprah is kindness. Oprah is all-knowing.*

Oprah is next to me.

"Three, two, one, go!" The stage manager pointed his finger like a gun, and the ON AIR signs lit up green and glowing around the studio. A breath of silence before the live audience exploded into applause.

"Welcome back." Oprah smiled warmly as the applause died down. "We're here today with Amy Burns, the Gypsy who has the power to tell a person the name of their One True Love." A pause as the cameras switched to close-up. "Ms. Burns, tell us it's true!" Oprah leaned forward.

Amy nodded as she soaked in Oprah's warmth. Talking to this woman was like chatting with your One True

Love. Not that Amy would know; she never heard the name of her *own* One True Love. Her sisters called this information gap the central tragedy of Amy's life. Amy called it irrelevant. Having her own True Love wouldn't have landed her on *Oprah,* that's for sure. You had to get your priorities straight. "I hear the voice of an all-knowing spirit," Amy told Oprah. "When willing, she can speak the name of a person's One True Love."

The audience murmured in appreciation. Some clapped. Some slunk back in their seats, not meeting the eyes of their companions.

"As we all know, Ms. Burns predicted the whirlwind love affair between Josh Toby, *People* magazine's sexiest man alive, and his new wife, who happens to be Amy's sister, Jasmine Toby."

Now, that was something the Oprahites could rally around. But were they applauding for superstar Josh Toby or for the power of True Love? Despite the lights roasting her, Amy felt the focus shift away from her as acutely as if the whole stage had gone dark.

"Ms. Burns also predicted the storybook love affair between Cleo Chan of the HBO series *Agent X* and her new fiancé, *right here on this stage.*"

The crowd went mad for the affair between the superstar and her new beau that had been smeared all over the tabloids for weeks. Amy sometimes rated a sidebar box on the third page. Sometimes, a grainy photo was attached. She sucked in her stomach farther. *I've got more psychic power in my big toe than Cleo Chan has in her entire bloodline.*

Oprah turned back to Amy, if possible more radiant and focused than before. If there was one person in the world who had a slice of True Love for every creature on earth, it was Oprah. Maybe that was *her* tragedy. "So," Oprah begged, "give us details. Does your spirit-voice have a name?"

Amy melted under Oprah's gaze. Or was it the hot-as-hell studio lights? "I call her Maddie, but I made the name up. She never says her name. She only speaks the names of others."

"And she's been with you your entire life?"

"On and off." A tremor of fear raced up Amy's spine, but she shook it off. These last few years, Maddie had been mostly off. *But she'll show today. She just has to.* She always showed when Amy needed her most.

Oprah threw back her head, held out her hands, and flashed her magnificent incisors. "So touch me, baby! Tell me the name of my One True Love!" The audience sat forward as one. "Just don't tell Steddy, okay?" She winked.

This woman was amazing. She had no fear. Her One True Love could be anyone—man, woman, black, white, drug addict, CEO . . .

Amy took Oprah's cool, smooth hands in her hot, wet ones. *Please, Mads. For Oprah. For America. For me.*

Silence. Amy closed her eyes. *One last time. I'll do anything.*

She felt a rustling, a disturbance in the energy patterns. *Yes. Thank you. I knew you'd come.* The warmth that signaled Maddie's presence rose in her. This was going to be the biggest moment on TV *ever.* Oprah's One True Love!

"She's smiling, ladies and gentlemen. Does that mean you're hearing the voice?" Oprah asked. The studio was silent with breathless anticipation. Dust particles hit the hot lights and exploded, microscopic portents of the fireworks that would explode when America knew Oprah's One True Love.

Amy held still, trying to empty herself so Maddie could enter her soul. *Talk to me, baby. Talk to Oprah.*

The heat intensified within her. First a pinprick, then the warmth of the spirit spread through her like an opening flower. *Oh, Mads. Thank you for coming! I love you. I really do. Sorry. I'll shut up. Go ahead. Give me the big lady's One True Love.*

The voice in Amy's head spoke in a soft but distinct whisper: "Good-bye."

Then there was nothing.

First Course

When working with a roux, liquids must be added very slowly
or the mixture will be lumpy and not properly thickened.
Like love, too fast or too cool, and all is ruined.
—JAMES LACHANCE, PROLOGUE, *The Meal of a Lifetime*

Chapter 1

Three months later

James stirred the melting butter counterclockwise, adding flour with a flick of his fingers, a snow flurry melting on the buttery sea. He watched the flour dissolve in the golden liquid, then handed the wooden spoon to Troy. He checked his watch. Three o'clock. Two hours to opening, three hours to rush, four hours to chaos. "Stir. No. The other direction. Counterclockwise."

"Why's it matter what direction I stir?" Troy asked. His question was laced with doubt and defiance.

James glanced at the boy. He was just a kid. Barely fifteen. James knew he shouldn't be hard on him, but this was a *roux*, the classic combination of butter and flour that formed the base of French cooking—the base of *life*. You couldn't go soft on essentials like this. "You wanna be a great chef, you honor the roux. Do *not* question the roux. I'm gonna check out front for the wine delivery."

Troy changed the direction of the spoon with a scowl that made James proud. A great student asked, but a great teacher never answered, because anyone worth his or her balls in the kitchen didn't give a shit what anyone else said. If Troy was going to be a great chef one day, he'd stir clockwise just to see what happened.

Besides, if James told the kid he stirred counterclockwise for luck, he'd lose face. And you never lost face in your own kitchen. Worse than death.

James passed through his restaurant's gleaming chrome kitchen, grunting in admiration for Raul's perfectly seasoned stock, for John-John's exquisite mise en place, for Craig's perfectly minced garlic. Each of his cooks told him to fuck off, a chorus in his wake. He loved these guys.

He grabbed a wooden spoon and stuck it into Pablo's soup of the day. "More salt," he muttered. Pablo gave him the finger but added the salt. James passed the Guatemalan boys husking corn on overturned milk crates. The corn was shit. He could tell at a glance, feel it in the tips of his fingers as surely as if he'd grown and harvested and detasseled each ear himself. "Throw that garbage to the rats," he commanded. "Then go across the street to Alma and *beg. Roges! Ahora!*"

Damn. Lousy corn *plus* his floor manager, Elliot, just told him that his best server, Roni, had gone AWOL. The night was shaping up to be a nuclear meltdown. A thrill of excitement raced through him. All good chefs were adrenaline freaks; it was in the job description. A meltdown was a test of manhood, of ability. It was all in a night's work.

James pushed through the swinging doors into the deserted, darkened dining room, thinking about the menu for the night. He was short a first-course special. A delivery of lust-inducing shiitakes had arrived that morning, but they'd keep. Better to use the broccoli rabe that was dying in the walk-in fridge downstairs.

His restaurant, Les Fleurs, was the only two-star French restaurant in Philly (besides Le Bec Fin, the bastards), as rated by *Le Guide des Restaurants*. That is to say, as rated by God. Two stars meant a six-month wait for reservations and a constant panic headache at the base of James's skull at the thought of losing even a fraction of one of his precious celestial bodies. Les Fleurs was going to be the death of him. And what a way to go. *Bury me in foie gras, white truffles, and red wine.* He loved the place like a woman.

No, more than a woman. He hadn't slept more than four hours a night since he'd opened his doors to rave reviews two years ago. No woman had ever been able to keep him up that long.

The windowless dining room was dark except for a single stream of snow-reflected daylight coming through the front door's glass panes, a reminder that, to the normal world, dinner was still a long-off event. He flicked on the bar lights, grabbed the seltzer siphon, and shot a stream of ice-cold liquid into his mouth.

"Can't a person get a bite to eat in this joint?"

He peered into the dimness. A woman stood in the darkness. He could just discern her outline in the shadows. *How had she gotten in here?* James reached behind the bar and flicked on the overhead work lights, throwing the room into garish display.

Hello.

Her face was a valentine heart, her eyes as black and slanted as a doe's, her lips a perfect bow. Sparkling snow-flakes dotted her tangled hair, blinking in and out like tiny SOS warning beacons. A surge of lust rose within him.

"I'm here for Roni." Her voice was sandpaper rough.

Right. She must be the temp server to replace Roni. James had overheard Elliot sweet-talking into his cell, trying to steal a server from La Fondue across town to replace Roni tonight. It was standard restaurant practice to pilfer help. No hard feelings. Three weeks ago, the scum at La Fondue had picked Louis, James's garde-manger, right out from under him in the middle of a Saturday-night rush. All was fair in love, war, and high-priced food.

James watched the woman closely. "Elliot told you the drill? We do a four-table split, under the table for tonight, on the books if this turns into a regular gig, and whatever bonus Elliot promised for jumping ship." He wasn't usually involved in front-of-house affairs, but he wanted to keep talking to this woman. Wanted to keep looking at her. In the sedate perfection of the tasteful white-on-beige dining room, she looked like a rosebush in the desert. A mirage.

She leveled her black eyes at him, watching him like a cat. Then, all at once, she swept her knee-length shearling coat behind her, a swish of her tail, and came straight toward him, smoky, dark, full-bodied, and confident. A silver-dollar-sized gold pendant swung between her breasts with pleasing effect. This woman was cayenne in a blush sauce. Hot and smooth.

She dumped her gloves and coat into his arms as she

glided past him to the deserted bar. The heat of her body rose off her discarded clothes.

"Do I look like the coat-check girl?" he asked, intrigued by her boldness. He raised her coat and inhaled her scent. Cinnamon and clove.

She ducked under the bar, looked him up and down, then tossed him a wicked smile. "You look like the coat-check girl's fantasy lay, Cheffie."

Her sexy, fuck-me smile almost knocked him off his feet. He put her coat onto the bar and slid onto a stool, watching her inspect his stock. He had dated the coat-check girl once. Maria. He had made a soup inspired by her, a tomato bisque. Spicy, with an acid undertone. But Maria was nothing next to this woman. A soup.

The woman continued to ransack his bar—an act no floor staff would ever dare. For a server from the Fondy, she sure didn't seem to know much about restaurants.

But he wasn't sure he cared. She wore a black fitted corset-type thing that cinched her waist, swelling to a stop just below her remarkable breasts. A white, off-the-shoulder peasant shirt spilled out from under the corset, covering her in a thin layer of fabric that did little to hide her black lace bra. Layers of long cotton skirts, some hanging low, some bunched at the hems, cascaded out from below the corset. She could have just exited stage right after the first scene of *Carmen*. She was shabby but gorgeous.

Wait, she was *really* shabby. Threads were loose on her shirt, hems undone on her skirts. Dangerously sexy, but no way was she from La Fondue. That was a classy operation, despite its asinine name. Where had Elliot found this woman?

She pulled out two glasses, then plucked the fifty-bucks-a-pour single malt off the shelf. "Drink?"

He shook off her offer. The pendant around her neck fell forward as she poured. It was a gold cross inside a red circle, surrounded by some sort of engraved writing. It seemed to glow, but that was most likely his overheated imagination. It had been a while since he'd been near a woman this sensuous.

Had he ever?

The woman poured two shots despite his refusal. "So where's Roni?"

"Why do you care?"

She threw back her shot. Considered a moment. Threw back his, too. Then repoured. "She's not here?" Her voice was flat.

"Why would I be hiring a temp server if she's here?" He struggled to follow the odd turn the conversation had just taken.

A pause. Something dark clouded her eyes. She licked her lips. "Oh. Yeah. Right. I get it now. That's what you were yakking about—books and tables. Right. I'm the temp server. To replace Roni." She dared him with her obvious lie.

A surge of energy spread through him. Okay, more than energy. Lust. This woman had nothing to lose, and she knew it. *Down, boy.* This was business. They needed a server tonight, and here was at least a warm body.

A hot body.

The sexiest woman he'd ever laid eyes on. Plus something else he couldn't put his finger on. The contrast between her bravado and her shabby clothes threw him. In the split second after the overhead lights had hit her, he *had* glimpsed something in her eyes that he recognized. But it was gone before he could place it. Or, more honestly, it was still there, but his interest had strayed elsewhere. He tried to keep his eyes off her chest. "Ever wait tables?"

She downed her drink. "For a few weeks. Mexican joint. Got fired for stealing from the register." She cocked her head and blinked her doe eyes, daring him.

"Did you?" He already knew the answer.

"Of course. Shit job." She licked her lips, the tip of her tongue a promise.

James checked his cell for a call from Elliot. If he hadn't looted a replacement server for Roni by now, he wasn't going to. James's other servers could handle an extra table each. But an extra set of hands—not to mention an extra set of what was so magnificently spilling over her black corset—would help with Dr. Trudeau, who came every Tuesday night for his one-night stand— consommé, bib salad, and roasted duck served wordlessly by Roni and only by Roni, the beautiful Gypsy with the big black eyes.

Wordless seemed unlikely with this woman, but at least Dr. Trudeau would have these cauldron-deep eyes to stare into as he slurped his broth.

I'll just have to keep an eye on her. The thought made his crotch jump. *An eye; only an eye.* "Do you have a name?" he asked.

She seemed to consider. "Amy," she said finally.

"Hi, Amy. I'm James." He wondered what her real name was. Well, if she stuck around, he'd find out eventually. Maybe.

Salade de Tres Fleurs
Lobster salad with ginger and tamarind reduction
—James LaChance, *The Meal of a Lifetime*

Chapter 2

The scotch scorched Amy's throat, but it didn't help ease her growing panic. For three months, she'd been searching for her missing spirit-voice, Maddie. Finally, after three well-placed, ever-increasing bribes to a corrupt high-level Gypsy elder in Yonkers, she had gotten word of a young Gypsy waitress in Philly who had mysteriously begun hearing a spirit-voice that spoke names and only names.

The voice just had to be Maddie. *Her* Maddie. *Her* voice. And she was getting Maddie back; that wasn't negotiable. The voice said only names in a woman's singsong; it appeared just last week out of nowhere; Roni, the waitress, was reportedly good and honest and pure—exactly the kind of Gypsy Maddie would want to inhabit after her obvious disappointment with Amy's more unconventional ways.

In other words, Roni was Amy's complete opposite.

Amy couldn't stand the woman already.

She still had no idea how she'd get Maddie back from this Roni. But the details would come to her; the cons always did.

It was the traveling that was killing her. She was getting too old for this nomadic life. Thirty-four sucked. The long trek to Philly began with a cross-country Greyhound ride from Chicago, her seatmate a two-hundred-fifty-pound man with a bad case of dandruff, and ended with a mile-long slog through the slush in her hole-laden boots.

And Roni was gone. She had missed the Rom by a day.

Amy was so tired and wet and cold, she wanted to cry.

No. She was no weeper. *Think. Make a plan.* She concentrated on the handsome chef. His ink-black, pinstraight hair was pulled back into a ponytail at the nape of his neck like a nineteenth-century nobleman. His angled cheekbones directed her eyes toward his carefully drawn mouth. In fact, every dark, angled plane of his face pointed toward that tempting, burgundy mouth—which was talking again. "You'll need different clothes. The floor staff wears uniforms. Black button-down shirt and black pants, but at this short notice—"

Bingo. A plan. "Front me fifty bucks and I'll match the look. Boring and uptight, right? No problem. I'll pay you back from tips." The idea of waiting tables in this stuffy joint made her whole body ache with fatigue. No way was that happening. She'd take this sexy chef's cash, get a lousy room, and sleep. Just sleep. Then, in the morning, she'd figure out how to find Roni.

The dark, handsome chef fished a roll of cash out of his pocket, and Amy watched him count twenties, her mouth watering at the sight of the bills. How her life had come to this, she didn't know. Finding Maddie had become a three-month obsession that was getting out of hand. But every day without Maddie, a hole deepened inside her that became harder and harder to fill. It was like Maddie had been a person—a friend, even—which was ridiculous. Amy watched the money—twenty dollars, forty, sixty.

He met her eyes, paused, then unrolled seven more twenties. He pushed the cash across the bar, holding her gaze as he did.

She broke his gaze to look at the cash. *I asked for fifty dollars and he gave me two hundred.* It was an act of trust that knocked her sideways to Tuesday for the simple reason that they both knew she didn't deserve it. She'd have to watch James; he was smart to tie her to him like that. It was harder to rip off a guy who made a point of trusting you.

Especially one who looked like a pirate on shore leave.

Never trust a Gypsy, Chef. She'd take the cash and split—

And then what, Einstein? She had no idea where this Roni lived or where she might have gone. All she knew was that she worked here and that she might have Maddie. Amy's toes were soaking wet and icy cold. She wished she could pull off her boots and warm her feet in her hands while she tried to think.

Amy shook off her doubt and fear. *I am Amy Burns! A powerful Gypsy who makes her way in the world on brains and guts—*

—and a spirit-voice that ditched me.

Okay. New plan. She'd take the cash, steal a new set of

clothes, work one night for the tips, learn what she could about Roni, *then* split.

She took the bills but hesitated. She hated owing people. She might be down on her luck, but she was never down on her pride. *Equals or nothing, Chef.* She reached behind her neck, unclasped her necklace, ducked under the bar, glided behind James, and draped the jewel around his neck. *I'll call your cash and raise you priceless jewels.* The clasp closed with an ominous snap. "Collateral until I pay you back," she said.

"Welcome to Les Fleurs," he said.

"Lays Florz," she said, anglicizing the French with exaggerated disregard. "Lays floors. Lays coat-check girls. Lays Roni?"

He didn't flinch at her brazen question or ask how she knew he'd slept with the coat-check girl; Amy had seen the flicker of memory in his eyes when she mentioned her. Gypsy Con 101: watch the eyes. She knew he'd slept with her and knew the woman had left him. *And,* more important, she knew he didn't know why.

"Not that my sex life is any of your business, but I don't sleep with the hired help," he said.

"Too bad," she said. She didn't believe him for a minute. She'd bet every dollar he gave her that his staff were the only people he knew. "So if you're not boffing Roni, why would she come back to this dump?" She tucked the bills into her bra.

His eyes followed the bills. "I'll take that as a compliment."

Amy felt a rush of excitement at their flirtation. *I may be a Gypsy with nothing, but I still have some power.* "Is she coming back?"

"She'll be back. I've got something of hers she can't live without."

"Hope it's not a dime-store necklace," she said.

His eyes hardened, and something seemed to shift deep inside him. "Four-thirty sharp for the staff meeting," he said. "Be there or never set foot through my doors again." He rose abruptly from his stool and made his way through the swinging doors into the kitchen, leaving her alone in the empty dining room, wondering what she had done to piss off that moody chef.

James was furious as he strode through his bustling kitchen. She might as well have punched him in the gut with that dime-store-necklace comment. Not because he believed her. The weight of the real-gold pendant resting against his chest gave her away. But her clumsy bluff said that she didn't trust him. Trust was everything in his restaurant. She was clearly an outsider who thought she was dealing with a fool. She was—

A taste-vision struck him: she was a lobster salad with wilted lettuce, candied ginger, and a wine and tamarind reduction.

He froze. *She had inspired a first course on first sight.* That had never happened before. Women inspired all his dishes. But for it to happen so fast, without even a kiss. A touch.

And he didn't even like her.

He stood in stunned silence. The dish was surprising, sexy, brash. *Just like her.*

Imagine if I kissed her, what I'd come up with.

Imagine if I made love to her . . .

James stirred from his fantasy to find Troy watching

him. Or rather, watching his chest. The kid's eyes were glued to the pendant, his spoon suspended over the steaming pot.

"Counterclockwise!" James commanded, proud of the boy but trying not to let it show. The last thing he needed was a cocky brat in his kitchen. The boy was too young to be in here, anyway.

But Troy didn't move; his eyes were fixed on the necklace.

James grabbed the spoon out of Troy's hand. "Have you ever *seen* a clock? Round thing? Ticks? Stir this way."

The boy shook his head. "I wouldn't wear that if I were you, Chef."

"Why not?" A chill rose up James's spine, but he kept stirring. What did that Gypsy want with Roni, anyway? And how had she known he had slept with Maria? "What is this thing? Gypsy voodoo?"

"Voodoo isn't Gypsy. It's Haitian, migrated over from Africa." Troy rolled his eyes as only a disgusted teenager could. "But that medallion, my man, is bad luck. The worst kind of shit-awful luck."

Yeah. Tell me something I don't know, James thought.

Because despite the steaming pots around him, all he could smell was cinnamon and clove.

What you put into cold storage will never be what you take out.
Often the change is for the better. A ripening. A master chef
will be aware of these changes at all times. Anticipate
them. And plan for them accordingly.
—JAMES LaCHANCE, *Meal of a Lifetime*

Chapter 3

An hour later, Amy stood in the center of the walk-in cooler, a refrigerator the size of a subway car, stacked floor to ceiling with color-coded plastic food containers of every size and shape. She had planned to change in the staff women's room, but it was jammed with crates of canned tomatoes. Anyway, this place was fine. Everyone was too busy in the upstairs kitchen to notice her. Not that she cared who saw her. Prudishness was hardly her thing.

She tugged off her shirt, wondering what James had that would make Roni return, besides his green-flecked caramel eyes and amazing puppy-huge hands. A flash of longing raced through her. *Sleeping with the boss sure would be a more fun way of getting info about Roni than waiting tables.* But she'd have to be careful; this guy wasn't her usual mark. He was smart.

"Didn't realize this was the dressing room at Loehmann's." James leaned against the open door to the enormous refrigerator, his white apron tied jauntily around his waist. It was surprisingly sexy, a man in an apron. Like a man in a kilt, only with promise of dinner afterward.

She studied him with the same lazy, slow once-over he was using to take her in. Now that she had a plan, she could focus on him better. His brown-green eyes radiated under black eyelashes a woman would kill for. He had the lean, well-formed muscles of a man who made his way in the world through precise, controlled physical labor. If she hadn't known he was a chef, she'd have guessed he was a quarterback: the wide shoulders, the narrow waist, and the intelligent, always-scanning eyes.

Amy refused to be cowed by his dark attraction. Or her lack of a shirt. She put her hands on her hips and faced him head-on. Well, more like breasts-on. He might be the boss of this restaurant, but she had some powers of her own, two of them, to be precise, and she intended to use them. Plus, she was wearing her best black-lace demi-cup. She knew what that could do to a man.

He didn't flinch or look away from her . . . eyes. *Strange man.* Without a word, he unclasped the pendant from around his neck and tossed it to her. "Here. I was told it's bad luck."

She caught it easily and draped it back around her neck. When she was satisfied that it was nestled perfectly between her breasts, she pulled James's cash out of her bra.

She came to him and tucked the bills into his apron. "Bad luck is better than no luck at all."

There, they were even. She felt at ease for the first time since they'd met.

He watched her wordlessly, his lips pursed. He didn't move to count the cash.

She went back to her new clothes and shrugged on her new black shirt, shoplifted along with a black skirt from the discount joint down the street. His eyes bored a hole into her as she buttoned. "Love to chat, but I've got a four-thirty staff meeting to get to. Whatever that is." She considered whether to finish changing here or to scurry to privacy. What the hell? It wasn't like she cared what he thought of her or her underwear. And if she could seduce him, she could find out more about Roni.

She turned her back to him, took a deep breath— *showtime*—and let her skirts drop to the floor. She stepped out of them gracefully, careful not to catch her black high-heeled ankle boot on a hem. She leaned down seductively and slowly, *slower, slower, milk it,* pulled on the black skirt. *Put that on your French baguette and spread it, Cheffie.*

She shoved the tags into the waistband so she could re-turn the skirt later (she was the queen of returning things without a receipt), then turned to face him, swinging her hips to test the skirt's movement. Not bad for a five-finger discount. It flowed to her ankles, just the way she liked it. She never could shake her Gypsy fashion genes.

James cocked his head and narrowed his eyes like a panther. "Nice pants."

Good start, kitty. She had dangled the string, but would he pounce? "So, don't just stand there," she said. "Tell me I look amazing."

"I didn't think you'd come back," he said. He folded his arms in front of him. He wore his simple cotton chef whites like a five-thousand-dollar Italian suit.

She considered her discarded clothes, glanced around, then stuffed them into an enormous empty stockpot on the floor. She replaced the lid, then sat on top of it and tossed her hair over her head, gathered it, then twisted it into a suitable, uptight-restaurant-worthy bun. It didn't escape her that he hadn't called her "amazing." Maybe apron-boy didn't like women. She glanced up at him and caught his cat-sharp eyes narrowing again. He was stalking for sure. He liked women fine.

Maybe he just doesn't like me.

The disturbing thought made her flinch. Losing Maddie was bad enough, but losing the power to seduce? Never.

James stared at her for a long moment, then strode into the walk-in cooler. *Oh, yeah.* Amy braced herself for him to crash against her. She closed her eyes and prepared for those burgundy lips.

She felt him brush past her. She opened her eyes and blinked. He was pulling a container off a high shelf. He opened the top with a flourish and spun around to face her. "You want to see amazing? Look at these."

Amy peered into the container.

Gray fish stared back at her with unblinking eyes.

He flashed them at her with the same jaunty spirit she had just flashed at him. *You show me yours; I'll show you mine.*

Only his was dead fish.

"Whatever turns you on," she said. His rejection stung her to the soles of her feet. Her skin was hot with shame. *I flashed you my red thong and you didn't jump me?* Moron. Jerk.

Foodie.

Maybe he had a girlfriend. Her thoughts flashed to

Roni. What did James have that she'd come back for? Did that woman have her spirit-voice *and* this dark chef?

He was staring at her again.

"What?" *Don't flash those green-rimmed eyes at me and then fondle fish.*

"Can you do me a favor?" He sounded sincere, like he was truly asking.

"I think you just dissed me for rotting fish flesh, so that would be a no." She tried to keep the hurt out of her voice but was aware that the hardness of her tone betrayed her.

"Can I kiss you?"

The chill of the cooler deepened, and she rubbed her bare arms. "You're a strange, strange man."

"I need the kind of kiss your great-aunt might give," he said.

"My great-aunt is a Gypsy hustler in Vegas. She kisses like a sailor."

He smiled, crooked and cocky, a sliver of pirate rowdiness showing from under his smooth polished surface. He rested the fish container against his hip. "This will be strictly work."

"I'll put it on my time sheet under 'face-munching with boss.'"

His eyes met hers straight on. "I get my inspiration for great food from beautiful women," he explained. "I need one more first-course special tonight. After you left earlier, I was struck with a vision, a lobster salad with wilted greens, candied ginger, and a wine and tamarind reduction. But I'm not sure about the herbs. Tarragon or just white pepper?"

"Kissing me will give you inspiration for grub?"

He winced at the word *grub,* as if she had smacked him

in the face. "For lobster salad with wilted greens, ginger, and a wine and tamarind reduction," he repeated.

Tam-a-what reduction? He wasn't making a lick of sense, but she wanted this dark, intense man to touch her. He was beautiful the way an animal was beautiful, sleek and mysterious. No way was she kissing him like an old-maid aunt.

I've been chasing Maddie for three months, and I was so close, and now I'm standing in a cooler with a hot, handsome chef who wants to kiss me for a sauce recipe like he's my nephew. No way, bad boy. My life sucks, but not that bad.

She crossed the cooler to him. Up close, she had expected some imperfection. But he only seemed to get smoother and taller and darker as she neared him. She rose to her full height and took a deep breath. Her forehead came to his lips. *Next time, I'm wearing my four-inch heels.* She clasped her hands behind her back, closed her eyes, and chastely lifted her face to his. *Get ready to meet Mrs. Robinson, Nephew James.*

The air stirred as he lowered his lips to hers. Lightly. Lips pressed against hers. Not a kiss so much as a touching. A connection.

She couldn't move.

She had planned to devour him. But his tenderness was so surprising, it turned her to stone. He smelled like a million good things to eat—roasted meat, olive oil, mustard seed, and man.

His lips warmed against hers, searching, softening, brushing as if he was reading Braille. Other than his lips, no part of him touched her, as if nothing outside of their lips existed.

After a long moment, he pulled away, separating so carefully she had the sense that he had left something fragile behind in her care.

She opened her eyes. His remained closed. He stood like that, breathing.

She could hear the air moving around her, feel it pass over her supercharged lips. His eyes were still closed, his long eyelashes casting jagged shadows onto his etched cheekbones. A hint of stubble added to his dark, earthy appeal.

"No herbs," he said. "Just the ginger, wine, and tamarind."

He opened his eyes, looked at her with such intensity she felt he had read her soul, then nodded curtly, the moment gone. He took his fish and an enormous sack of onions, and left.

Amy plopped onto the stockpot.

No herbs, just the ginger, wine, and tamarind.

Inexplicably, that was the nicest thing anyone had said to her in ages.

*How a person approaches food says everything about them.
Is he a nibbler? A wolfer? A watcher, who doesn't
partake of the feast at all?*
—JAMES LACHANCE, *Meal of a Lifetime*

Chapter 4

Troy sat at a corner booth watching James brief the servers, plus the new temp chick. He couldn't wait until he was old enough to be a server—which could happen *years* before he was allowed into a kitchen. Servers got to sleep late, *and* they raked in the major cash.

He looked at James. Now, chefs, they rocked. Especially owner-chefs. Arrogant pricks, sure. That much Troy had learned while watching his mom serve for most of her life. (He didn't watch the other part—when she danced. That was too, well, whatever. He didn't like it.) But who wouldn't want to be an arrogant prick?

James said he'd consider Troy for a server job when he was eighteen and not a day sooner. Three years! Consider! Hardass. Troy knew enough about the business to work the job already. But then, with a few more hundred times like earlier this afternoon, when James had let him into his kitchen to lend a hand, maybe he could skip the wait gig and go straight to line cook. His skin tingled at the bliss of it.

Until then, busing wasn't bad. Had its perks. Like easy swiping from handbags dangling off the backs of chairs. His mom had caught him once, but he split the twenty-three bucks with her and it was cool. He never got caught again. *Just take what you need.* That was his motto. These rich stiffs never missed a few bucks. He didn't spend it on junk. He had a secret bank account that paid interest. *The Stuffed Shirts Scholarship Fund* he called it. Someday, he was going to be famous and rich and arrogant. *And good.*

Like James.

The five servers sat around the big table in the back, listening while James ran through the specials for the night. He had prepared a sample of each special so they could remember it and answer questions. *Oh, yes, the sauce au snobbo is piquant with just a hint of bullshit.*

Dan took a bite from the fish and passed the plate to Stu, who asked about the sorrel pesto before passing it down the line. When the dish reached the new lady, *she ate the whole thing*, wolfing it down like she hadn't eaten in weeks.

The other servers and James stared at her like she was downing a bowl of slugs. She shrugged and smiled and said, "What? There are starving Gypsies in Romania, you know."

Troy sat up straighter at the word *Gypsy.* Was she? Was she the one who had given James the pendant? Gypsy or not, Troy liked the way the woman shrugged. It said, "Screw you" and "I'd love to screw you" all in the same motion. He wished his mom were at that table. He wished he knew where she was. Of course, then she would have made him go to school today, and he wouldn't have gotten to watch James make his roux. *Counterclockwise my ass*.

He forced down the lump that was rising in his throat. Troy didn't care. It'd been one night. His mom would be back. She always came back. A week was the longest she'd ever been gone. She knew he could take care of himself.

But she'd been acting so funky before she split. The whispers on the phone, that strange old Gypsy, Madame Prizzo, coming and going. Mumbling about "names" and "never-ending names." Something was up, and it was weird, and his mom wasn't telling him shit.

Concentrate on the present. Prep chefs chopping garlic in the kitchen. Veal stock set to simmer. Brown crushed velvet chairs and little white candles that would glow yellow when he lit them at four fifty-nine. Les Fleurs was white-tablecloth stuffy up the ass, sure, but it was home.

Well, not exactly home, but—yeah, it was home. Who was he kidding? It was where he ate and did his homework. And where he got to watch James cook.

He locked his attention onto his two favorite servers, Stu and Dan. Stu was fifty-four and hairless except for his gray goatee. The man's life was consumed by his bowling league and his boring family, and you knew it—or at least something like it—just by looking at him. Dan was twenty-nine and a drummer in a band called "Darkness." You knew that, too, in a glance.

But when those two dudes, *Stuart and Daniel*, were on the job, they became blank slates. Invisible waitrons, barely noticed, forgiving and docile and in love with whomever they served as if they served them alone, personally, every night, lords and ladies, masters all.

They were no dummies—none of the servers were. There was major cash to be made if you oozed servitude just right. But that new temp server. All hair and tits and skirts. She'd play her game different. Sex and food. Food and sex. No difference except that paying for sex was way cheaper than the food in this joint. Not that Troy had ever paid for sex. But he'd had it. Once. Andrea Pruis from third-period bio.

He was ready if the opportunity ever presented itself again.

A mixture of terror and anticipation washed through him. *Please, God, one more time before I turn sixteen. This time, I'll open my eyes.*

Meanwhile, he listened carefully to the kitchen warriors who came and went. Troy knew what was what in this town and this biz, *and* he kept his grades up. He was going to go to culinary school the day he graduated and make the big bucks and have a family where people didn't disappear for days on end.

A wave of sadness passed over him. For a split second, when he had come into the dining room, Troy thought the new server was his mom, proof he was losing it. He sank deeper into his corner chair. It was an honest mistake; she sure did look Gypsy. Hey, maybe she was Rom and his mom had sent her with a message for him.

Troy sat up straighter. *Maybe. It was possible.* His mom knew how he worried when she split.

He shook away the crazy thought. With all those skirts and bangles on sale at The Gap, every other chick looked Rom. You couldn't be sure. Better to lay low.

James and the maybe-Gypsy kept locking eyes and staring each other down as James blah-blahed on. It

wasn't like James to go on and on like this. Usually, Elliot, the floor manager, took over so James could get back
to the kitchen. Was it the new server that kept him blab-
bing? James and that new waitress side by side looked
like one of those evening news clips after a tornado: one
house pristine and perfect, every blade of grass in place;
the other with no roof, timber strewn everywhere, all
hanging out.

Shit. Was James hot for the temp chick already? Troy
loved his mother to death, but he couldn't get how she
never managed to catch James's eye. If she had, then they
could get married, and then James would be his . . .

"Roni had tables five, six, nine, ten, and twelve,"
James said. "Stu, you take five. Dan, you take nine. Amy,
can you handle the rest in that section? We're full straight
through two seatings. One fifty on the books."

Troy startled out of his daydream at the mention of his
mother's name.

The woman saluted. "Got it, Jimmy."

"James."

"No prob." She paused and leaned forward. The pendant James had been wearing earlier fell out of her shirt,
dangling from her neck. "Jimmy."

She was Gypsy. And not just any Rom but a Kalderash
who wore the cross of The Triumph. Did his mother send
her to look after him? Was this stranger waiting for him
to come in at five like he usually did when he bothered to
show at school and meanwhile she figured she'd make a
few bucks?

Well, Troy would show himself to his mom's messenger when he was good and ready. After all, maybe he
didn't want a message from his mother. At least, not a

message delivered by a stranger, Gypsy or no. No big deal where his mother was. She'd be back. Always was. He'd rather wait and hear the excuses from her own mouth. Not from some stand-in, no matter how scared he had been last night in their empty apartment, alone, praying for his mom to come home.

Great cooking makes us remember great times.
—JAMES LaCHANCE, *The Meal of a Lifetime*

Chapter 5

*I*s it worse to have psychic power and lose it or to never have power at all?" Oprah asked, leaning forward slightly, her voice breathy and expectant.

Amy smiled sweetly at the napkins she was folding. Ever since her humiliation on national TV, she had a continuous, imaginary feed of Oprah in her head, even when she was in some uptight restaurant in Philadelphia facing a pile of cloth napkins rising before her like Everest.

She grabbed a napkin and folded. *"It's much worse to lose it,"* Amy said to her imaginary Oprah. She was pretty sure everyone had an inner Oprah they talked to in their head. How else could you sort out your life? Especially now, when the one presence Amy usually counted on, Maddie, was gone. *"Because then you realize how lame the world is on the surface."* Amy stiffened at the sadness the truth of her words sparked inside her.

"But kissing James wasn't lame. Maybe Maddie chose

Roni as her new medium in order to lure me to this man. Maybe James is my One True Love. If I believe in soul mates, I must believe in destiny and fate. Nothing is just chance."

Amy turned her best side to the pretend left camera as she imagined it zooming in for its close-up. The idea that James was her soul mate had occurred to her the minute she laid eyes on him.

But, then, she was afraid everyone she met was her soul mate. The Gypsy lore that swirled around Maddie, handed down generation to generation, was that once you fell for your soul mate, your spirit-voice left you. Forever. Supposedly it had happened to Natasha Cooper, the Gypsy who had Maddie before Amy, in 1978 when she met Cyrus Kern and went on to have his six children. And to Magda Orpheleous twenty years before that, even though she set sail to America to avoid finding her One True Love and losing her power. But her One True Love, Seymour Smith, had signed onto the ship as cabin boy, and, well, the rest was history.

Once those women—both powerful and respected psychic seers—spoke the fateful words "I love you" to their soul mates, *poof,* Maddie split to another Gypsy.

For years, this wasn't a problem for Amy. After all, she just had to touch a person. If she heard another person's name, Amy knew that she hadn't stumbled onto her own soul mate, and she could relax. If she heard nothing, as Maddie would never tell Amy her own True Love's name, she was in trouble. Not that that ever happened in the beginning.

But then, over the years, Maddie had become less reliable. Sometimes Amy could get a name, sometimes not.

She had to be more careful. Whenever she felt a deeper pull for someone, any affinity at all, she split. If she liked their purple Converse sneakers, their dirty jokes, the way they played bass guitar—she was gone. No way was she going to be tricked into falling in love and losing Maddie like Natasha or Magda. Losing her power.

Not that it had mattered. Maddie ended up leaving her, anyway. Had Amy wasted the best years of her life, when she could have been with all those funny, sneaker-clad guitarists?

Amy shook her thoughts away. Gypsy legend was probably bullshit, anyway. Who knew if Natasha Cooper really existed? Magda Orpheleous might have been a bed-time story, made up by Amy's father to keep her from having a boyfriend.

Still, Amy was superstitious. You couldn't take chances with these sorts of things. In her experience, there was always at least some truth in every fairy tale.

Oprah was waiting for a reply. What had they been talking about? Right, James maybe being her One True Love and Maddie leading her here on purpose. Nothing doing. No spirit could con a con-woman as practiced as Amy. *"I'm here for one reason and one reason only: to get Maddie back."*

"How are you going to do that?" Oprah was breath-less for the inside scoop.

Amy felt a twinge of pride at being such a stimulat-ing guest—even if it was all in her head. Still, she knew she was born for the camera, for fame, for success, for Maddie. "I'm going to wait patiently by Roni's side. I'll be her teacher in the ways of the voice. Her best friend. Then, when she realizes what a curse Maddie is, she'll try to banish her. And I'll be here waiting to help. Maddie will see that Roni hates her guts and that I have always been the perfect Gypsy for her." Was that a plan or a wish? Amy felt the weakness of her situation and cursed it.

"But why not just move on?"

Amy shook her head in confusion. *"Move on? To what?"*

Oprah's eyes melted with warmth. She said gently, as if talking to a child, "To whatever you could be without Maddie."

This was so not in the preinterview script. "I'm nothing without Maddie. Look at me. Maddie is my calling. This is bullshit." She gestured to the pile of napkins.

Oprah shook her head sadly. "Yeah, those napkins suck."

The word *suck* coming out of Oprah's mouth startled Amy back to reality. Oprah hadn't said *suck*. A teenager stood before Amy, dark and sullen.

"Sorry, but it's true. Worst napkin side-work I've ever seen. And I've seen my share," the dark boy said, nodding at her uneven napkin sculptures. He carried a case of Stoli on his hip, and the dissonance made him seem even younger than he probably was. Pink, plump lips like his came only on a kid.

"Troy, come on, man. Stop yapping with the ladies. Get those to James before customers come," the bartender called from across the restaurant. As he spoke, the night's first customers pushed through the door, loosening their ties and settling gratefully on the plush barstools.

"Later," the boy said. He moved across the room under

the heavy load, looking back at her with his enormous black eyes as if he had something more to say.

Just what she needed, a teenage napkin critic.

An hour later, Amy stood just inside the kitchen doors, watching for her chance while the cooks did their crazy dance. She was leaving. She'd had it. The consommé she had spilled in Dr. Trudeau's lap was the last straw. She felt her face heat with shame. She wasn't cut out to serve. She had at least forty bucks in tips. She could get a cheapo room for the night. She was so out of here.

But she couldn't go out the front, past Elliot. He was like an eagle at the door. Plus, Dan and Stu had been so good to her all night, she didn't want them to see her slink away in shame.

The kitchen, in marked contrast to the floor, was a madhouse filled with psycho, shouting lunatics. She could slip out the kitchen door to the back alley without anyone noticing. Her heart pounded as she worked her way to the door.

A runner blocked her path as he shouted for a roasted duck, and she pretended to be with him, waiting, too. What a night. She had never worked a place where people ordered three courses, *in French*, from a menu that each and every customer wanted to have described down to the dumbest detail. Amy mostly made stuff up. How could she remember if the oxtail was braised or roasted, since she didn't know the difference between the two?

The tail of an ox? God, she hoped no one asked her about *that*. Just think where that thing had been.

The runner got his duck and darted past her. She made her way forward carefully, past Burt Jobs, the expeditor. Burt was the oddest part of this odd kitchen. She'd only worked in one other kitchen, but still, even she knew that no one writing orders down was strange. The servers screamed everything to the cooks, who nodded or cursed in reply. Burt, a squat man with no hair, stood in the corner of the kitchen behind a small computer that looked like a cash register. He typed everything the waiters called out into his computer, but only to produce a computer-generated check for the customer. Burt didn't let a scrap of paper near the cooks. He called the orders to James and the other cooks in his accountant's flat tone if anyone asked him for a reminder or if he noticed something not right. But mostly he just stood, eyes everywhere while his fingers flew blindly over his keyboard.

Dan smashed through the swinging doors into the kitchen. "Table two. Trudy, Amanda—rare, and two Iggie's."

"Got it," James shouted back.

Burt typed, nodding.

She had made it to the door. She put her hand on the handle at the exact moment James spun to face her.

"Leaving?"

"Yes." *Damn*. Had he smelled her or something? She stood as tall as she could.

He narrowed his eyes. "Coward."

"I am not."

"Are too."

She put her hands on her hips. "Am not." She felt like she was five years old.

"Then I dare you to stay," he said.

"Why?"

"Why? Because you should. Because it's the right thing to do. Not to bail on your mates."

"You've got to be kidding." The kitchen seemed to have quieted around her. Couldn't he see that appeals to honor wouldn't work with her? It was like he thought she was trustworthy. Her, a Gypsy hanging around until his flaky waitress showed up. A klutz who spilled soup in his best customer's lap. What was wrong with this guy?

"I don't kid. Look, I threw you in too deep. Just get them bedded, wetted, and breaded." He tore his eyes from her. Then he yelled into the steam, "Dan and Stuey, take Amy's tables. She's your runner. Grab the kid. Go, go, go. Table four is up." He went back to slamming pans around his eight-burner stove like everything was settled. The kitchen was instantly back in high gear. Maybe she had imagined the pause? His hands flew, grabbing from already-assembled bowls of chopped whatnot.

"Got it, Chef," Dan called. "I'll tell Stu." Dan grabbed two plates from under the warmer and swept back out to the floor.

"Baby blues are up," James called. "Pablo, fire the Josies."

Amy considered heading back for the door. After all, what was with this place? Couldn't they just call the dishes what they were on the menu without the kitchen patois? Each dish transformed into a woman's name—

Oh, hell. The tama-whatever-reduction kiss. Each dish on this menu represented a woman that James had—kissed? Or had—

Ewwww . . . it was too gross and masculine and testosterone-laden to contemplate. She looked around the steaming, pulsing madness that was her new job. How could she have been so blind? *I'm the only woman here.* No wonder the staff women's room was filled with provisions. Roni was probably too nice ever to say anything.

James spared her a glance. "Grab those plates from the window. Run 'em to table six. Then get back. You'll be a runner. Don't sweat it. We may be the *Titanic*, but if we're going down, we're all going down together." His movements at the enormous stove were fluid and studied, not a wasted motion.

Stu crashed into the kitchen. "Table nine. Big Sally twice up no sauce, Susan and a round of Denise times four."

"Got it," James called as Burt's fingers flew over the keyboard.

James's sous-chef, Manuel, nodded as he tossed things into pans. Other men careened around the kitchen, somehow never touching despite the chaos.

Amy made her way carefully to James's stove. Earlier in the night, she had seen firsthand what happened to anyone who touched one of the cooks in the kitchen when a runner accidentally nudged John-John and got a knee in the groin and a stream of vile curses in the face. She reached James's side after dodging two runners and a manic Manuel. "Does Denise know about Susan?" she demanded.

James didn't turn. "Do you always leave at the first sign of trouble?"

She scowled at him. *Yes.* "If I'm the lobster salad, then why is it called Josie and not Amy?"

"You wanna go public?" He was tossing chopped-up white things in a pan.

Right. He had a point. "But why Josie?"

He spared her a glance, and a wicked smile leapt across his face like the flames on his stove. "Like the pussycat. From the cartoon. She reminds me of you."

Now it was Amy's turn to blush. Josie was a rock star. The leader. The smart one. Maybe he saw that in her, despite the fact that, at the moment, she was the loser sneaking out the back door.

Stu grabbed three plates, laying the third in the crook of his arm like a precious child. "You heard him, honey," Stu said. "Grab the plates. We've got your back. Don't think, just *run*." He swept out the doors just as another server careened back in, yelling into the chaos.

Amy took a deep breath. Right. Run. That was such a better plan. It was only eight o'clock. She could take her tips and get a crappy room for the night. Find the local Gypsies first thing tomorrow and track Roni's trail instead of hanging around waiting for her like a wuss.

James thinks I'm Josie from Josie and the Pussycats.

Stu has my back.

We're shipmates, going down together.

James was immersed in his pans. He looked so sexy and happy behind his flaming stove.

Show-off.

He was in full pirate mode, his hands flying from pan to pan. He was drunk on the chaos, swinging from the rigging, rain from the storm bouncing off his gorgeous grin.

It looked like Roni had already taken the last lifeboat off this hulk. For some inane reason, Amy almost liked the idea of sinking with a crew.

Three months alone, adrift on a wooden raft, made a person soft like that.

She grabbed the plates and went back to work.

With every new flavor, you improve your palate.
—James LaChance, *The Meal of a Lifetime*

Chapter 6

Amy inhaled the first cigarette she'd had in five years as she leaned against the brick wall of the alley behind the kit-chen. She had bummed it off the bartender, who nodded sympathetically and said, "Today one cig. Tomorrow, I'll bring you your very own vial of crack. Welcome to Les Fleurs."

Seventy-three dollars in tips was tucked into the waistband of her skirt. If she hadn't been bounced to runner, she would have made way more.

Not so shabby. She was kind of proud of herself for sticking it out.

She checked herself. *No, I'm not getting off on being a good runner.*

Well, a semi-passable runner.

Okay, so I was a lousy runner, too.

Whatever. I'm getting Maddie back . . . somehow. Once I find Roni, I'll know what to do. The plan she had outlined to Oprah wasn't tight enough and she knew it.

She looked up at the stars. The biting cold felt good against her skin. One more puff and she'd go and get her coat and see if she could find a cheap place to sleep tonight. God, she was bone tired.

An alley cat rubbed against her legs. She patted its sleek black fur. "You and me both, kitty. Who needs homes, right? We do just fine on our own."

Just then, the kid pushed through the kitchen door into the alley. The cute little busboy with the supermodel lips and the intense eyes. He had seemed to be trying to talk to her all night. But things were so crazy in there, it was impossible to say anything other than, "Out of my way, asshole!"

He threw himself against the wall next to her and patted down his pockets for a cigarette while casting her shy glances from under his floppy black bangs. He found his pack and began another pat-down for matches. "Don't pet the cats. James hates them. They drive him nuts."

Amy offered him what was left of her lit stub before she remembered he was a minor. "Someone's feeding them." Amy nodded to three small dishes lined up neatly along the wall, the same dishes they used to serve dessert.

He shrugged, took her stub, and lit his cigarette, inhaling deeply. "Thanks."

"You're too young to smoke."

He shrugged. "I'm twenty-one."

"Can't lie to a liar." She studied him carefully. "Twelve."

"Fifteen!" he cried, indignant.

Amy raised her eyebrows and grinned.

He stared, confused for a half second until he realized

she'd tricked him into admitting his real age. He huffed and took a long drag.

"No sweat," Amy reassured him. "Fifteen is a great age to destroy your lungs and drop dead. Forget I said a thing." The cigarette in her hand suddenly seemed terribly wrong. Good thing she wasn't on to the crack just yet. She threw the butt on the ground and stubbed it out with her heel.

He kept looking up at her from under his fringe, as if he had something to say.

"So did my mom send you or what?" he blurted finally. He kicked at the old butts littering the alley.

His mom? Black eyes, black hair, olive skin. Lips like a supermodel. No, lips like a *Gypsy.* This was Roni's son? Amy brightened. *If Roni had a son, then she'd be back.* That was what James had meant when he said he had something of hers. *Was he James's son, too?* She studied the boy's round face. He and James had the same olive coloring, although the boy was darker, but that was the only similarity. She filed the possibility away for later, though. "I've been trying to talk to you all night," she hedged.

His eyes lit up. Wide and wet and exposed. That was the problem with kids; they were too out there. Nothing held back. "You're Rom, right?" he asked, using the traditional term for Gypsy.

"Of course."

"We're Kalderash. Mom and me." He named his tribe.

Her mind clicked through the possibilities. If Roni was anything like her kid, she was sweet and kind and vulnerable as hell. Just the kind of medium Maddie would choose to hang with. Someone who would be good and decent and spread True Love like daisies. Until, of course, poor sweet Roni found out that True Love was the last thing people really wanted. Amy licked her lips. This was going to be too easy. "I'm Kalderash, too. That's how I know your mom."

The boy turned his face to hers. She recoiled at the intensity in his eyes. Kid should wear sunglasses. *I could teach him a few things about being a Gypsy.*

"I *knew* she sent you."

The trust in his eyes pierced through her. She had to remember his name. The servers and kitchen staff had been messing around with him all night. Tony? Tom? Hell, she was getting old. She didn't need Maddie to tell her people's soul mates' names anymore; she needed Maddie to tell her *everyone's* name. "Well of course she sent me. What, did you think I'm here to waitress?"

"No. You sucked at that."

Amy's stomach tightened. Honesty was another thing she hated about kids. She pushed the truth to the back of her mind. She didn't need to be a good server, because she was getting Maddie back. She studied the boy. Tim? Thomas? *When in doubt, go on the offense.* "How do I know you're Roni's son?"

"Look." The boy pulled a wallet out of his back pocket. He handed her a Pennsylvania driver's license. *Troy Valentine. 243 23rd Street, Philadelphia. Black eyes. Black hair.*

She handed it back to him. "Says here you're twenty-two, Troy."

"Yeah, well, don't tell my mom, okay?"

"No problem. Us Rom have to stick together." Especially Rom with a place to crash and possibly even a car.

He nodded, serious and intent.

"Your mom said that I should look out for you. You know, like, babysit. Just till she gets back." Amy felt only a mild tug of guilt at the lie. After all, the kid obviously needed looking after, and it wasn't like any of those strutting, cursing men in there were going to notice him. Her back straightened a notch in female indignation. It *was* required that she look after a Gypsy in need.

"You can sleep on the couch. Or in Mom's room, I guess." The boy looked relieved.

Amy wished she had her cigarette back for one last drag as she tried to sort out her feelings—her *motherly* feelings—toward this boy. Not that she'd ever been a mother. But she'd had a gerbil once. The tenderness felt cobwebbed and rusty, and airing it felt kind of good, like stretching after a too-long séance. "The couch is fine."

"So let's get out of this freezing alley and you can tell me where my mom is."

"You got it, buddy." A flash of inspiration, sparked by a distant memory of her youngest sister, Jasmine, surprised her. Maybe the tenderness wasn't motherly; it was sisterly. Jasmine had come to live with Amy for a few months after a lifetime apart when the girl was just sixteen, about Troy's age. Amy had secretly enjoyed looking after Jasmine. But she had messed it up by bringing Jasmine into her scams. Poor kid couldn't handle it.

This time, Amy had the urge to get it right. Just because she was lying to the kid about knowing his mom didn't mean she couldn't really help him out. "Your mom said I had to report to her when she gets back."

"Yeah? Whatever."

"So no smoking. And no cutting school. Or lifting

from the customers' purses." He looked surprised but softened when she shook off his worried look. "I'm not a cop. Don't sweat it. But I notice things. So don't make a liar out of me."

Again, Troy looked relieved. "Okay. Whatever. I'm beat and freezing, and I still have a book report on *Silas Marner* to finish for tomorrow." He dropped his butt on the ground and snuffed it out with his boot.

"Lead on, brave Troy."

The kid smiled at her, and her stomach jumped with a kind of joy she hadn't experienced in a long time. Everyone in this loopy restaurant was so . . . trusting. She felt almost—what was the word for what was tingling her nerve endings? For the feelings this kid was dragging out of the dark recesses of her emotional closet?

I feel like I might belong. Like they might like me.

Either that or it was food poisoning from the ox butt she had finally deigned to taste.

She looked at the boy.

Definitely ox butt fever. She wasn't going to let her defenses down and let this boy under her skin any more than she was going to let herself fall for James. She was here on a mission—to get Maddie back from Roni. That was it.

She really had to watch herself. Trust no one. Find Roni. Fast.

Then get the hell out.

Great chefs cook to please only themselves.
—James LaChance, *The Meal of a Lifetime*

Chapter 7

Two days later, still no Roni, and Les Fleurs was going mad. The rush didn't let up from five until after ten. It was nuts, but Amy was getting better at running plates and watering suits. Not much better, but enough that James let her hang around. She figured the chaste cooler kiss had something to do with that. The lobster salad, Josie, was flying out of the kitchen like nothing else on the menu. He was probably keeping her around for another kiss for another inspired dish.

Not that they had kissed again.

In fact, they had barely spoken. He was busy all the time, racing between the prep kitchen and the main kitchen, tasting and stirring and shouting and waving his arms.

It was all very sexy, actually. Like watching an artist paint. He was possessed, immersed, passionate. And intimidating. It was clear his staff loved and feared him.

Mostly feared. Lovely in a man who looked (and cooked) as good as James.

Unless you wanted to kiss him. Then his passion for the restaurant was a major pain in the butt.

Not that Amy wanted to kiss him.

Okay, so she did. But it didn't mean anything more than the fact that it had been such a rotten three months since she lost Maddie, the warmth of any human touch would turn her to jelly. Just look how soft she'd been getting around Troy, and all they did was play checkers and talk.

She refilled the breadbaskets, her back to the chaos. There were so many things she still had to ask Troy about Les Fleurs. Like, why was there no sign outside, just three red tulips carved into the doorjamb? *Fleurs,* she knew, was French for "flowers." But still—no sign? And what was with the bare-bones menu? "Chicken, $29," the menu read. "Duck Breast, $37." "Soup du Jour, $12." The servers had to describe the sauces and the sides over and over and had to memorize the specials down to their ingredients. They even had to know the name of the duck farm and that it was organic and humane. As if anything in South Jersey could be humane.

Okay, so she really shouldn't have told the couple at table three that the ducks bedded down on three-hundred-thread-count sheets dyed to match their tail feathers while a violinist played Mozart to them. But the snobs didn't blink an eye, even when she offered to bring out live bunnies in a basket so they could choose one for their *lapin* soup.

Although, come to think of it, they did order the veggie cassoulet.

God, she was exhausted. Amy was sure the servers must recite the dishes in their sleep. It was almost as if James couldn't bear for the diners to have to read, as if that was too much work for someone spending three hundred dollars on dinner for two.

Come to think of it, maybe it was. For those prices, the food should come prechewed.

She put bread on tables six and four, then scurried back for more, pausing to arch her back. Sleeping on Troy's couch wasn't helping her performance, but the kid was starting to talk about his mom, and the info was priceless. *Nice, sweet, good, gentle, kind*—the woman was exactly what Maddie would want in a Gypsy.

And exactly the kind of person who wouldn't be able to handle screwing up nice people's lives with the chaos of discovering their One True Love.

She prepared another breadbasket with enough food to take a Gypsy family through a whole day: three whole-wheat walnut rolls, three brioche, and three thick slabs sawed from a simple crusty French loaf—her favorite.

She glanced from side to side, broke off a crust, and stuffed it into her mouth. Everyone scarfed the bread, but Stu had warned her it was a major taboo to do it on the floor, where a customer might see. Too bad. She couldn't help it; even though the staff all shared a huge predinner meal around four o'clock, she still couldn't resist the temptation of James's heavenly bread.

She tossed two herbed butter tubs into the basket and went to table four, bread in one hand, ice-water pitcher in the other.

The men at the table barely glanced at her as she put down the basket. She filled the glasses as she listened halfheartedly to their real-estate talk. Leases, subleases, square feet, to hell with tenants' rights . . .

"Hey! I know you." One of the men at the table, dark-haired and blue-suited with a red tie, grabbed her wrist midpour. "How do I know you?"

Amy gulped down her bite of bread, but it stuck in her throat. She cast her eyes around the table as she coughed, trying to remember this man. She didn't doubt for a moment that she knew him.

She needed the upper hand until she figured out who he was. Plus, she needed to not choke to death. Forget taboos. She grabbed his water glass, washed down the crust, and then smiled sweetly. "Are you the man with that enormous . . ." She paused for full effect as she focused her gaze on his lap. One. Two. Three. She looked him in the eye. "SUV?"

The man didn't let go of her arm. His eyes narrowed. "You're that Gypsy psychic." His grip tightened. "From Baltimore."

The image of this man in a neon-lit, red-velvet-draped storefront came to her like a scene from a movie. *Why'd he have to spot me here?* Her stomach dove for cover, but she held her voice steady, her eyes hard. "I have no idea what you're talking about. I've never been to Baltimore."

The man stood, his grip still tight on her arm. "You swindled me." He was starting to huff and color around the gills.

Easy, big boy. Amy's heart ran cold as conversations at the nearest tables stopped. She could handle this guy, no problem, but she didn't want a scene. James would kick her out for sure.

She could sense a kernel of doubt in the blundering

man, his two-martini-addled brain trying to reconcile this fancy schmancy eatery with their last encounter in the shabby storefront on Porno Row in Baltimore. She *had* swindled this guy, but what were the details? He was one of so many. There wasn't time to figure it out. She considered dumping the ice water on him and running.

But that probably counted as a scene in an uptight joint like this.

She could go the seduction route. That would be quiet and smooth and hopefully tempt him out of the dining room and into the street where they could talk. Amy let her eyes go wide.

But just as she was about to speak, he jerked her wrist, sending water splashing onto the pristine wooden floor, the ice cubes skidding in all directions like frightened mice.

Nice job, mister. Now they had the full attention of the entire place, staff and diners, everyone frozen except for a flash of black—Stu slipping into the kitchen.

The man's eyes widened as he studied the tattoo on the underside of her arm. "That snake. I still see it in my dreams. No, my nightmares. It is you." He pulled her close to him and whispered fiercely, "You told me my One True Love was named Susan Lord. Then, wouldn't you know, I run into a Susan Lord *the very next day?* But she was working for you, wasn't she? You two swindled me—"

Amy continued her blinking innocent-doe-caught-in-the-headlights act while her mind focused like a laser. Bob Stutz was his name. Scummy land developer. When he wasn't tearing down the old-growth forests for shopping malls, he turned his attentions to tearing down whole neighborhoods, ripping the poor of East Baltimore out like trees; their roots were deep but were no defense against his bulldozers. Amy didn't pick her marks randomly. She always made sure they were scum. Rich scum, true. But she never swindled anyone who didn't deserve it.

Or who didn't need it.

She remembered scamming Bob with civic pride. Mayor Dixon should have given her a ribbon.

Conning this guy had been child's play, if she remembered correctly. The usual. She had hired a young Gypsy, Amelia Denton, to pose as Susan Lord, Bob's One True Love. Didn't take much to persuade him Amelia was the one. After all, sensual, beautiful young women like Amelia didn't let fat, stubby, puffy men like Bob near them in the real world. But Amelia's great-aunt had been forced out of her building on Biddle Street by this prick, so Amelia put on the charm full force, had Bob eating out of her hand.

Anyway, Susan Lord *was* the real name of Bob's One True Love; Amy always told the real name. Of course, Amelia was no Susan Lord. A night or two of flirting, straight vodka for Bob while the bartender funneled Amelia water, then an hour or two of searching while Bob slept. Bank numbers, credit card numbers, jewelry, car keys—it was too easy when you were inside. Worked like a charm.

Until it came back at you when you least expected it. Like now. The restaurant around them was silent except for the giddy whispers of diners who, up until this moment, were sure the truffle potatoes were the most exciting thing that would happen to them in their entire, boring, sheltered lives.

Troy appeared with three towels draped over his arm. He dropped a towel, moved it with his foot, then replaced it with a dry one, removing every last drop of water. If you weren't watching closely, you might have thought he was just standing there. He had used the same effortless grace to clean up when she had spilled the soup on Dr. Trudeau on her first night.

If only Bob could be cleaned away so easily. "Didn't you read my note?" Amy hissed at Bob. Her wrist was starting to hurt, but she pretended otherwise. She had to calm him down and get him outside so they could discuss this rationally. "We left you a note on your bed stand. Susan Lord is really your One True Love. You need to find her. The real her. It's your only hope of not being an asshole for the rest of your life."

"Why should I believe you after—?"

"Is there a problem here?" It was James, at her side, looking as calm as if he were inquiring about the doneness of a steak. James nodded at Troy, and the boy withdrew to join the rest of the kitchen staff, who had assembled around the kitchen door. John-John had an enormous black frying pan in his hand, and he looked as if he was prepared to use it.

A flutter of relief moved through her, which dissipated into dismay. Everyone in the entire restaurant had come to a halt and was staring at their odd triangle—Bob, flustered and puffing in his conservative suit; James, menacingly calm, in his pristine chef's whites; and her, playing the innocent.

It wasn't her strongest role.

Bob looked James up and down. His face had gone red with anger. "This waitress is a lying, conning—"

James held up a hand. "Let this woman's arm go. Now." His voice was icy but calm.

"Who the hell are you?" the man asked James. He

still gripped her arm, but his eyes darted around the room nervously.

Chef whites? Apron? Two guesses, Bob. A rush of triumph gripped her.

James pulled his chef's knife out of his apron. "Me? Who am I?" He studied the blade.

Off with his head! James was going to risk dinging his precious knife on this anvil-head? For her? She felt like a pure, innocent maiden.

What an odd feeling.

"Who I am doesn't matter," James said to Bob. He was still looking over his knife, turning it this way and that. "It's who you are that's important. Are you a person touching a member of my staff? Are you a person upsetting diners in my dining room? Disturbing these fine people's meals?" He expanded his arms to take in the room, the knife catching the light. James's face was eerily still. He met Bob's eyes and held them.

Bob yanked his bloodshot eyeballs away and glanced uneasily at his tablemates.

They stared into their sweating water glasses. Checked their watches. One manically stuffed roast chicken into his mouth, as if he knew this was the last shot he was getting at James's two-star food.

Harmless boobs, Amy thought. But what about Bob? Amy could see that he was trying to gauge whose side James was on. He was obviously confused that James—a *man* and the boss of this classy establishment—was siding with a female underling. It didn't jive with Bob's sense of order in a male-dominated, money-dominated world.

"I think you should go," James said. His words hung in the air, heavy with the weight of his unspoken threat.

Bob backed away a step, keeping his eyes on James's knife, dropping her arm. "I think I might have . . . you know . . . She just looks like someone I used to know." Bob began to tuck himself back into his seat. "My mistake."

James caught Bob's arm before he sank into the chair. "Perhaps you didn't hear me?" James looked angry enough to flip him like a pancake, despite the other man's heft.

The other two men looked at each other, befuddled. One of them grabbed a shrimp from his plate, but James plucked it from his hand and tossed it onto the table. "Dinner's over."

They looked at each other in shock.

"Now." James looked from his knife blade to each of them in turn.

As one, the three men scuttled from the table, casting wary glances back at James. They hustled into their coats, which Joey, the maître d', had waiting by the door. "You'll be sorry," Bob called, just before he scurried through the door into the cold night. "I know people. I control this town."

"Susan Lord," Amy called after him. "Look her up."

Joey shut the door firmly behind them.

Then all was silent.

James tucked his knife back into his apron. He raised his voice into the void so the whole dining room could hear. "So sorry about that little mix-up. Espresso and dessert on the house for everyone."

The room buzzed with its good luck—a scene by a famous chef *and* free dessert.

Trust your instincts over your recipe.
—JAMES LACHANCE, *The Meal of a Lifetime*

Chapter 8

Amy and James retreated to the barista station. Now that the crisis was over, it bugged Amy that she needed to thank James for saving her. She liked running her own show, thank you very much. "Thanks, but that wasn't necessary. I could have handled that schmuck. That guy was just—"

James held up his hand. "Don't want to know."

But Amy wanted to explain herself. She wanted James to know that she ate jerks like Bob for breakfast. "But don't you want to know why he—?"

James turned to her. "I don't care if you killed his mother. If he messes with you in my dining room, he's gone. This is a business, and a business can't operate if we're not a team. Always. Whatever happens. If you screw up, you're gone. If you do your job, then you stay, and that lardass is gone no matter what you've done in your past. My kitchen is filled with ex-cons, ex-drug-addicts, ex-hustlers. But I stand by them. Always. And in turn, they do the same for me. Always." He paused, searching her face. "I'm not sure you get that."

She was stunned. When had anyone ever stood by her like that? Not her mother, who split the moment she learned that her soul mate was not Amy's father. And certainly not Maddie, who split, too.

Fact was, after that encounter with Bob, Amy was ready to split herself. What was she doing hanging around this place, anyway, waiting for a woman who might or might not show up? Who might or might not have her spirit-voice? It was so not her style. She had a code of her own: When the going gets rough, set sail for calmer waters till the storm's over. The Gypsy way. She had enough in tips to last her a while, and she could stay with Troy for free. She didn't need to owe James anything. "Don't worry, I'm leaving."

His eyes hardened, just the way they had the first day, after she had given him her necklace.

She felt all the anger of the last three months well up inside her. "Why do you care, James? Don't give me that trust bullshit. Or that teamwork bullshit. I'm not a member of this dysfunctional restaurant family you're trying to make here, with you as Papa Chef. I had a papa, and I don't need that shit." She shook off the emotions that always flooded her when she thought of her father.

He shook his head. "You don't get it at all, do you?" Then he straightened his apron and strode away from her, moving from table to table, greeting thrilled diners, shaking hands, not looking back.

Amy watched him with frustration. What had she expected, that he'd beg her to stay? She sucked at this job, and he clearly hated her guts.

She spotted Troy, who was watching her from across the room, his face dark and suspicious. His eyes bored into hers, full of questions. Full of doubt.

She felt sick to her stomach. For the last few days, he had thought she was the good one, the rescuer come to save him from his flaky mom. It had felt embarrassingly good to play that role.

Just like it felt kinda good to play the role of damsel in distress for James.

But they were just that, roles. Not who she was. Just who she was pretending to be. Just like James was pretending. He could yap about his crew all he wanted; live for his imaginary family of cooks and servers, but in the end, in this world, you're on your own.

Even if once, a sexy chef stood up for you.

In front of everyone.

For no good reason.

James went back to his stove, aware that his line was watching him uneasily. He was so mad he couldn't speak. Not without blowing up. And he had to keep his cool. It had been exhilarating standing beside Amy, the two of them against the world. He hadn't experienced that kind of rush since the main water pipe exploded halfway through second service three months ago, and they managed to stick it out with a bucket brigade from Alma and free wine for everyone in the house.

But then she said she was leaving. Just like that. *Hey, thanks for saving my butt, bye-bye.*

He threw some shallots into his pan and tossed them

over the high heat, trying not to acknowledge the memories that were accosting him. Amy was just like his father, always leaving, off to another three-month-long business trip, to another affair. Even after James's mother died and an endless string of servants raised James, his dad still left, as if a kid didn't mind being alone with strangers who were paid to be there.

Your dysfunctional restaurant family . . . with you as Papa Chef. So, he was used to paying people to stand by him. He wasn't an idiot; he knew his staff wasn't his real family.

Thank God. His real family was his father, and that man was a constant disappointment. It had taken a long time for James to learn that his behavior didn't matter a whit; his father left no matter what young James did. In fact, the more dependence and need James showed, the *faster* his dad split.

Which was why James never showed any weakness. Never let on that he needed a thing.

He flicked the shallots with a jerk of his wrist, and one flew out of the pan and into the fire. It sizzled and then was gone in an instant.

James stared after it, then shook himself from its spell.

He didn't need anything except his restaurant. The food and work had become like a drug, blocking everything else out. He wasn't blind; he knew that his life was lacking a certain, well, normality. He had heard his staff wonder about him when they thought he wasn't around: why he had no family; why he showed up every single night, without fail; why he cared so deeply about every garnish, every pat of butter. But he had it figured out; Les Fleurs filled him. It was enough. It was solid. It was constant.

But, then, why could he not get Amy out of his head? So she'd quit? She sucked at her job. She had no sense of loyalty or responsibility. She didn't belong here.

Or did she?

She inspired the best dish I've created in years.

The lobster salad wasn't a dish; it was a revelation.

He splashed red wine into his pan, and the whole thing burst into flames that disappeared as quickly as they came.

If he could keep Amy here, what else could they make together? If he had a whole menu of dishes as inspired as the lobster salad, he could go for a third star.

I could get my third star.

He looked around his kitchen. It was good. But who wouldn't be hungry for more? It would help all of his staff, make everyone's life better.

But it was too late for that; Amy was gone. And no way was he chasing after a woman who was so unstable, so disloyal, so willing to flee at the first shadow. Plus, he wasn't his father. He didn't use people for his own ends. He wouldn't use her. It was good she was gone.

But then why did he feel so bad?

Technique is everything.
—JAMES LaCHANCE, *The Meal of a Lifetime*

Chapter 9

Amy had her head deep in a kitchen cabinet when she heard Troy wake up. It wasn't even six in the morning, the day after she quit, but she hadn't been able to sleep. Her body knew when it was time to go. And now she must have woken up the boy, as here he came padding down the hall, still half-asleep.

"What are you doing?" Troy asked. He was in his sweatpants, his hair tousled from bed. Amy snuck the pen she was holding into her sleeve. "Nothing." She stood, moving away from the cabinet she had been rifling through.

Troy pushed past her to the cabinet and threw it open. He knelt down. "Then what's that?" He pointed to a small upside-down horseshoe with an *A* in it. "Are you tagging our apartment? I found one of these in the bathroom, too." He looked around. "Hey, you're dressed. You're packed. You're leaving."

Amy shook her head. Stupid observant kid. She ignored his accusations. She had spent the last hour searching the apartment for clues as to where Roni might have gone, and, yes, leaving her mark with her trusty black Bic permanent pen. It was an old habit, leaving a sign that she had been somewhere. It was what she did before she split. She wasn't sure why. Maybe all her wandering made her want to leave some kind of proof that she had existed.

"Yes, I'm leaving, Troy. I'm going to get your mother."

Troy rubbed the sleep out of his eyes. "Because of that guy? Bob? The guy at the restaurant? You think he's after you?"

"No. I'm not scared of him," she scoffed. "I just think it's time your mother came back, that's all. And I'm not the type to hang around and wait. I'm going to get her."

"But you told her you'd stay with me," Troy said. It was the first time since their conversation in the alley that he sounded like a little kid. He sat down at the kitchen table and ran his hand through his bed-headed hair.

Yeah, well, that was a lie. I'm a liar. Deal with it. "I'm only leaving so I can get her back faster, Troy. It's better than me waiting around."

"But you said—"

"Well, I'm sorry."

He shrugged. "I'm going back to sleep. Search the apartment all you want. Believe me, I've already been through it. There's no clue where she split to." He met her eyes straight on. "I don't know why I believed you when you said you knew where she was."

"I do know. I just—"

"I don't care," Troy said. "Split. I never asked you to be here. I don't need you any more than James does."

* * *

From the front seat of her old beat-up Chevy Malibu, Roni watched Amy leave her apartment. She sank down low in the seat, pressing a magazine to her face in case Amy came her way. Her hands were shaking with fear.

Amy Burns is after me.

She tried to stop her shakes. Everything was going fine. This was the plan. Step one complete: Roni had carefully let out word through the Rom network that she had Amy's spirit-voice, which was a lie.

And Amy had come.

Roni took a huge breath and pulled herself back up so she could watch the retreating Gypsy. She wished she could race inside and tell Troy where she was and what she was doing for him and why. Or even just give him a big hug and then run away before either of them could speak.

She felt nauseous.

Her hand went to her stomach, where the tiny new life had started to grow. The moment she had realized she was pregnant, she knew her life had to change. She had to quit being the nice guy and be tough, be brave, be ruthless. She had come home from the Gypsy midwife with her folic acid pills, a worn copy of *What to Expect When You're Expecting,* and the most important thing of all from the used bookstore on Market Street, *The Art of the Con.*

It was time for the new Roni. The one who wasn't sweet and good, the one who went after what she wanted.

And she didn't want Amy's spirit-voice, that was for sure. This con game lifestyle wasn't her style. She put her hand to her throbbing heart. How anyone could live like this was beyond her. Between the nausea and the fear, she could hardly sleep.

No, she didn't want the voice. She wanted money—real money, stay-home-and-raise-two-kids money—and this was her one chance. Roni had seen Amy on *Oprah*. She had seen pictures of Amy's movie-star brother-in-law, Josh Toby. She had read about how he routinely gave away money—big money—to people in need.

Roni reached for *The Art of the Con*. She flipped to a dog-eared, much-read page: *You can only make a person do what they want to do already.*

Step two of the plan was working beautifully. Now that Amy had been lured here by Roni's lie, Roni had to disappear so that Amy would bond with Troy. Then, Amy would *want* to help him.

Only Roni hadn't expected step two would be so hard on her. She felt awful leaving her son with that woman, but it was just for a few more days. It was all for Troy. Troy and the new life inside her.

This was the chance of a lifetime. The con of a lifetime. She couldn't believe her good luck so far. But, then, hadn't she deserved it, being good and nice her whole life? Didn't she deserve something? Didn't Troy?

She caught a glimpse of Troy in the window, watching Amy disappear around the corner.

Roni sank back down in the seat; it was too dangerous being here. She couldn't tell Troy what was going on. Not yet. And he was sure to spot their car if she lingered.

She couldn't wait much longer for step three: to return, mild and meek, and tell Amy that the Gypsy she had run to for advice told her that the voice would go back to Amy if she helped Troy. And Amy would want to because she would be fond of Troy. Who wouldn't be fond of Troy? Of course, since Roni didn't really have the voice, she couldn't give Amy anything. But by then, they'd be long gone, the three of them, to a new life.

The thought made Roni weak with fear. She hoped she could pull it off. She had to learn to control her shaking hands.

Roni could tell from the way she walked that Amy Burns was nobody's fool.

A half hour later, Les Fleurs was dark and empty as Amy pushed silently from the alley into the kitchen, careful to keep the circling cats out. Someone had fed them recently, and they purred against her legs, hoping for more. Thankfully the key had been where she'd seen the kitchen boys stow it: third brick up, fourth brick over behind the trashcans.

Not a soul stirred in the deserted kitchen. The transformation from last night, when it had been filled with slop-slinging, bellowing barbarians, was remarkable. Now it was like a gleaming chrome temple, shining and silent as if she had imagined the chaos. *Ghost chefs.*

She had come to get something worth pawning before she split to find Roni. She made her way through the dark dining room and straight to the three jade flowers in their decorative alcove. She'd been eyeing them for days. She slipped the largest flower off its stem and into her bag.

Her stomach growled. Maybe the walk-in downstairs would be unlocked. Might as well get some provisions while she was here.

She stole carefully down the dark back steps.

Someone was in the basement prep kitchen, the secondary kitchen that was outfitted with expansive chrome counters and enormous stockpots. She could hear the chopping of a single knife, could see it flashing in the slash of yellow light that spilled into the dark hallway. Hear its rapid beat as it hit the cutting board.

She crept toward the walk-in. It was open. She grabbed a few apples and a hunk of plastic-wrapped cheese. Then she took out her Bic and left her mark on the wall, low to the ground. The horseshoe with an *A*.

Okay, now she could split.

But the rhythmic chopping seemed to call to her. Maybe the early morning crew would have some information as to where Roni had gone. Anyone who worked at this hour just had to be a low-paid sucker, willing to spill for a price. Plus, just thinking about going back out into the freezing morning with no leads made her toes ache with anticipated cold.

She hesitated in the hall, then peeked around the doorframe into the kitchen.

James.

He was stooped over a cutting board, his profile to her, chopping carrots.

She ducked back into the shadow, breathing hard. The scene made her think of those pictures in the National Gallery in D.C. where she had gone sometimes to pick pockets when she had lived in Baltimore. They were small oils with varnished surfaces where people stood by windows, thinking thoughts so personal you had to look away. The people in those pictures were always alone, doing menial tasks, but in the presence of something holy. Vermeer was the name of the guy who painted them. Or something like that. Johannes Vermeer. *Johannes*. Some language for "James," maybe?

"I smell you, Amy. Cinnamon and clove."

Damn foodies. Why was she constantly underestimating this man?

She peered around the doorframe. He didn't look up but kept his head down, chopping. "I was just—" She paused. *Just pilfering your restaurant, just rooting around for free info, just lonely in a strange town . . .* "Leaving."

Without stopping his work, he eyed the apple in her hand with narrowed eyes. "Thought you quit." There was a hardness in his voice, the same one from the previous day.

"I did." She came into the room and leaned against the counter next to his chopping board. Her heart was pounding madly, as if she cared about getting caught by this dark chef. "Just had to get something I forgot."

"My designer, citron-scented, New York State Arpeggio apples? Those babies are grown only in one orchard outside Albany. I have them FedExed down in a brown, unmarked box so the spies from Le Bec Fin can't steal my sources." He was transforming the carrots into tiny, diced squares like a machine, his hand moving independent of any conscious effort. The effect was remarkably sexy, a craftsman at work. *What else can you do with those hands?*

"Hmm. I thought they were pretty good. For apples, anyway."

He scowled, as if considering something grave. "Can you handle a knife?"

"I guess."

"I don't suppose you have a knife?"

"In my boot," she said. "Right next to my handgun."

His eyes traveled down the length of her. Was she imagining it, or did they travel slowly, lingering? They stopped at her high-heeled black boot.

Chop, chop, chop a wee bit faster.

"Kidding," she said, pleased that she was arousing him.

His eyes traveled back up her body and stopped at her chest. They definitely lingered. She inhaled and straightened, feeling his gaze like a caress.

He stopped chopping, and the room fell silent. He didn't smile. "Sammy, my prep guy, should have been here twenty minutes ago. You want a new job? A job away from the customers?"

"I don't know." He was offering her a second chance. What if she stayed? If even for just one more day? Maybe she could get something right. She was obviously better suited for the manic, obscenity-laden kitchen than for that stuffy floor job.

"If you take it, you can't quit on me again. If I teach you how to use a knife, you'll owe me. Big time. There are people who would kill to have a lesson like this from me."

She rolled her eyes. "You want help or not?" *Please say yes.* She wanted another chance to be near this man. She didn't want to go back out into the freezing morning searching for a woman she wasn't sure she wanted to find.

What if Roni hates me for lying to Troy? What if Roni wants to keep Maddie? What if my one goal in life—getting Maddie back—is impossible? What if this is my future? Being awful at everything I try and owing strangers more and more?

Could she chop? Could she learn something new? She'd never been taught anything in her life, except how to con and steal. Maybe it wasn't her fault that she stunk at everything else.

"You can use my knife today. But tomorrow you've gotta bring your own. And promise me you'll never, ever, put it anywhere near your boot." James rooted around in an enormous drawer that had a set of keys hanging out of its lock. "No chef shares his knives lightly," he said. He pulled out a canvas cloth that looked like the kind of case her grandmother used to hold paintbrushes. He pulled a tie and unrolled it to reveal gleaming knives of every shape and size. He handed her an identical knife to his: long with a straight blade and a wooden handle. He watched her take it as if he were entrusting her with Baby Jesus.

It was surprisingly light.

He picked up his own knife and a carrot. "The carrot is round, but you must produce perfect squares." He paused and leaned toward her. "*Perfect* squares. Called a *brunoise*. I'm not messing around about how good they have to be. Each square has to be like a tiny orange die. With numbers carved in the side. Weighted to roll six every time." He proceeded to chop the round edges off the carrot in four swift movements. "It's like harvesting wood. The tree becomes flat planks. Then two-by-fours, then—"

"Lumberjack analogies are lost on me," Amy interrupted. "You were on the mark with the dice, though." She picked up the knife.

"Wait—protection!"

"Are we cutting tubers or having sex?"

"It's the same thing." He tossed her a towel. "Technique, technique, technique, and good hygiene. Wash the hands up to the elbow."

"Remind me never to sleep with you." While she washed her hands in the enormous sink, her stomach coiled in disappointment. How could a man who kissed like James equate sex with root vegetables and hygiene? It was like James was two men, the Iron Chef on the surface, the wicked pirate buried beneath.

I could get below his iron surface, expose the real man begging to get out.

When she came back to the counter, he pulled out a huge wooden chopping board and laid it before her, a shield for battle. She stood beside him and grabbed a carrot. Trying to imitate his swift strokes, she cut off the round edges and ended up with a sapling of still-roundish carrot. She glanced up at him, but he continued chopping, not saying a word. She chopped the carrot into thinner slivers, not nearly as regular or thin as his.

A door slammed above, then footsteps stumbled down the stairs. A blond, bed-headed, gangly man with a five-o'clock shadow and an untucked shirt barreled into the room. "Sorry, boss." He stopped short when he saw Amy. "I'm twenty minutes late, Chef. You're not gonna can me for less than half an hour?" He was panting, his face still red from the cold outside.

"Twenty-*five* minutes. Which throws everything, Sammy. You should be here twenty minutes *early*. This is the third time this week. Get lost."

A chill went up Amy's spine. *You're part of the team until you fuck up,* James had said. Guess he meant it.

Sammy came to the counter. "My dog can do better brunoise than that, dude. Er. Dudette. That's like, a *chop*, not a dice." He pulled out his knife roll and unwrapped his knives. Amy wondered if the general public had any idea there were an army of cooks out there, armed with gleaming, razor-sharp knives roaming the city. "I won't be late again." He stank of beer and cigarettes. "You want me to trash those, Chef?" He nodded at Amy's carrots.

"Why are you still here?" James was chopping again, his back to Sammy.

For an instant, Amy thought James might be referring to her and her awful *chopped* carrots. When she realized he was talking to Sammy, a brightness rose within her so brilliant, she was afraid if she opened her mouth, her teeth would glow. *He's on my side. Again.*

Sammy stared at her with building hatred. Then he relaxed. "Hey, you're the new temp server for Roni." He sneered and leaned in close to Amy. "Heard you've been fucking Troy."

James's knife stopped.

Her internal light snapped off, throwing her into darkness. Amy turned instinctively, raising her knife to Sammy's throat. "Heard you've been fucking your mother."

Sammy jerked away. His hand flew to his throat, as if to test if the flesh was still intact. "You slept at his place," he fumbled. "She did, Chef. At Troy's. Manuel saw them fix it up and split together like three or four nights now. She told the kid she knew Roni. Which was, like, a total lie."

"I thought the man told you to split." Amy was tickled that Sammy looked so scared. Like she'd really slit his throat. This guy was obviously a moron. But she really had to shut him up. She snuck a look at James. *He* didn't look like an idiot. He looked like he had a lot on his mind—anger, confusion, *questions*.

"Go," James said.

Sammy and Amy glanced at each other, not sure which one of them he meant. But when Amy looked back at James, his eyes were blazing at Sammy. Relief and gratitude filled her. *I'm back on the team.*

And I want to sleep with the coach. Uh-oh.

She could kiss James.

She really could.

She really should.

Sammy backed out of the room, away from her knife and James's icy stare. "Cradle robber," he muttered as he made for the stairs.

She lunged forward with the knife, as if she planned to come after him.

He upped his retreat. "You couldn't fine-dice if your life depended on it," he shouted back at her. "You, you— chopper!" He fled up the stairs and out of sight.

When all is said and done, it's time to cook.
—James LaChance, *The Meal of a Lifetime*

Chapter 10

James went back to dicing, not looking at Amy. He didn't believe for a minute that she had touched Troy. But had she lied to Troy about knowing his mom? What was she doing at his place?

He glanced at her. She did dice like a child. "You're going to lop off a finger," he said. "Knife tip never leaves the board. Watch. It rocks, like a cradle." *Ooh, bad word choice.*

"I wouldn't know about cradles." She shot him an anger-laden glare.

"Like a boat."

"Aye-aye, Captain," she harrumphed, and tried to mimic his movements, chopping, occasionally even *dicing* the slivers into smaller bits. Her knife was more controlled now, but her carrot pieces still looked like a kindergartener's next to his.

James shook his head and moved behind her. He put

his arms around her and covered her hands with his. A shock of heat and lust rocked through him at the softness of her. "Don't resist. Let your hands relax in mine." He began dicing with her knife, her hands enclosed in his, his arms circling her, every breath laden with the scent of her. Cinnamon and clove and carrots.

The heat of her so close was going to cook him and those damn carrots both. Her muscles relaxed into his, and he wondered how long he could stand being this close without kissing her. The knife rocked with pleasing quickness, his hands light over hers but controlling. He bit his lip.

Even if she's just lying to Troy, she has to go. It's about trust and honesty and loyalty, none of which she seems to know a thing about. Hell, last time he'd seen her, he'd thrown Bob out for her, and all she said was, *Hey, thanks for saving my butt. Bye-bye.*

Time to stuff his lust into a pillowcase and drown it in a lake.

They diced a second carrot while he whacked through his thoughts with a machete. His mind was mush, because he wanted to get her into his bed. To hell with the bed. He wanted to have her on this bed of carrots. Now. He wanted to make her his muse. The food they could make together could be spectacular.

But she was a Gypsy, a wanderer, a person with no sense of place or loyalty. *She will leave me. Like my father.* He had to watch himself. *Control.*

The rhythm of his hands was becoming her rhythm, and he lightened his touch. "Why'd you lie to the kid?" The gleaming knife flashed, his voice a growl. He stopped the knife abruptly and let her go.

She spun around to face him, her eyes flashing with anger. She pointed the knife at him. He backed away, unsure if she understood how sharp it was. "What have you done for Troy since his mom split? Do you know what a dump he lives in?"

James was mute with surprise. No one attacked him in his own kitchen. It was unheard of.

She continued, waving the knife to emphasize her words. "You're all 'teamwork' and high and mighty boss man, but I'm the one who washed the pile of moldy dishes in that kid's rat-hole apartment last night. I'm the one who made sure he wasn't stuck there by himself. I might not really know his mom. I might have lied to him, sure. But it's no lie that he's scared and doesn't want to be alone. He's a *kid*." She ended her speech with the tip of her knife lodged against his heart.

God, that was sexy.

Her eyes softened as she lowered the knife. "You gadje never get the worth of a good lie."

"Gadje?"

"Non-Gypsy." Her voice was softer now, her anger spent. "*The Easter Bunny is real. The Tooth Fairy is coming as soon as you fall asleep. You're above average. Everything's gonna be all right.* Lies are a part of parenting." She leaned against the counter, staring into the distance.

"I wouldn't know." He leaned next to her, a little disappointed that her anger had cooled. He had enjoyed her passionate outburst more than he wanted to admit. "The Easter bunny never came anywhere near my house. Probably afraid that my father would send him off to an egg-painting assembly line in China. Not that my father had ever bothered to be around on Easter." Why was he telling her this?

"My house either," she said. Her loneliness spiraled around her like something you could smell. "Not that we had a house. Mostly, we just had shitty apartments and shittier hotel rooms."

"Believe me, a nice house doesn't make up for a self-absorbed, workaholic, cheating father who's never around."

"Where was your mom?" she asked him, as if it were perfectly normal to be having a conversation in his kitchen, when there were things to do. Important things. Like carrot dicing. Where he was the *executive chef.* Feared and respected, but not *talked to.* This was not the kind of relationship he knew what to do with.

And yet, he found himself answering her. "She died when I was twelve. I was raised by a series of servants. They sucked, but at least we always had a cook on staff. I learned everything from the cooks. They were bored to death, cooking for a twelve-year-old and the occasional business party." He looked at the carrots, wishing them gone so he could be completely alone with Amy. "What about your mom?" Damn, why had he asked her that? They had stock to make and mise en place to prepare, and he was already behind on the prep work.

"She split when I was six. Comes back now and again to pretend nothing bad ever happened in our storybook life. As if it wasn't too late. Hah." She turned her attention back to the carrots and began to chop. "What's with Roni, anyway, leaving Troy? The kid said she's done it once before."

He heard the heat of her own memories in her tone,

and he realized how much she and Troy had in common. Of course she would try to help him—she practically *was* him. "Once that I know of. Rumor said she was pregnant and went off to get an abortion." He watched her hands. Her dice still sucked. "Rumor had it that it was true. Took it pretty hard."

"Did Troy know?" She examined a carrot that she'd cut into one of those shapes he never could remember in school—a hexahedron, maybe. You'd think cubes would be easier than her multiplaned creations.

He started dicing again. "I don't think so. It was two years ago. I hope that's not what's up now. She should have known she could come to me for anything." His knife slipped, and he cut a triangle. He stared at it in disbelief. He tossed it into the trash before he could think too much about how this woman was messing with his morning. "Roni wasn't the type to ask, you know? She never asked for anything. Not a day off. Nothing. Ever."

"Of course she didn't. She was terrified of you."

"Terrified? Of me?"

She bit into an unchopped carrot. "James, you're kind of intimidating."

"Doesn't seem to bother you."

"No one intimidates me."

Except me, when I had my arms around you. He had felt her longing and felt her fight it. He wondered why she fought it. She didn't seem the type to care about a stray caress. "This restaurant is a family; we're a team."

"Tell that to Sammy." She pointed the carrot at him.

"Sammy fucked up."

"So did I. The soup in Dr. Trudeau's lap? You didn't fire me. Face it, James, you're a loose cannon."

He stopped chopping. "I'm completely rational."

"You're random. That's good. It's good to have people afraid of you. It keeps fear in people's hearts. Keeps 'em on their toes."

James felt dizzy. He steadied his hands on the counter. *It's good to have people afraid of you.* That was what his father always said. James broke out in a cold sweat. She was wrong. He didn't want his staff to be afraid of him. To respect him, sure. He had to keep some semblance of order. But they knew they were like his family. He wouldn't treat his family the way his father treated him.

Or did he? Was he acting exactly like his father—an irrational tyrant leaving everyone quaking in fear, and he was too blind to see it? His stomach clenched like a fist.

Amy was watching him carefully. She seemed to be sizing him up, filing information away for later.

He felt the need to explain, more to himself than to her. "Look, there are two kinds of ways people fuck up. The ways they can control and the ways they can't. I never blame people for stuff they can't control. Never. Sammy didn't have to be late. But—"

"But I can't control that I spill soup on the customers? Or that I suck with this knife?"

"No. You *can* control that. You just need practice and someone to teach you. I can teach you all that stuff. C'mon. You know what I mean. Isn't there something in your life that you can't control? Even if you try, you're stuck. Dead in the water." He paused. "Like leaving, quitting every time something happens that touches an emotion?"

She stiffened, but she didn't back down. He liked that in a woman. Er, in an employee. "What's your weakness, Chef?" she asked.

"You." He surprised himself and her equally. There was truth in that word, but he was also covering for his real secret, the one no soul in his kitchen could ever know.

The air grew heavy around them as she absorbed what he had said. And what he hadn't.

"But that doesn't mean that you can dice worth shit," he said. This was still his kitchen. He was still the chef. He still had to keep control. "So I still need you on the floor bussing with Troy until you can handle that knife. It'll take at least a month. Till then, you'll do both—dice with Denny and bus with Troy."

She turned back to hacking her carrots, more intent now. They diced side by side for a while, until she said softly, almost gently, "I know you have a deeper secret now, James. One you're not letting on to. Don't think you can flatter me into believing that I'm your weakness. I'll figure you out. I'm no one's fool."

He smiled. Amy was starting to fit right in. Of course, he'd have to trash her carrot dice. But he'd do it later. When she wasn't around, holding a knife.

James had gone to inspect the produce delivery, leaving Amy with the Mt. Everest of carrots.

As soon as he left the kitchen, she dropped his knife and let her head fall to the cool, chrome counter. What was she doing?

Okay, so James was sexy. Pressed up against her, her hands dwarfed in his, it was all she could do to stop herself from turning the knife on his chef whites, shredding them off like in those *Zorro* movies.

Well, maybe she'd have to get a little better with the knife first. Otherwise, that could be nasty.

Still, his body against hers had been electric. She was sure he had felt it, too. *Is that a carrot in your pocket or . . .*

And he had given her a second chance to stick around. Who ever got a second chance?

And a knife lesson.

She looked down at her carrots, which looked like they'd been hacked to death by a mob of angry preschoolers. It was hard to dice carrots with a man like James around.

Or maybe she just sucked at this, too.

A month to learn, he had said. Like she'd still be here in a month.

She wondered what his flaw was. The deep, dark secret that he couldn't control. No way it was really her. It was something deeper. Something that was keeping him from kissing her, from giving in to her. Because the truth was, if he had really wanted her, he could have had her right there in the prep kitchen, and they both knew it. No, something was holding James back, and she intended to find out what it was.

She hoped it was something truly awful but fun. Kleptomania, maybe. Now, that would even the playing field between them. Make them a perfect match.

Perfect match. Her interior alarm system went off, sirens wailing, just like they always did when she was considering getting close to someone. *Don't risk losing Maddie for a klepto knife fanatic.*

She hacked a carrot clear in two like an angry ninja, sending one of the pieces skidding across the kitchen. She had to stay away from James whether she liked it or not. Far away. If Maddie lured her here to be sure she could ditch Amy for good, it was Amy's job not to fall for the con.

I lasted thirty-four years without love. Now that I know how bad life is without Maddie, I'm certainly not going to cave now for a cute chef. No matter how good his body feels pressed against mine.

Ten hours later, James sat in the empty restaurant, catching his breath. Another wild night of a double-booked full house. A successful, first-rate kitchen was energizing. Like war, except that the only casualties were sides of beef and weak chefs.

It was almost one in the morning, but he didn't feel like going home. As he was changing out of his whites and into his jeans in the back after the last customer had left, his saucier, Denny, had invited him out to meet a crew of off-duty chefs from restaurants all over town, still revved up from the night, unable to sleep, at a diner down in Flourtown. Maybe he'd go. Maybe not.

Amy and Troy had cut out as soon as they could, around ten. They had a long talk in the alley first, and Troy seemed mad but agreed to whatever Amy proposed in the end. "We're heading straight home to study for that math test," James had heard Amy say in a mom voice as they slipped away, down the alley and out of sight.

She'd been right—she did more for the kid by staying with him than he had teaching him how to make a roux. Okay, maybe her company didn't help Troy in the long run like knowing the secrets of the roux would, but in the short run, a fifteen-year-old boy needed an adult.

Maybe he'd just swing past Roni's place to check on them. It was on his way to meet the boys, so why not? He owed Troy at least that. The kid might be a wiseass pain in the butt, but as long as he pulled a paycheck from Les Fleurs, he was James's wiseass pain in the butt.

"Charlie, I'm gone," he called to his night porter. Night porter was a shitty job, but someone had to clean the restaurant after the kitchen shut down after midnight and before James returned before dawn the next day. Night porters were singular people. Luckily, there was a place for every lost soul in a restaurant.

Even for me.

He listened for Charlie's grunt, then grabbed his black leather coat and swung out the door, locking up behind him.

The lights were blazing in Roni's second-floor apartment, illuminating Amy, sitting at the kitchen table. James remembered how beautiful she had been the first time he saw her, snow twinkling in her hair. How she had struck him instantly as intense and unreal.

And sexy as hell.

And alone. He had glimpsed that in her on the first day they'd met, in that split second as the lights came on: loneliness. Piercing, soul-eating loneliness.

It was an emotion he recognized.

Absorbed in his memories, he realized too late that she had stood and walked to the window. He almost ducked behind one of the massive sycamore trees that lined the street but didn't. Hell, he must look pretty pathetic and alone, too, standing on the street in the dead of winter.

He adjusted his features. *I'm not afraid of you.*

Okay, he was a little afraid. But a good kind of afraid,

like a hunter spotting his prey. His whole body was already bathed in adrenaline. The hunt had begun.

She stared down at him. He didn't break their gaze as she pressed her forehead against the window, her breath condensing on the glass. A slow, easy smile spread over her face. She nodded her head toward the downstairs entry.

His blood surged. What the hell? He didn't really feel like hanging with the guys. And he'd kick himself if he didn't check in with Troy. *I'm just going up there to check on the kid.*

Oh, what a load of crap.

Easy, boy. He had to remember how she had quit on a dime. How she casually lied to the kid. How she was completely hopeless with the napkins, and the soup, and the knife.

How she felt pressed against me.

How her lips felt on mine.

How she had inspired me to create maybe the most successful dish of my life, just by standing near me.

Scallops a la Tres Fleurs
Seared diver scallops in wild mushroom sauce with
braised endive and roasted asparagus
—JAMES LACHANCE, *The Meal of a Lifetime*

Chapter 11

She met him at the apartment door dressed in a black T-shirt and black skirt, her feet bare, her hair long and loose.

"You're late," she said.

Another surge of adrenaline shot through him. So much for small talk. "I got held up."

She moved into the apartment, her hips swinging as she moved away from him.

Each rock of her hips sent him spinning into a tighter and tighter orbit.

"I thought you wouldn't come." She turned to him and lifted off her shirt in one swift movement.

"Where's Troy?" He knew her intentions—and his own—the instant he had met her eyes from the street below. Still, he had expected . . . hell, who cared about expectations? This woman wasn't about expectations. She was pure impulse.

"Troy's gone to his friend's for the night. Study sleepover. Which of course is a lie. But the kid's been so good, I let him go. I think his girlfriend's mom is out of town. He deserves a little fun, too." By the time she finished her speech, she stood before him in only her skirt, her bra on the floor behind her. "You threw out my carrots."

He watched her step out of her skirt. "Carrots?" The skirt joined the bra.

"Carrots," her black lace thong said. Er, she said. Where was he? What was he doing? "There are starving bunnies, you know, who would have killed for those." She carefully laid herself onto the couch.

"Bunnies?" She was long and curved and glowing in the soft light. He was going to join her discarded clothes on the floor in a minute if he didn't pull himself together.

"Forget the bunnies. I forgive you. Finish what you started this morning, carrot boy."

"Oh, right. Carrots." His head cleared briefly. "Listen, I still need you front of house. Until your knife-work improves."

"Don't pretend you came here to talk restaurant. I'll bus. Whatever. Who cares? Just shut up and make love to me. Now."

Now, there was an excellent idea. His heart was beating a mad rhythm of desire. He studied her elaborate tattoos while he let it calm. A snake curled around her upper arm and down to her wrist. A rose vine curved around her thigh. A band of black twists wound around her ankle. She rolled over to reveal an elaborate dragon at the small of her back.

It was the sexiest thing he'd ever seen on the sexiest woman he'd ever seen. Her gently curved back, the dragon, the naked skin peeking from between its bold black and green lines as if she were sheltering behind the protection of the beast. His blood crashed through his body so violently, he could hear the torrent. *Try to stop me, dragon.*

He dropped to his knees in front of the couch. She laid her head on her hands, watching him, a playful look in her eyes. He traced the scrolled dragon with his finger, and a smile curled her lips, daring him further.

As if he could stop now even if he had wanted to.

He traced the dragon with his tongue, enjoying her murmurs of delight, holding her hips down firmly so she couldn't squirm.

The scent of clove and cinnamon, underlain by carrot, swirled around her. He rolled her over, and she complied willingly, arching her back like a cat.

"How did you know I'd come?" His voice felt thick with desire.

"I'm a Gypsy," she said, pulling him toward her. "We're psychics. We know everything."

The urge to taste her further flooded him. "So you know what I intend to do to you?"

"I sure hope so."

His body flared and he kissed her, and her warmth spread through him, carried by a sea of images: the fire dragon on her back, the fire of her black eyes, the smoke of her swollen lips. Each memory ignited its own spark until he was inflamed with her. *Her, in his restaurant like a vision, snow in her wild hair. A mirage,* he had thought on first sight. *Too good to be true.*

He pulled himself from her, just to check, and the bliss

on her face matched his. *Sweet God.* He kicked the coffee table out of his way with a swift jab of his foot. *What's wrong with a mirage? Something temporary. Something unreal. Magic. Is that so bad?*

Being fully clothed with a naked woman, especially this naked woman, was unbearably sexy. The power of it surged through his veins. He wouldn't undress. He'd pleasure her, holding himself back. He'd break through her facade of power and control. If he gave her more, he'd never see her again. He knew that as surely as he knew that he had to see her again. All of her.

He traced her body, from toe tip to forehead, with his finger, an inventory of smooth flesh and curves. Then he turned to her breasts. His finger circled each nipple; then he bent down to take them one by one into his mouth. She let her hands run through his hair as she threw back her head with a soft moan, then pulled him to her. He hadn't wanted a woman this badly since . . . when? Maria, his last girlfriend? But that was different. Maria had been all lust. With this woman, even though she was sexy as hell, he felt something more intense—

"Stop thinking about other women," she said.

"Stop reading my mind." Could she read his mind? He didn't believe in psychics.

She laughed, using the break to shimmy out of her panties so she lay before him completely naked and exposed. "Every man thinks of all women past, present, and future when he fucks. You're imprinted. You can't help yourself." She lay luxuriously against the couch cushions, her hands raised above her head, her hair splayed on the pillow behind her.

She reached behind the pillows and pulled out a condom. She tossed it to him. "Nothing better than a house with a teenage male. These are stashed everywhere. Now, c'mere."

He regarded her flashing, laughing eyes; her give-me-more mouth; her hips and legs like there was no tomorrow. Forget the stay-dressed plan—he had to have her. Now. This was too much control, even for him. He stood and unbuckled his jeans. Then stopped. What was he doing? She was temporary, not the least bit serious.

If I make love to her, she'll leave.

He thought back to the last time he'd given everything for her, throwing out Bob. It had scared her to death and she fled. Was that it? If he reached out, she'd be gone?

"Want to wash up to your elbows first?" she teased.

And that was when he saw it. The same flash he had seen when he first saw her in his restaurant. It was the fleeting expression of pain behind her eyes. *She's lying. She doesn't want to make love. She wants a reason to leave me.* She was as alone in this world as Troy.

As me.

And she hated it.

He was standing, his jeans half undone. His busboy's condom in his hand. He looked around the apartment— the place was filthy, small, dark, awful. What the hell was he doing?

He had missed all the signs of his busboy needing a hand, and even if he had seen them, he wouldn't have had the first idea how to help the boy. But maybe here, with Amy, he could redeem himself. Show her something human and lasting. Show her something of herself before she ran off like the alley cats he fed every morning before anyone else showed at Les Fleurs.

He rebuttoned his jeans. "Tonight, I just want to hold you."

She eyed his erection pushing against his jeans. "Liar."

He felt the pain of not making love to her like a knife wound, but he didn't care. "Lying is good," he said. "A mysterious Gypsy told me that."

"She lied," she said, but she rearranged to make room for him when he lowered himself onto the couch. He wrapped her in his arms and stroked her naked skin, glowing in the moonlight. He was nuts. Completely, madly insane. If his crew ever found out about this, he'd never hear the end of it.

And he didn't care. He inhaled her hair, pulling her closer. To his surprise, she complied. It was late, and he saw that she was as tired as he was. He tried to memorize this moment—the taste, the smell, the feeling. *She was seared diver scallops in wild mushroom sauce with braised endive and roasted asparagus.* If he could get diver's scallops this late in the season, it could be on the specials menu tomorrow.

An entrée. She had inspired an entrée, just lying naked in his arms. This was more than the Josie first course. This was amazing. Unheard of. And they hadn't gotten past foreplay.

"What are you smiling about?" she asked.

He kissed her. "Nothing. Just you."

"Enough with the lies." She whacked him on the chest, but her body had softened, and he could feel sleep overtaking her as she settled her head on his shoulder. "You're thinking about your stupid restaurant. I know what turns you on. I'm no dummy."

The melting scallops in his imagination and the sensation of her melting beside him conflated into one sensation. Was she right? Did the food turn him on? With
a few more dishes this inspired, Les Fleurs could get a
third star.

"Don't think you're getting away with this," she said to
him. "You owe me."

"Well, you'll just have to stick around, then, to collect,
won't you?" he said.

And she bit him on the shoulder. Hard.

"Well, well, well, what do we have here?"

James's eyes sprang open. It was pitch dark outside
the windows, but the single light on in the hall clearly
outlined Troy, a silhouette in the doorway.

Oh, hell. He had fallen asleep. James reached down, relieved to find himself covered in a pink comforter, alone.
The blanket smelled like stale beer. He nodded at Troy
and sat up. "I thought you were at a friend's house." He
felt stiff and sour from sleeping in his clothes.

Where was Amy? He looked at his watch. It was six-
thirty in the morning. He was going to miss the fish man
from Anthony's if he didn't get on it. He needed those
scallops.

"Why would you think that?" Troy plopped onto the
end of the couch.

"Because"—he paused—"never mind. I gotta get to
the Fleurs and call Anthony."

Troy reached around behind the pillows. "As I suspected. You owe me a condom."

James pushed out from under the comforter. He was
starting to rack up the IOUs. He needed liquid. He made

his way to the crappy kitchen and opened the fridge. Yellow industrial-strength mustard, off-brand ketchup, neon-green relish—all the major condiment groups. He shut the door.

Troy followed him into the room. The kid was already dressed for school. Ripped jeans and a faded, purple, stretched-out T-shirt. He looked younger without his busboy uniform. "Watch out for her, Chef," Troy said. "She lies. She said she knew my mom, knew where she was, but she doesn't."

James regarded the boy. His hair was still tousled from sleep. "So why don't you kick her out? This is your place." *And then she could stay with me.*

"She's not all bad," Troy said with a shrug. "I'm just saying she lies. That's all. I still like her. Plus, she's genuine Rom. I can't kick her out. It's a tribal thing."

It tugged at him to see this tender, vulnerable side of his busboy. *His mom's a flake, so he'll trust anyone who'll pull mom duty, even if she's a liar.* Troy couldn't be over fifteen. But fifteen. Hell, when James was fifteen, he was living in his dad's four-thousand-square-foot Connecticut Tudor with servants and cooks and chauffeurs.

But he knew, as did Troy, that it was all shit without a mother.

"I gotta split," Troy said.

"Me too," James said. "I'll get us a cab."

"Nah. I like to walk. That's why I leave so early. Gives me time to think."

Again, James's gut tightened. *To think about his shitty life.* He hoped Roni would show soon. But then would Amy leave? Or had he convinced her to stay? It bothered him that he still didn't know why exactly she was hanging around, waiting for Roni.

His hand went to the bite mark he was sure was imprinted on his shoulder. Yeah, he'd made some kind of impression on her. She sure had made one on him. "I ought to say good-bye to Amy." He went down the hall and looked into the bedroom, where Amy slept, coiled deep under the comforter, looking serene. Peaceful, even. James realized that awake, she never looked this way. She looked like she might have found a place for herself here with Troy.

With me, too?

James bent and kissed her cheek lightly, but she only moaned and curled deeper into the covers.

As James and Troy walked through the early morning chill, it occurred to James that a stranger might mistake the two of them for father and son. But the stranger wouldn't know the part where Troy had caught him splayed out like a fillet on the couch. He hoped the boy would keep his mouth shut.

Troy stopped in front of the CVS at the corner of Nineteenth and Chestnut, startling James out of his thoughts. "This is where I leave you, my man."

"See you at five o'clock. Sharp. We have almost a hundred fifty on the books tonight, so don't be late."

Troy nodded, but neither of them moved.

Troy kicked a stone on the ground.

"Why is Amy waiting for your mother?" James asked.

"I dunno." Troy met James's eye. "I'm not worried or anything. Not scared, I mean. Just, the lies. You gotta be careful."

"I think Amy's okay." James couldn't support his belief, but Troy nodded.

"I think so, too. Sometimes. But, you know. Anyway, I gotta split."

The boy shot him some sort of hand gesture—three fingers outstretched.

James had no idea what it meant, but he flashed it back. It felt kind of father-and-sonish, like they had some sort of inside signal, a secret communication.

James blushed. What was he thinking? He wasn't the kid's dad. Never would be. He was glad Troy had already turned away and started down the street. It was too stupid; fathers didn't take advice from their kids about their sex lives. That hand signal probably meant *old guys suck.*

I have no idea what goes on between fathers and sons besides disgust and neglect.

He watched Troy disappear around the corner. *Go get 'em, kid,* he thought.

Maybe tonight he'd let Troy help with the stock.

Only when a person decides to cook for others does he discover the true meaning of the act.
—JAMES LaCHANCE, *The Meal of a Lifetime*

Chapter 12

Amy padded out of Roni's bedroom and glanced at the kitchen clock. Twelve-thirty in the afternoon. Troy and James were both gone, and she was starved. She opened the fridge.

Ketchup. She loved ketchup. Especially Pathmark brand, which was pleasantly sweet. She pulled out the bottle and rooted around in the cabinets. Ritz crackers. A little stale, but no mold. She assembled a cracker/ketchup sandwich and ate, washing it down with splashes of water from her cupped hands held under the tap.

Okay, now that she'd eaten, she could think about what an idiot she'd been last night. She closed her eyes and tried to center herself.

What have I done?

James had ambushed her. He had caught her by surprise. He looked so good down on the sidewalk, looking up at her. So she had decided—*idiot, idiot, idiot*—they could just screw around. Keep it light. She wouldn't even give him time to talk. She'd seduce him, get him out of her system, and then move on.

But then he ruined everything.

Why'd he have to ruin everything?

When he stopped, it was like death.

It was like heaven.

Gah! She shoved more crackers into her mouth. Drank more water out of her cupped hands. Then sat at the kitchen table and let her forehead fall to its cool surface.

Maddie led me here to fall in love with James. Amy had suspected it before, but she was sure of it after last night. She had seen people try to resist their soul mates, and it was always like this. They let down their guard for a split second, and they were lost. Devoured. In Romany, the language of the Gypsies, *I love you* literally meant "I eat you." And this man had swallowed her whole. Stupid, beautiful chef, she was missing him already.

"Oprah, what am I going to do?"

"Buy the man a ring?" Oprah nibbled at the corner of a cracker, then put it down. "Then let him teach you to cook. Forget Maddie. It's all settled!"

"Be serious, please!" Amy knocked her head against the table, but it didn't work. She couldn't shake the warmth of James out of her system.

"You're imagining things. You have no proof that Maddie has anything to do with this. You have no proof that he's your One True Love."

"Except for the way I feel. I've got to find Roni."

"Then quit stuffing your face and lolling around feeling sorry for yourself and get to work!"

Right. No time to think about that man's hands on her

hips. The look in his eyes as he devoured her. The intense tenderness when he told her no.

No one *ever* said no to her.

Last night, she had laid with him for hours, unable to sleep, her head on his chest, listening to him breathe deep and even. It felt so good to be held by a man like James. A man who wasn't a jerk. A man she wasn't even conning.

Which is why she panicked and fled to Roni's bedroom. Terrified of what she had felt in his arms. *Leave first, before he can leave you.*

She had never felt so at peace with a man.

Which is why I have to find Roni, get Maddie, and get the hell out of here.

Oh, please don't let James be my One True Love. If he was, and she fell, Gypsy lore said Maddie would be forbidden to her forever. She had to think of Natasha. Think of Magda. She had to think of herself and her future.

An hour later, Amy pushed through the doors of the dusty pawnshop. The store was empty but was so cluttered that Amy had to turn sideways to move down the narrow alley to the counter. A full set of leather Gucci luggage brushed her legs. Luggage. Now there was something that no self-respecting Gypsy would ever carry. Wear what you need on your back, then steal the rest when you arrive.

"Hello? Anybody home?" Amy leaned over the counter.

Footsteps, then a man. Potbelly. Bald spot. Whiff of Budweiser cologne.

In a word, perfect.

He looked her over lazily. "Help ya?"

Amy could tell from his sleepy blue eyes that she had him at hello. No one better for info than a horny middle-aged male. It almost wasn't fair.

A memory of James rose in her mind, his eyes on hers.

Oh, for crying out loud. I'm not flirting; I'm conducting business, she chided herself, mortified that she felt responsibility toward James.

"I'm looking for gold," she said, fingering the feathers on an Indian headdress hanging over the cash register. The man didn't need to know she was really looking for the town's most desperate Gypsies so she could get a lead on Roni. And the most desperate Gypsies always came to pawnshops—standard operating procedure from the Gypsy survival manual. The closest shop to Roni's house would mark the beginning of her trail.

Amy looked around at the amazing display of electric guitars. Musicians were even worse at keeping their money than Gypsies. Too bad there was no musician survival guide.

The man behind the counter hesitated, sucking his lips to his teeth with an annoying chirping sound.

Amy leaned forward to study the digital cameras and elaborately carved knives in the counter display case. A little more forward. An inch more. Perfect.

The man gaped into her cleavage.

Amy gave him her best bedroom-slow smile and nodded.

He rushed to unlock the display case and fished out a tray of bling-bling chains and diamond rings.

Amy barely glanced at it. "I was looking for something a little more exotic." She looked at him as if he, with his fringe of graying-yellowed hair and wet, pale eyes, was the most exotic hunk of man she'd ever laid eyes on. "What's your name?" she asked.

"Um."

In his mind, he was already making love to her. She urged him on with her eyes. *That's right. Right there. I like it like that, you big strong man.* "Bubba? Buddy?"

"Oh. What? No. Um. Dave."

"Davey, I want to see jewelry with a woman's head in profile. Or anything with a horseshoe that has the ends pointing up. I want a piece that has raised flowers or filigree. Do you know what that is, Davey? Filigree?"

"Sure. Um—"

"It's twisted metal, honey. Metal that winds around and around and around." She demonstrated by taking his hand and drawing the twist on his palm with one bright red fingernail. She described as many Gypsy motifs as she could think of until she could see the sweat rise on his palm. *Bingo.*

It's not cheating on James because this is fake. It's a means to an end. It's okay. But then why did her stomach feel so constricted?

"I have something, but I can't—that is, I promised—" Davey stumbled.

"Who did you promise, sweetie?" Amy had to use every ounce of her energy not to vault over the counter and throttle the guy. "Here's the thing, darling. I don't want the jewelry."

"No?"

I want you, you gorgeous specimen of pure testosterone, she said with her eyes. With her mouth she said, "I want to know, *if* you have a piece like that, who it belongs to, and if she said anything about when she was coming back or where she was going."

"Um."

Amy sighed. This was getting tiresome.

Dave looked doubtful but willing to be persuaded. No Gypsy wanted to give up their jewelry; that brought on the worst rotten luck. *Been there. Done that.* So whoever had brought in whatever it was Davey didn't want to give up had made him promise to try to hold on to it. Good. A desperate Gypsy was a Gypsy Amy could work with.

"My promise is golden if I seal it with this." Amy reached over the counter and grabbed poor Davey by the scruff of his shirt.

"I have a gun—" he began.

She winked. "I bet you do, big boy. I bet it's a big one." She was about to press her lips to his, when she thought of James. Something stirred in her gut. Guilt? Who cared if she kissed this slob for info? Certainly not James. Plus, she didn't owe him a thing.

And yet.

She pulled Davey closer. She could see the individual beads of sweat drip down his forehead. *Kiss the fool and get this done.*

But she couldn't.

Oh, hell.

She let Davey go. "Tell me who gave you this jewelry," she said angrily. Her anger was completely at herself for wimping out because of James, but Davey didn't know that. He turned white, then red, then started to talk.

Two minutes later, she left the store with an address and directions scribbled on her palm. Now she just had to find this Madame Prizzo who had come in with Roni to sell Davey the jewelry.

She'd know everything she needed to know about Roni by the end of the day.

The old Gypsy who had helped Roni pawn the gold, Madame Prizzo, lived in a trailer wedged under the Schuylkill expressway just outside of Philadelphia, exit 338. Follow the abandoned R6 train tracks; veer off past the cemetery, down the abandoned streambed and to the river.

What a mess. And that wasn't just the trailer. Madame Prizzo must have been eighty, and she looked every day of it and then some.

"Why are you looking for Roni, my child?" the old woman cooed. She collected skulls, and they covered every surface. Birds, squirrels, dogs . . . humans? Yep, in the corner, its dome shiny as if it'd been rubbed repeatedly for good luck.

Amy shivered and focused on a tiny bird skull. Its bones were like spiderwebs. "She's got something that belongs to me. I want it back."

"Ah . . ." Madame Prizzo closed her eyes and touched her fingers to her temples.

Oh, give me a break. Did this woman really think Amy would fall for pretend-Gypsy hocus-pocus?

"She has something you desire," the old woman sang.

No shit. Amy had to get to Les Fleurs to chop, a task she was getting disturbingly fond of. Was James right? She could learn the restaurant biz? "Roni has a spirit-voice that used to belong to me."

Madame Prizzo's eyes went wide.

Good. The woman seemed genuinely surprised. Amy waited.

"I don't know where Roni is, but the spirit-voice I can find." She held out a shaking hand holding a smudged business card: MADAME ALEXANDRIA PRIZZO, CHANNELER. UNDER I-76, EXIT 338. FOLLOW THE SIGNS. FOLLOW YOUR SOUL.

Could this old hag really channel Maddie? Now, there was an intriguing thought.

Amy studied the card. *Madame Alexandria Prizzo.* This woman was one of the most renowned channelers on the East Coast. Amy tried to keep her face neutral as she took in the new possibilities opening before her. If she talked to Maddie, maybe she wouldn't have to find Roni. Hope rose in Amy's gut, then fell. Maddie had never said a word that wasn't a name.

Except once, unforgettably, when she said, "Good-bye."

Why would Maddie start talking now, even to Madame Alexandria Prizzo?

But what if she did? Amy carefully put down the bird skull. The bones that hinged the beak blew in the breeze of the small movement, as if the bones themselves could still fly. "Okay. Let's do it."

"Cash. One thousand dollars."

Amy expressed proper shock and indignation, although she wasn't really in the mood to bargain.

"Okay. For you"—Madame Prizzo took Amy's hand— "five hundred."

"I don't have it on me." Amy had left her stash of tips at Roni's, taped under the silverware drawer. It wasn't even close to five hundred dollars. "You get me Maddie now, I'll bring the cash tonight." To come up with the money, she'd have to resteal the jade flower she had put back after chopping carrots with James.

The old woman smiled. She had four brown teeth interspersed between the yellow ones. "You bring the cash, *then* I'll get you your precious voice. Friday. Midnight. We do it then."

Amy rolled her eyes at the notion of midnight. Imbuing the proceedings with details like *midnight* was straight out of the con-a-gadje handbook. Plus, making her wait until Friday was pure con. The passage of time heightened the suspense and the desire to know. She'd raise the price back up to a grand when Amy showed up on Friday.

Amy couldn't stand the charade another moment. "You don't have to play Gypsy with me," Amy said. She pulled out her pendant and flashed it at Madame Prizzo. "Let's do it now. I'm good for it."

Madame Prizzo studied the pendant while Amy enjoyed the shock on the old woman's face.

Then it was Amy's turn to be shocked when the old woman reached into her mouth and, with an effortless click, pulled out her fake teeth to reveal a gorgeous set of pearly, bleached-white teeth that smiled up at Amy. "Why didn't you say you were Rom in the first place?" Her voice had lost most of its rasp, although it was still rough from cigarettes. She strode across the trailer, discarding padding as she went—her enormous heaving bosom, her butt pads, her hump.

By the time she had reached the opposite side of the trailer to flick on the overhead lights, Madame Prizzo was the paragon of vigor and health. "Call me Alex." She moved from surface to surface, blowing out candles.

"When Davey called and said he sent you, he didn't mention you were Rom. Probably had no clue."

"By the time I left Davey, I don't think he knew who he was himself," Amy bragged.

Madame Prizzo nodded in approval as she unwrapped layers of skirts to expose a pair of tight gym leggings. She shrugged out of her black polyester grandma blouse to reveal a body-hugging white athletic jersey. The last thing to go was the gray wig, which Madame Prizzo—Alex—arranged carefully on the human skull. The stylish, peroxide-blond buzz cut made the transformation from hag-Gypsy to lunch-at-the-club Grandma Alex almost complete. "I play tennis this afternoon with the girls. In fact, I ought to be on my way there now. We're getting Chinese takeout after. Lunch special from Susanna Foo. Do you play doubles? What did you say your name was?" She was bending over the sink, washing off her stage makeup.

"Amy Burns. From Baltimore." She waited for her name to register, but apparently Madame Prizzo had never heard of her. Guess she didn't watch *Oprah*. She shook off her disappointment. "The channeling," she reminded Madame Prizzo.

The older woman pulled her BlackBerry out of a Coach purse that had been stashed under the sink and pushed a few buttons. "I have twenty minutes till we lose the court. No time now. Come back tonight. Why don't you meet me at my condo downtown? I have a place with a view of Rittenhouse Square. This place is just for clients. Oh, no, shoot. I have a channeling with a manicurist from Wayne here at ten. So meet me here, afterward. I want to discuss Roni. It's very worrying, the voice. It's all we've been talking about for days, except for—" She stopped, then pulled on a pair of Nike tennis shoes and laced them up. "I couldn't channel the voice for Roni. I tried but no dice. But if it was your spirit-voice before it came to Roni, maybe it will show for you. It's worth a try. What does the voice want, anyway? All those names. It's maddening. I told Roni to go to Pittsburgh to meet with an expert. We raised the money for her to go by selling her gold."

"Does the voice sound like an old woman? English accent? Did Roni say?" Amy asked, trying to catch Madame Prizzo in a lie.

"No. She said it sounded young, kind of singsong. She didn't mention British."

Amy felt dizzy. She tried to hide the emotions that were flooding her by staring out the dingy window into the gray winter sky. Everything she had suspected was being confirmed. It was one thing to guess at it, but another to know it: Roni had Maddie, and she didn't know what to do with her. None of the local Roms did. So she had set off for expert advice.

She was so close.

Which meant it was doubly important to keep James far, far away. At least until Roni could tell Amy the name of her One True Love.

Amy looked at her watch. "I gotta split. I'll come after work. I'll get here as quick as I can."

"Great. C'mon. I'll give you a ride back to town."

Amy followed Madame Prizzo to her car, a white Mercedes hidden behind a mountain of discarded railroad ties.

As Amy climbed into Madame Prizzo's spotless car, she thought about how it was all starting to come together.

So why did she feel so empty and gray?

Roni watched Amy get into Madame Prizzo's car, then stepped out from behind the trailer. Her fingers were numb from cold, but they were shaking from fear. It was all starting to come together. So why did she feel so terrified?

Was it because Amy had found Davey and then Madame Prizzo in the blink of an eye? That was so not part of the plan. Amy was smart. Terrifyingly smart.

Especially with men. Seeing James leave her apartment this morning had shocked Roni to her toes. Again, *not* part of the plan.

Roni had spent the morning trying to figure out if James being with Amy mattered. She reread whole sections of *The Art of the Con*, her new Bible, finally finding what she was looking for: *The intended mark must be as vulnerable as possible.*

No woman could feel vulnerable with James by her side. Not that Roni would know from experience; James had never given her more than a glance. Jealousy at Amy's easy power over James filled her. Roni never got the good ones. She got the scum who said they loved her and then split, leaving her with nothing.

Her hand patted her stomach.

Well, not nothing. Something. Something she had to hold on to this time.

Which was why it was time to bring Madame Prizzo into the con. She had hoped she wouldn't have to do that, because then she'd have to split her earnings. She and Troy and the baby needed everything. But Roni knew she was floundering. Amy was too smart. She had maneuvered into Troy's and James's lives like a shadow, pushing Roni out as if she'd never even existed. Then, Amy had found Madame Prizzo as if a trail of breadcrumbs had been left for her. Amy was like her complete opposite, the one who got what she wanted, fearlessly.

Oh, stop feeling sorry for yourself. Amy was the enemy. She had to remember that.

Madame Prizzo would know what to do.

At least Roni hoped so, as she couldn't stand this tension, or her shaking hands, much longer.

Chapter 13

Amy pushed through the front door of Les Fleurs at four thirty-seven, the exact same moment James pushed through the kitchen door into the dining room. John-John was behind him, carrying samples of the night's specials. Dan and Stu were already waiting at the huge back table with other servers. They had just finished the giant pre-service staff meal, but you wouldn't know it by the way everyone stared hungrily at the newly brought food. The busers and runners, who were standing around the bar being lectured by Elliot, all descended on the table like animals drawn by the smell.

"Late," James said to Amy as the plates were placed on the table.

Sexy, Amy thought, watching James in action. The contrast between his bleached chef's whites and his dark olive skin made her want him more than ever. Why was this man always in clothes?

The reverence of his staff vibrated around the room, all eyes on James and his food. The man towered above everyone, not just because of his height, but because of his intensity and focus. He was the star of his own show.

Amy missed that feeling. She was a nobody runner. Or was she? At least she had something with James. But what?

A heat of a blush crept up her neck, betraying her unease. She couldn't get a read on how James was feeling about last night, but to her dismay, she cared. Deeply. She willed away the tension in her stomach. He was fun. He was sexy. *He told me no. He held me tight.*

The amazing smells wafting off the night's special dishes swirled around her. She hadn't eaten since the ketchup and crackers that morning, and her hunger made her feel even edgier than she already felt at the memory of his hands on her hips. His mouth on hers.

Elliot ran through the special guests and large parties expected that night; then James reviewed the appetizer specials. Amy didn't hear a word of it. What if she could speak to Maddie tonight? What if Maddie spoke in sentences, words other than names? It would be freakish, like hearing a baby sing opera. Maybe this whole thing was a terrible idea. What if Maddie said something Amy didn't want to hear? What if she said James wasn't her One True Love and Amy could have him, no strings attached?

What if she said James was her One True Love and she had to give up her power forever if she wanted to have him?

"We're doing the Josie again," James said. His lips tried not to quirk into a smile as his eyes met Amy's.

"Awesome," Dan said. "Josie's huge. I can barely walk it across the floor without getting molested."

"I think it'll be even better today," James said. "I have some new ideas about making the sauce a little smokier, more complex." His eyes were smokier, more complex.

He likes me, too.

"And, the entrée special is divers scallops," James said. He pointed to a plate on the center of the table. Elliot passed it, everyone spearing a scallop greedily. "Pan-seared with wild mushrooms, Belgian endives on the side, braised with fish stock, butter, vermouth, and sugar."

Stu chewed thoughtfully, then swallowed. "Hey, you get laid last night, man? 'Cause this is good!"

Dan ate carefully. "Oh, yes. It's been a while, Chef. Spill. Who's the babe?"

James met Amy's eyes. The entire staff turned to her, and she felt herself go hot with embarrassment.

But Dan misunderstood her blush. "Oh. Hey. Sorry, Ames. Just. Nothing. We forgot there was a woman present," Dan sputtered. He was bright red.

The staff seemed to come around to Dan's misunderstanding that they were embarrassing Amy by talking about sex, and they all hemmed and hawed and looked away.

But Dan went on. "Aw, hell, if she works here, she ought to know that James names all his dishes after women. He gets his inspiration from, well—"

"Fucking?" Amy asked sweetly. She was thrilled that she had inspired another dish—without fucking. Almost thrilled enough to forget her unease at not knowing what was going on behind James's inscrutable expression. "I'd like to hear about James's lay, too." She reached in and took a scallop with her fingers. She leaned her head back and dropped the morsel into her mouth. The flesh melted on her tongue as the flavors exploded one by one. James watched her. "She must have been very, very good, James."

"It's all right there. Soft, trembling flesh. Amazingly fresh. Almost raw."

"What's the code name, Chef?" Stu asked. "Lulu? Betty? Who is she? Do we know her?"

"My little secret. Let's call her"—he hesitated—"Fiona."

Amy felt her body heat down to her toes. Fiona was her second favorite Pussycat. She snatched the last scallop just before a buser got it. The man shot her the evil eye. But Amy didn't care. The scallop was so luxurious, so sensuous. Her whole body went hot with desire. *Was this what sex was like for a man?*

Was this what sex would be like with James? She wanted to find out; Maddie could go to hell.

Amy fell into a chair at that unexpected thought. *Did she want James more than Maddie?* Oh, she had to watch herself. He was just a man. Maddie was her life, her power, her world.

Elliot took over. He ran through most of the server sections for the night, then turned to Amy. "Ready for your own table tonight? Number eight. And run for Stuey and Danno. And bus with Troy."

Elliot met James's eye, and Amy knew that James had given her the table. A thrill ran through her, chased by apprehension.

"You'll get it," Stu said, catching her uncertainty. "It took Danno here at least a week to learn what a reduction was."

"Yeah. No sweat," Dan added. "What's a reduction again?"

Stu swatted him and James looked appalled.

I'm not going to be here another week, Amy thought. *I've got to grab Maddie and go.* And yet, she still wanted to know what a reduction was. She wanted to get it right.

What if for once in her life she could get something right besides conning people?

"Okay, kids, back to work," James said. "Let's get this room ready." James rose and Amy tried not to watch the length of him uncurl from the chair. *Lovely.* "Sell the hell out of Fiona tonight. I got a deal on scallops, but they won't keep."

"Not a long-term relationship, huh?" Dan asked.

"We'll see," James said. He looked right at Amy. "I hope so, but you know how some dishes are. They come and go on a whim."

"If I just sleep with him once, to get him out of my system, is that so bad?" Amy asked her imaginary Oprah. They were at the barista station near the kitchen door, checking the glassware for spots.

"That makes no sense at all, hon. But, then, you've never been one to follow reason; why start now?"

"Because this is serious. I can't love this man. Oh, don't give me that look, Oprah. You'd never give up your power for a man."

Oprah clamped her lips shut. They were silent for a while. But just as Oprah was about to respond, Stu walked into the space Oprah was occupying, and the imaginary host disintegrated into nothing.

*   *   *

"You okay?" he asked. "You look like you saw a ghost."

Amy was back at the restaurant. "I think I'm allergic to scallops."

Stu shook his head. "On the contrary. I believe scallops suit you to a T. Congratulations are in order. An entrée so fast is a record, Fiona."

Amy clamped her teeth together to keep her mouth from flying open in surprise.

Stu must have misunderstood her rigid jaw, because he patted her hand sympathetically. "Jamesey didn't spill. But I'm no dummy. I notice these things. That's what happens when you're happily married for twenty years with a kid about to go into college. You watch other people. They're way more interesting. My life is stable and dull."

"It was a one-night stand. Not even," Amy said. A pang of curiosity shot through her at the thought of stable and dull. Stu might have been the happiest-looking man she'd ever seen. Except for James, last night.

Last night. James holding her. She had felt so totally . . . stable.

And it had felt good. Was that what it felt like to be normal? It was like a secret no one had ever let on to her about: *being held was better than sex.*

No way. She was losing it. Completely losing it.

"He's downstairs in the walk-in," Stu said. "If you want to keep it going."

"Did he put you up to this?" *I hope so.* Amy wasn't sure what to make of Stu. With his bald head and paunchy middle, he looked like the kind of nice, beer-drinking, everybody's-best-friend captain of the bowling team.

"A happy chef makes happy diners, and happy diners leave good tips."

"So I should fuck the chef in the fridge so we make more money? Is that what you're saying?"

"Take one for the team, so to speak," Stu said.

Stu had a little more edge than he showed in his soft, blue eyes.

Don't sleep with James for yourself; do it for everyone else. Now, there was an excellent rationalization she could latch on to.

Stu went on, "I'm also saying that James is a good guy, and we all depend on him. And I could be wrong, but I think you might be good for him. Let me tell you something about James that you might have noticed: He never leaves this place. Comes at the break of dawn. Leaves after midnight. It's good for us; we make a killing. But it's not normal. A man needs more than that kind of life."

Amy didn't want to think about what James needed. She was here to get what she needed. And yet, she couldn't shake the idea of James needing her. It felt so warm and right. "Does everyone know everything about everyone in this place?"

"Yup." Stu smiled at her. "Red thong first day here," he added, winking at her, in case she needed proof.

"I'm gonna kill James—"

"Nah. Denny was down there for cannelloni beans, and he caught the show. Let me tell you, the kitchen boys have been way happier than usual to schlep to the walk-in. It's six-to-one today on green. When are you changing?"

"Bet a hundred on yellow. We'll split the winnings."

"Sixty-forty."

"Hey, it's my butt in the underwear."

"But it's my ass if I get caught cheating."

"Ten minutes from now, in the walk-in." Amy was anxious to get Stu on her side. They sat for a few minutes, inspecting the glasses. "So where is Roni?" Amy asked as casually as she could.

"That I don't know." He met her eyes. His face was creased with worry, like a dad.

Good, Roni didn't share Gypsy business with the staff. That was excellent news, since nothing else seemed to be a secret around this place.

More good news was that Stu had a soft spot. That might come in handy later. *He's smart but soft. Family man—a big weakness where kids and wives are concerned.* Stu was one of those rare men who truly seemed to love his wife and kid.

Amy imagined what that might be like, living with people you loved and who loved you back. Staying put, in one place, building a home. Stu was like an alien from another planet that she had never even wanted to visit. *Until she met James.* "Troy said she disappears a lot."

"Not a lot. Once since I've been here. But this time is weird."

"Why?" Amy strained to hear every detail. Maybe there'd be a clue. Something she could use to find Roni.

Stu stood up, smoothed back his nonexistent hair, then stroked his graying goatee. "Because this time there's a beautiful gypsy named Amy chasing her. And Amy seems kind of dangerous. You know what I mean? Shows up out of nowhere. Lies to the busboy and gets into his apartment. Gets the boss in her bed and inspires an entrée before we even learn her name." He held up a hand to stop her from responding. "I like you and so does James. Which means whatever you're up to, I don't want to know. I just want this restaurant to keep filling the seats so that I can send my kid to college and keep my beautiful wife the happiest woman in the world."

"Got it." Amy felt kind of sorry for the guy, wanting so little.

But she sure didn't feel sorry for his wife. Amy imagined what her life would be like if James felt that way about her.

Then she caught herself. What was wrong with her? She didn't need a man. She needed Maddie. Fast.

The first bite must contain the promise of the entire meal.
—JAMES LACHANCE, *The Meal of a Lifetime*

Chapter 14

Three hours to Madame Prizzo and Amy was hunting the walk-in for a hunk of cheese that had to reach room temperature before it could be served.

Getting sent to the walk-in during second service by the entremettier was like being sent to the spa. She loved diving into the swimming pool–cool noiselessness of the tiny room. Everyone upstairs was running around like organic, roasted chickens ($29) with their heads cut off. But here she could breathe. She searched halfheartedly for the Stilton she had been sent for. Cheese for dessert didn't make a lick of sense to her, especially warm cheese, but it seemed to be a big thing with Frenchie wannabes.

Third bin on the left, needs to come out now. Smelly, tinged blue, and crumbly. As if Amy didn't know what Stilton was. Which she didn't, although she wasn't about to admit that to anyone.

Or admit to anyone that she had had a few mishaps out

on the floor tonight. But with only one table to look after, it had gone better. She was managing the second seating, even though the loner guy who was ordering way more than any man had a right to eat was rude and curt, even when she flashed him some extra cleavage to make up for the late arrival of his second salad. Who ate two salads?

"This is Stilton." James appeared at the walk-in door. He grabbed a tub and showed her the scribbled label. Then with a devilish smile, he tossed it over his shoulder and pulled her into his arms. He smelled like scallion and seared beef and garlic. The tub of abandoned cheese clunked to a stop against the far shelves.

"Hmm . . . I sort of recall a man kissing me here once. Kinda looked like you."

"Did it feel like this?" His lips touched hers as gently as sleep, and she let her eyes flutter closed. *I'll just shut up now.* The restaurant was gone. Thoughts of missing Maddie were gone. The chilled air around them was gone, replaced with the warmth of him. His arms wrapped her like a blanket. He inhaled her deeply and murmured, "I've been waiting all night to kiss you. I haven't been able to see straight since last night. I can't even cook. All I can taste is you."

The strain of the night drained out of her. The strain of not knowing where Roni was or when she was coming back. The strain of still being bad at her job.

"Later tonight," he commanded. He was nibbling down her neck. "Come to my place. I'll be there by midnight. Well, by one. Two at the latest."

"So you can leave me hanging again? No thanks, James."

"I was a total idiot last night. A first-class moron. Tonight—"

"Can't," she protested. She had to be at Madame Prizzo's. "Maybe tomorrow—wait, can't. I have to stay with Troy."

"I'll come there, then. You can lie to me again about him being gone, and I'll pretend to believe you." He pulled her into him, her hips crushing against his. His hand moved down her back and he sighed. "All I've been thinking about since last night is you."

It was lovely to hear him like this and yet completely terrifying that his thoughts matched her own. If she could talk to Maddie tonight, then maybe she could find out more about this man.

His eyes flicked to his watch. "I have three and a half minutes until I've gotta fire four lambs for table nine."

"Then shut the hell up and get to work, Chef." She pulled him closer. The Stilton could wait. This was too good to pass up; after all, how could she possibly fall in love with him in three and a half minutes?

He freed her shirt from her skirt, and she shuddered from the warmth of his skin on hers. His hand found its way to her breast. "Oh, God. Amy." His mouth was on her neck.

"I know. I know. Just shut up." *This could be our last time together*. If Maddie came to Madame Prizzo tonight and told her that James was her One True Love, this was their last chance to be together. She had to be firm about that, no matter how he was making her feel right now, in his arms, his hands rough against her, pulling her close.

She had to keep her eyes on the prize. She pulled his

face to hers and kissed him hard. *Note to self: He is not the prize.*

His other hand drew her in to him, the length of him against her bringing her whole body to high alert. He murmured, "I can't get enough of you. I taste you all the time."

Why was he wearing so much clothing? His chef's shirt was like a straitjacket, his apron a ten-foot wall between her and what she needed from him. Needed so badly that she felt as if she might die without it. Now or never. "James."

"Sorry, lovebirds, but we've got a problem." It was Stu. The urgency in his tone broke them apart like a crowbar. "Scottie Jones is at table eight. We missed him 'cause it was Amy's table. He's halfway done with his entrée."

James fell away from her, and Amy experienced the parting like he'd ripped a piece off of her. James's face had gone pale. "Where's Joey?" James asked, his voice barely there. Joey was the maître d'. "Why didn't Joe spot him?"

Had James forgotten her? She was still panting with desire. Why didn't James tell Stu to get lost? They still had at least two minutes.

"Joey was in back taking a call, and Scottie strong-armed Eddie into seating him," Stu said.

"He snuck in," James said. He paced the walk-in like a tiger.

Hello? Who cares! But James's face was rigid with anger.

"Are we talking about the little jerk at table eight? That asshole—" Amy began.

"—is the most important food critic on the East Coast.

He writes for *Le Guide des Restaurants*. What's he back for?" James raged. He kicked the tub of Stilton, and it burst open against the wall. "My stars should be good for one more year at least."

Precious seconds were ticking away, but James was lost to her. A cloud of tension surrounded him. Whatever was going on here, James thought it was somehow her fault. She had missed Scottie, the bestower of magic stars, whoever the hell he was. But how could she have known that little tub of a man was important?

Stu spoke quietly. "I have heard a few rumors . . ."

James spun around. "Tell me." He jumped at Stu and instantly had him by the scruff of his shirt. "What did you hear? Why didn't you tell me?"

"I didn't think it was important."

James looked like he was going to slit Stu's throat. Amy backed away from the two men, feeling jilted and forgotten.

"What wasn't important?" James growled.

"Raul and John-John were whispering a few days ago," Stu began, "that some of the cooks from the Fondy were gossiping after hours at the Lido. They said that you pissed off someone important . . ." He paused and Amy didn't blame him. James looked like a devil. "That you"—Stu gulped as James tightened his grip—"that Bob guy. The guy who went nuts on Amy. He knew someone, an investor at the media group that runs *Les Guides*. They own some chalet time-share deal in France together." Stu paled as James's grip tightened. "Hey, I'm just the messenger."

James let him go, and Stu had to catch himself from falling.

Stu took a deep breath. This time he spoke quietly,

almost gently, like a doctor giving a regretful prognosis. "Bo over at the Fondy said the Bob dude is in tight with this investor guy." He didn't meet James's eyes. "I dunno. Maybe they sent Scottie because they were pissed at being thrown out."

Amy flashed back to James's fearful scene in the dining room, when he threw out Bob. *When he threw out Bob for her.* She tucked in her shirt.

"You should have told me," James said.

"Bo's an idiot." Stu defended himself, but he looked pale, as if now he understood that maybe Bo wasn't such an idiot after all.

James stood silently, emotions playing over his face like shadows.

Amy thought it through. No problem, it wasn't her fault. James would understand. He'd stand by her. Loyalty and teamwork and ships going down together and all that.

"When someone orders more than a human can eat, you gotta tell someone. Fast. That's how you know they're a critic."

Amy realized he was talking to her. The fury in James's voice drained her blood until she felt like a statue. "I didn't know—"

His flashing eyes met hers. "I knew you were bad luck the first time I met you. You've spent your whole life a loner con-woman, haven't you? I should have listened to Bob. I knew I should have thrown you out and not looked back. You know nothing about loyalty and teamwork. You're just here for yourself, and you don't give a damn about anyone else. How could you miss Scottie Jones?

I thought you were a Gypsy," James spat. "Could read minds, know-it-all."

Amy felt as if she'd been slapped. "Obviously not. I didn't know you were an asshole." *But maybe I found out just in time.* Trust and teamwork bullshit. James only cared about his restaurant. Three and a half minutes. She had almost thrown away her life for three and a half minutes of bliss. *If this asshole is my One True Love, I escaped his clutches just in time.*

They glared at each other as fiercely as they'd groped at each other just a moment before.

Stu coughed.

James jumped up, his nervous energy uncoiling his long body like a spring as he barked at Stu, "Tell me what he ordered. Tell me what's up next. Get Amy off the table! Get Dan on it, stat." He bounded up the stairs, calling back to Amy without stopping, "Don't just stand there like an idiot. Use your Gypsy powers to figure out what this asshole is gonna write about me, then cast a spell so we can fix it."

A deep pain sliced through Amy. She held her sides, trying to stay in one piece.

I will not break down in a fridge because a man I started to trust just totally dissed me. I will learn from this and never, ever make that mistake again.

Better to leave first. Better to leave before you got left. Staying meant helplessness. It meant losing her power. Hadn't her whole life taught her that?

God, this felt awful. She had experienced pain this intense only once before, at the Baltimore airport, watching her mother board the plane to India to find Emeril

Livingstone, the man Maddie said was her mother's One True Love. Amy had been six years old. Memories of that awful day assaulted her. Her sister, Cecelia, weeping by her side. Her father, forlorn, his head hanging. Her mother leaving with Jasmine, the baby, who was too young to be left behind.

But what about me? What did I do to deserve being left behind? "You shouldn't have told your mother that name, Amy," her father had muttered, over and over, looking at a spot on the filthy floor.

She had learned at that moment that lies were good; it was the truth that should be feared.

They had stood in that airport for hours, long after the plane had left, just standing, watching the rain fall, not having any idea where to go.

Better to leave first. Before everything falls apart. Before you do something so dumb, you ruin everything. Better to just keep moving.

She breathed deeply, trying to calm her pounding heart. A cold sweat coated her skin, and the chill was piercing.

If you leave before they can hurt you, you don't get hurt. If you leave before they can hurt you, you don't hurt them by screwing up.

Fuck you, Maddie. It was all Maddie's fault. Why did she want that stupid voice back, anyway? Her mother had abandoned her. Maddie had abandoned her. James had abandoned her. If she was going to chase one of them, why was she chasing Maddie? She should run from Maddie like she ran from the rest of them. Maddie was the cause of all her pain. Maddie had ruined her childhood by breaking up her parents with her prophecies, and now she had brought Bob, and Bob had brought Scottie, and Scottie was going to ruin James's restaurant.

I don't want you back, Maddie. Ever.

I want James.

But James had just dissed her to overstuff a little fat man. He was a slave to his restaurant. The man had never had a relationship in his life except with a side of beef.

God, she was so confused.

She felt arms around her. For a second, she thought it was James, and she almost wept with relief.

But it was Stu, who had come back to check on her. "It'll be all right, hon. Don't give up on him. It'll be okay. He'll come around. Shhh . . . It'll be all right."

That was when she realized she was crying.

"This is the best appetizer you've ever made," Scottie Jones said.

James nodded his thanks. He was furious at Scottie for sneaking in, and yet, he couldn't show his anger and risk alienating the little man.

"And these scallops. James, do you have a new sous-chef?" Scottie ran his finger around the rim of his plate and licked it.

"No." James felt everyone's eyes on him, the celebrity chef, especially Scottie's little beady ones.

"A new girlfriend?" Nothing, including James's methods, could stay a secret in the tight Philly restaurant scene.

James ignored Scottie's insinuation. Especially because it was true. "My stars should be good at least another year, Scottie. What are you doing here?"

"James, forget your two stars." Scottie leaned forward and grinned up at him.

James felt his stomach fall. His restaurant. His life. He felt it slipping away. Amy had brought this on. Amy was bad luck.

"Look, a couple of uptight, idiot suits sent me here to stir you up a bit. Guess you pissed off someone important. Nothing I can do about it. Corporate stuff, you know." He rolled his eyes. "But their plan is gonna backfire, James. Go for three stars, my boy. These new dishes are amazing. You're on to something here that could be huge. Philly never had anything like those scallops. I'll be back in a month. You have the talent. This is your chance. James, I could make you big. Huge. More famous than ever." Scottie sat back so Stu could place the next course on the table. "This is your old stuff, right? I've had this before. Compared to the scallops, James, c'mon! Think about what you want, boy. Think about what you could have. One month. I'll hold off the corporate offices till then."

To see into a man's soul, watch what he eats.
—JAMES LACHANCE, *The Meal of a Lifetime*

Chapter 15

Two hours later, Amy and Troy walked home, heads down against the cold. She planned on dropping the boy off at the apartment, then going to Madame Prizzo's.

She also planned on never going back to Les Fleurs. After Stu had ushered her out of the fridge and given her about a hundred tissues, one after the other, she had pulled herself together. She tried to explain to Stu that it wasn't James, that it was something else, something James reminded her of. Stu just nodded and handed her tissues and said that James was an asshole but he'd come around.

As if she wanted him to ever come around again.

It was so unlike her to break down, especially over ancient history. Since Maddie had left her, she'd been so fragile.

So there. She wasn't upset over James. He was nothing. A man. Just someone who triggered deeper emotions.

She and Troy waited at a corner for the light to change.

It seemed as if the whole town was depressed, brown and gray. Even the snowflakes that had started to descend around them were gloomy and heavy, melting to nothing the instant they landed, like kamikaze snowflakes.

"That dude Scottie can use his stars to kill a business faster than an E. coli outbreak," Troy said into the silence. He sounded worried.

Amy looked up at the cloud-darkened sky. "Who cares about a stupid critic?" *Or a stupid chef.*

Troy kicked a hunk of ice. "James has two stars." The kid said it like he was saying James could fly.

"That doesn't sound so hot to me," Amy huffed. *Not as good as me, naked, in his bed.* God, she was such a fool. They hadn't ever gotten anywhere near a bed. What they had was almost-tawdry-couch sex and almost-sneaky-three-minute workplace sex. She was going to throw away her whole life for that? When had she become such an idiot? Why had she thought their fleeting encounters might count for anything even remotely resembling a relationship?

Maybe because she never had anything remotely resembling a relationship? How could she? Always on the move. One scam to the next. The key was to keep moving. To never stop long enough to be tricked into loving someone, to let them leave you first.

The light changed, and they hurried across the street, anxious to get out of the way of the aggressive SUVs that seemed to enjoy splashing them with filthy slush.

"John-John says that a man should have two balls and two stars," Troy said. He thought she really cared about James's stupid stars. "Anything less is deformed. Anything more is a freakish bonus. See, most places don't even get in the guide. Then like a hundred get in but without a single star. A bunch get one. A dozen get two. Maybe twenty places on this coast get three. Four is almost impossible unless you're in France. Five is, like, maybe two places in the world."

"I like my stars better. I get zillions every night just opening the curtain." She looked again to the sky. Nothing but clouds.

"That's why you're always broke." Troy stuffed his chin deeper into the collar of his too-thin coat. "My mom, too."

"You're mad at me, too, aren't you?" Amy asked, incredulous. She let people under her skin and what happened? They turned on her. "You think I screwed up tonight. Well how was I supposed to know that fat blob of a human, Scottie Jones, was a big shot?"

Troy shoved his hands deeper into his pockets. "You brought him. Everyone said. It was that guy Bob who was pissed at you that made him come. I knew you were bad luck." He punted a hunk of ice out of his way, and it smashed into a telephone pole and exploded into a million pieces. Troy upped his pace.

She picked up her own pace, her heels sliding perilously on the icy sidewalk. "The place is always packed. Why would people stop coming just because one guy said they should?" And why was she defending herself to a petulant kid who right now sounded like mini-James?

"Those fancy foodies are like lemmings. They'll go over a cliff if the critics say the foie gras is better at the bottom. They're too dumb to know for themselves."

The streets got quieter and darker as they neared Troy's place. People on the street moved by them more slowly, as if they didn't have anywhere they particularly wanted to go, despite the deep nighttime chill.

"What do you care about James, anyway?" She stopped in front of an all-night diner and turned to challenge Troy. Cabs idled on the curb as their drivers drank coffee behind the diner's dingy window.

Troy's voice became hard and his eyes flashed. "Because James is the only person around here who gets it."

"Gets what?" The intensity in the boy's eyes alarmed her.

"James always puts his restaurant first. Always! He doesn't give in to women or drugs or"—the boy's voice ratcheted up an octave—"stupid Gypsy mumbo jumbo."

The boy worshipped James. Of course. How had she missed that? Poor kid without a dad. With a flaky missing mom. Troy was mad at her because she had brought out the awful truth: You messed with James's restaurant, and he dropped you like a stone. She and the boy were in the same boat—falling for a guy who put you, if you were lucky, a distant second and third to a stubby, pale idiot who ate too much.

Which sucked if you wanted James to be your lover. Or your dad.

Her thoughts flashed back to James, furious at her over Scottie Jones. To Sammy getting fired in the prep kitchen. Even to Bob, crossing an invisible line in the dining room. James stood by his restaurant. They weren't a team; it was his place, and that was what mattered. It was best to learn that fast and move on.

She leaned in close to Troy, her nose almost touching his. "That restaurant is a gadje job serving uptight gadje. If people eating there are really so dumb that they have to listen to a little jerk named Scottie tell them what to put in their mouths, what's the difference between fortune-telling and fine dining? It's all a show to make people feel important and coddled, theater to ease their souls. James and his restaurant aren't any more solid than what we have. Don't dis your roots, Troy. That restaurant and James aren't the be-all and end-all. They're nothing."

Troy spun away from her and started walking again.

She watched him go. Life among the gadje. It never worked. Troy would have to realize that. Just like she'd have to accept that as long as James loved his restaurant, he'd never truly love her.

Not that she would ever truly love him.

Sheesh. What was she going on about? Love?

It was good that she saw James for who he really was. Good for her and good that she could tell the kid before he got hurt.

Anyway, she had her own show to pull together. She glanced at the dark night sky. She had a Gypsy to visit. Madame Prizzo was waiting.

She watched Troy's back, his shoulders hunched against the cold.

This was all good. They were Rom, and they had to stick together. She and Troy and Madame Prizzo and even Roni when she came back. They might not have a fancy restaurant, but they had their own power, and they never turned their backs on each other. That was the Gypsy code. Con a gadje, sure. But Gypsies were a huge, extended family.

Forget James and Les Fleurs. She caught up with Troy and walked him silently the rest of the way home.

If something doesn't taste right, it's usually because it's not right.
—JAMES LaCHANCE, *The Meal of a Lifetime*

Chapter 16

Amy Abigail Lester Burns."

Amy fell back in shock. Madame Prizzo had summoned Maddie. No one knew Amy's middle names. No one. Especially the unfortunate "Lester," after her great-great-uncle Lester, the legendary con man from Tulsa. Plus, more tellingly, Amy could feel Maddie's presence in her bones. She always could sense when her spirit was present—a warmth that started deep inside her. Madame Prizzo was the real thing.

Amy let out her breath and inhaled the rank but reassuring aroma of stale tobacco, soothing and familiar. She was with her people. With a true pro. It felt like home.

Madame Prizzo rolled her closed eyes, a repulsive burrowing of eyeballs under paper-thin lids. Eighty-two-year-olds really shouldn't wear blue eye shadow, but Madame Prizzo still hadn't washed off her costume makeup from her channeling for the manicurist, who had kept Amy waiting twenty minutes in the freezing rain.

Madame Prizzo, or rather Maddie, spoke again. "Now that I am no longer your spirit guide, you can know the name of your One True Love."

They were more words than Amy had ever heard Maddie utter. The shock of it almost undid her. Who knew Maddie could speak in sentences? Why hadn't she ever done it before? She looked around the trailer for signs of a con, but the place was clean.

Well, metaphorically speaking.

I miss you, Maddie, was what Amy longed to say. She longed to drop to her knees and beg Maddie to come back.

And yet, Maddie was finally speaking to her, and *this* is what she had to say? That Amy should be happy Maddie split because now she can have True Love? Amy pushed her longing for Maddie aside and focused on her three and a half months of pent-up rage, held in since the *Oprah* debacle. She let it ooze to the surface, to cover her pain with self-righteous pleasure. "I don't want my soul mate. I want you."

Maddie was silent. A fly landed on Madame Prizzo's nose. It cleaned its face like a cat. But the woman was so entranced, she didn't budge.

Amy was pacing now, her feet crunching on the filthy carpet. She could feel the fly's million eyes following her. "Okay, tell me the name of my One True Love if you're so hot to. I don't care. I'm not going after him. Get it over with," Amy said. Minutia to get out of the way so they could get on with business.

What if it was James?

What if it wasn't James?

I don't care, I'm getting Maddie back. I can resist James.

She pushed the thoughts away, irritated at herself for letting her mind wander off business at a time like this.

I am through with James.

"You must hear the name from the mouth of the one chosen to tell."

"Fucking ass-backward fairy rules." First the rule about not being about to know her own True Love's name when she had the voice; then the rule that if she fell for her True Love, she'd never get Maddie back; and now, this nonsense of who tells. Maddie was such a rule-following wuss. Maddie was obviously no Gypsy, Amy was beginning to realize. No wonder they had never gotten along. She had always assumed Maddie was Rom. But assumptions were for chumps. Maddie was probably—Amy looked around the trailer, her eyes resting on a horse skull—*Amish.*

She closed her eyes. She envisioned a horse and buggy with a prim, skinny woman perched in the back, her spine straight and her hands folded on her lap. Gag.

Amy sat back down and tapped her foot against the leg of the metal folding chair. "Look, Maddie. I'm no fool. You want to get rid of me. This isn't about my One True Love at all. It's about you leaving me for keeps. If I know my True Love's name, I'll be tempted to find him. And when I do, I won't be able to resist him, and you get to split for good, by the rules. You brought me to Roni so she could lay it on me—and you could set yourself free. I'm not an idiot."

Silence.

Amy paced. "You like Roni better. She's a pushover who'll do your bidding. You want to ditch me. You've always wanted to. It's true, isn't it? And it's true that once I find my One True Love, you can't come back to me. Right? Backward spirit-dumb-ass rule number 6,412."

"Yes."

Amy felt the trap close around her. "Do I have to really love him or just, you know, boff him?"

"The physical act is of no importance—"

"Well, that's what an Amish spirit with no body might think—"

"Are you ever silent?" Maddie boomed. Then her voice lowered. "Spiritual love. You must say out loud that you love him."

"Is my soul mate James?"

There was no answer. "Right. The rules. Roni has to tell me." Anger and frustration rose in Amy's throat. She stood, turning her back to Madame Prizzo and staring out the smeared window at night sky. For a minute, she thought she saw something duck into the shadows, like someone was out there. But who'd be out on this awful night? Probably the wind and her imagination playing tricks.

Amy focused back on the problem at hand. So, she'd made some mistakes, used Maddie to con a few assholes and turn a tidy profit back when things were good. So what? This was America. You had to take your opportunities. "Roni doesn't have the balls for this work. You know True Love isn't all goodness and light. You know True Love breaks up families and ruins friendships. You need a Gypsy like me. I have the guts to go where it's darkest and pry people out of their satisfied lives so they can find love. People who really need love."

"People like you, Amy?"

Amy froze. That little spirit bitch. How could she?

Madame Prizzo began to rock.

Maddie was breaking free. Panic rose in Amy's throat. She jumped for the old Gypsy. "Coward! Don't go! Hear me out!" Amy felt the warmth drain from the room, the familiar inhale of loss, leaving her cold and drained.

Madame Prizzo shuddered, opened her eyes, and looked around with that stunned look channelers always got when they were set free.

Amy carefully removed her hands from around Madame Prizzo's throat, took a step back, and fell into a dilapidated chair by the window, dislodging an angry black cat with yellow eyes. The cat hissed at her. Amy hissed back. Black cat, nice touch. *I could learn a lot from this Gypsy if a gaping hole wasn't opening inside me, threatening to swallow me alive.*

Maddie wants to ditch me. She's conning me, just like I conned people. Well, I won't let her. I won't ever hear the name of my One True Love. I'll find Roni and get Maddie back without ever hearing. Sweet little Roni won't last a month with Maddie ruining nice people's lives with her crazy mixed-up names. Everything is fine. Better than fine.

Madame Prizzo lit a Marlboro. "One fifty, for you, dear. Professional courtesy." She held out a wrinkled hand.

Amy felt in her bra for her cash. She counted out the bills and handed them to Madame Prizzo, who smiled, now sweet as pie with the cash in her fist. She unlocked a strongbox, tucked Amy's money inside, and then lit a second cigarette. The first was still dangling from the other side of her mouth. Channeling was exhausting, difficult work, and Madame Prizzo looked more like the ancient Gypsy she pretended to be than the tennis-court gym rat she was. *Always a little truth in any fiction*, Amy thought.

"Did you find out what you needed to know?" Madame Prizzo asked.

"Sort of." She wasn't about to tell Madame Prizzo her business.

Madame Prizzo waited, but when Amy didn't say any more, she stubbed out a cigarette and sighed. "Roni called me today to see if I had heard anything about how Troy was doing. I wasn't sure if you were the real thing before. You can't be too careful, you know, with strangers. But now that I see the voice really was yours—or at least that it responds to you—I see that you are the one sent to help Roni. I'll call her back. Call her home."

Amy tried to keep her mind on Madame Prizzo's good news. *She trusts me; Roni's coming back.* But the pain of Maddie's betrayal threatened to overcome her. As she fought it down, the ache of James's betrayal joined the tide swirling around her, pulling her further down. If her childhood memories piled on, she was done for. She blocked them with all her psychic might. Stay in the present. Deal with what can still be changed.

The first real conversation I've ever had with Maddie, and it sucked.

Madame Prizzo stubbed out the second cigarette. "She's a good girl, my niece Roni. She doesn't understand what's going on. That's why I sent her to Pittsburgh for a cleansing. To Madame de Guize. Do you know her?

The best. But now I see that the spirits have sent you to help her. What does this voice want?"

Niece? Well, that was interesting. But what was most interesting was that the old Gypsy hadn't heard a word of the channeling; the channeler usually didn't, but you couldn't be too sure.

"Helping Roni is why I came to this town," Amy said.

"Roni doesn't like it," Madame Prizzo said. "Madame de Guize has gotten rid of hundreds of pesky spirits."

"Only I can make it disappear by taking it back."

The old Gypsy nodded, unsurprised. "Take it away with you. Roni doesn't have the strength to endure it. She's a good girl."

That's what I'm banking on. "I'll take care of Roni, Auntie. Don't you worry about a thing."

Madame Prizzo was at the sink, washing the circus-show makeup off her face. "Did you say that you play tennis? I'd adore you to join us. There are some Rom I think you'd like. And I'd like to beat them in doubles next week."

Amy tried to hide the happiness she felt at being invited. Madame Prizzo was her people. She didn't need James and his restaurant crew. "Troy's alone in the apartment. I should get back."

"Good girl." Madame Prizzo nodded.

Oh, if she only knew.

"You have to hold it together," Madame Prizzo warned Roni later that night. They were at the counter of an all-night diner. Madame Prizzo was downing bitter coffee while Roni pushed scrambled eggs around her plate. "You made up a good plan, but then life threw you a curveball.

You need to adjust. So, the real voice came? It's an unexpected event, but we can work with it. It's good you came to me so I could help you through this. And so you could listen in on the channeling. We learned so much."

Roni felt like throwing up. That was pretty much how she always felt these last few weeks, but this was worse. If the real voice showed up for a channeling, what was to stop it from jumping right back into Amy's head and telling the names again? Or worse, to tell Amy she was being conned? All her planning for nothing. The fork in her hand was shaking so hard, it banged against the plate, tapping out a nervous rhythm. "Why didn't the voice tell Amy she was being conned? Or that I'm lying about being her new medium?" A wave of nausea rolled through Roni.

Madame Prizzo smiled. "Don't you see? The spirit is on our side. Amy is right—the spirit doesn't want her. Hell, would you? She's a major con artist, Roni. One of the best. But she's so weak now, it's almost a shame to con her. She's too easy. We should go for more. Go for everything."

A surge of pity welled up inside Roni, but she fought it down. *No more being nice. Yeah, let's go for everything!*

If only she didn't feel so sick.

Madame Prizzo was talking again. "So, let's put it all together. From what you told me about the channeling, we know that Amy and James are getting it on and that Amy thinks James is her soul mate. Now, thanks to Maddie showing up, we know that Amy can't have her soul mate and get her precious voice back. So, tell me, Roni, what's the next step?"

"Next?" Roni pulled out her book. Inside was the worn piece of paper on which she had scribbled her new plan now that Madame Prizzo was involved. She read from it. "Step four is to fake a channeling and pretend that Maddie says the only way she'll come back to Amy is if she proves herself by helping Troy."

The old woman scowled. "Child, that was the plan *before* we found out how crucial James is. Think, Roni. There's a new person involved. How does he affect the plan? If you want in to this business, you need to stop being afraid and start being logical." She eyed Roni's shaking hands and squinched her lips in disappointment.

Roni flipped through *The Art of the Con*.

Madame Prizzo snatched it out of her hands. "Use your head, girl." She smacked Roni on the head with the book.

Roni sat on her shaking hands. Sometimes she hated her aunt. So coarse and rough. She missed Les Fleurs, where for a few hours a night, when they served dinner, everything was beautiful and serene and perfect. If only life could always be like that—delicious, orderly, smooth, peaceful.

Madame Prizzo was watching her, her thin lips twitching with impatience. It wasn't the first time it occurred to Roni that the hag-Gypsy Madame Prizzo pretended to be for clients was closer to the real Alexandria Prizzo than the stylish woman who spent her afternoons at the tennis club. The two sides of Madame Prizzo converged into one as she scowled at Roni.

"We make James and Amy split up?" Roni ventured.

"Too hard. Have you seen that man's hands? Plus, he can cook." Madame Prizzo got a faraway look in her eyes. "Who would ever leave him? Try again."

Roni inhaled, glad that Madame Prizzo didn't smack

her with the book again. "We make sure that Amy thinks James isn't her soul mate," Roni said in a small voice.

Madame Prizzo nodded. "Very good. How?"

"I tell her someone else is." Roni put her fork down and fought off a wave of nausea. "She won't believe me."

"The woman is *desperate*, honey. She has absolutely nothing. Don't you see, that voice was all she had. She's so wrapped around your little finger, she'll believe anything you say."

"That's because she hasn't seen me yet." Roni held up her hands. Even her little finger quivered.

"Hmm. Yes. Here." Madame Prizzo fished a bottle of pills out of her bag. "These will calm your nerves."

"Can't." She patted her stomach to indicate the baby.

"I didn't forget your condition, Roni. These are fine. They're herbal. Natural Gypsy remedies from the old country. You don't have to worry about a thing. You know, of course, that your nervousness is much worse for the baby than some herbs."

Roni put the bottle in her purse next to her book, which she'd grabbed back the moment Madame Prizzo had turned her attention elsewhere. She'd think about them later.

"Now, let's think about what more we can get from Amy. We know her brother-in-law the movie star is loaded and will hand over major bucks for a good cause like Troy. We know from the Rom network that she's not above stealing what she needs if the brother-in-law doesn't come through. What about that necklace she's wearing? We should try to get that, too. It's worth a pretty penny. And we have to think about James. Is he ripe to be conned, too?"

Roni's head was spinning. "I'll think about it, Aunt Alex." She was desperate to get away. Tomorrow, she'd see Troy again. Only one more night in that awful skid-row hotel. She didn't want to con James, who'd been so good to her and Troy.

Madame Prizzo looked around the diner. "Hey, you, what's you're name?" she called to an unshaven, thin man restacking glasses behind the counter.

"Abbot."

"Abbot what?"

The man looked confused, but he answered. "Abbot Figes."

"Okay. There it is." Madame Prizzo turned back to Roni. "Amy's soul mate is named Abbot Figes. Now she can be with James and still think she can get her precious voice back. Make sure you tell her. Fast. Since we've summoned the real spirit-voice, we may not have much time. We have to shift this con into high gear."

*The first act of cooking for guests is
offering the proper invitation.*
—JAMES LaCHANCE, *The Meal of a Lifetime*

Chapter 17

James paced the sidewalk across the street from Troy's apartment. It was the middle of the night, he was freezing, and he could tell from Troy's unmoving lone form in front of the blue flickering light of the TV that if Amy was even there, she was long asleep.

If she was even there. Knowing Amy, she was long gone.

Which was good because this was crazy. He had meant everything he had said in the walk-in. He had no idea what he was doing here.

Or rather, maybe he knew all too well what he was doing here.

I want Amy Burns.

He was sure of it in a way he was sure of only one other thing: *I want that third star.*

This was bad. It was all getting mixed up, Amy and Les Fleurs, Les Fleurs and Amy. His head hurt just thinking about his two desires: did they conflict, or were they one?

The idea of asking her to be his muse to create a whole new menu had been circling in the back of his mind since the day he met her. She inspired him beyond any previous inspiration, and not just for food. At first, he had thought that she was completely alone in the world and didn't give a shit. She just kept fighting, holding on to her pride even though she had nothing—no home, no job, no skills, no family as far as he could tell. She was the loneliest person he'd ever met—and the fiercest. Nothing tied her down; she was completely independent.

Which was why he hadn't asked her to be his muse. She was just like his father—no loyalty, always ready to split. He had spent his life insulating himself from the whims of people like Amy. Did he want that third star badly enough to risk falling for a woman who had no loyalty, no sense of place, no problem with leaving people behind at the drop of a hat, as if they had never existed?

Then, tonight in the walk-in, his opinion of her changed. He had seen it in her eyes. He was glad he had wounded her with his idiotic, panicked tirade, because he had blundered into penetrating somewhere deep and protected inside her. He had seen that she had the capacity to care about him, that she didn't want to be completely alone. By shattering the facade that all she wanted from him was sex, he had exposed that she yearned for more.

If only he could coax her back to him. She was like the alley cats he fed every morning behind Les Fleurs. *Those cats still don't trust me, and it's been years. They're wild. Like Amy. Completely focused on survival above all else.*

But what if he could build her facade back up by asking her to be his muse? She might be tempted closer. He could keep her from fleeing. He'd let her believe it was only sex and food if that's what she needed to believe to stay. If he showed her anything deeper, he was sure she would bolt.

And then together, slowly, they could see if there was anything more or if he was being a total moron, mistaking his lust and ambition for something deeper.

For love.

He kicked a snowbank, sending the dirty snow flying to expose the pure snow underneath. Had he completely lost his mind? Confusion swirled around him as he paced. This might be the dumbest thing he'd ever done.

And yet, he had to give her a reason to stay. He had to see if she was for real. *I want her more than anything I've ever wanted.*

More than the third star from Scottie Jones.

And she was as good as gone if he didn't figure out a way to step in and stop her from leaving.

Amy spotted a man hovering in the shadows of the sycamore tree by the front door of Troy's building. James's knife was in her boot, and she reached down and palmed it. *C'mon, buddy, make my day.* She was so in the mood for a fight.

The man stepped out of the shadows.

James.

"Too bad I recognized you before I slit your throat," she said, still palming the knife. Her body had gone electric under his gaze, but she scolded it harshly. *This man is the bait for my destruction.* Amy's head was still swimming from the channeling. Maddie speaking in full sentences out of the mouth of that ancient Gypsy was ghoulish. Even though part of her was glad that everything was unfolding as she had expected—she had called every shot—it was still too much to take in.

James was watching her. "You okay?"

"Fine." Except that in the lamplight, James looked good enough to eat, his black wool peacoat unbuttoned casually, as if it weren't twenty degrees below Antarctica. It was only the second time she'd seen him without an apron, in his street clothes. His blue jeans hung perfectly to his scuffed black boots. A few strands escaped from his tied-back gleaming hair.

"So," James said. His breath condensed in the cold air. He rubbed his bare hands together.

She held out the knife, handle first, for him to take. "So, I quit."

He didn't take the knife. "I came to apologize."

Amy felt like stabbing him with the knife. This would be so much easier if he'd just be a jerk. "Didn't you get the script? You blame me for not noticing your scumbag food critic. Then you fire me, because you're too embarrassed at your enormous gaffe to ever look me in the eyes again."

He looked her in the eyes. "I'm sorry I freaked out on you. I was an ass. You can't quit. I won't let you."

"Let me?" Why did he have to be so smolderingly hot just below the surface? No wonder kitchen boy didn't have to button his coat. He was a walking furnace.

To hell with Maddie, I want this man. Hope that maybe they had something real together flooded through her, and she tried to damn the bubbling tide with reason. *This man is a trap set by Maddie, and I am not falling into it.*

Into him.

Oh, to fall into him.

"Are you gonna put the knife away?" he asked.

"How sorry are you really?" she asked. "Ever hear of hara-kiri?"

"I'm not *that* sorry," he said.

"Too bad. I would have enjoyed a little ritual disembowelment." She slipped the knife into her boot and tried not to notice the way the wind whipped a single escaped strand of hair over his face. Tried not to notice the way he had stepped between the wind and her, sheltering her, without even thinking about it. Tried not to climb a little closer into the warmth of him.

"It's my job to handle Scottie, and it's Joey's job to spot him," James said. "We fucked up and I freaked on you. I'm sorry. It wasn't your fault. I was a first-class asshole."

"You were." *Okay, let's go to bed. Now.* She exhaled, trying to banish her idiotic thoughts. *Don't nibble the man bait.*

"So?" he asked. "Am I forgiven?"

Well, her body had certainly forgiven him. His face was ruddy with the cold. He looked at her with his earnest eyes, and her mind caved, too. No, not all of her mind. Just the stupid-ass part. The other part would never forgive him. She had to guard her anger at him like a jewel. It was what would keep them apart. Keep her from loving—

Loving?

Good God, that wasn't what she meant. She could still smell the permeating scent of Madame Prizzo's cigarettes on her coat, wafting up to her like a warning.

Trusting. That was it. She would keep her anger at him

like a prize, keep her defenses up and not trust him. Ever. He had shown with his Scottie Jones freak-out that he didn't deserve to be trusted. "Don't worry about being forgiven, James. I'm not coming back to Les Fleurs. Roni will be back tomorrow."

And then what? What if everything goes wrong?

His eyes went dark, the green disappearing, the brown intensifying to black, chameleon eyes changing to his mood. At least his lips were constant. Constantly tempting. "Is that how you operate?" he asked, his voice gruff. "Get what you want and then scram?"

"I'm a Gypsy, James. It's what we do. Wander. Sticking around is not my style." A blast of cold wind blew off her hat, and he snatched it out of the air without seeming to even look. He handed it to her, and she shoved it back on her muddled head. Why did this feel so lousy when it was so obviously for the best? Why did she feel like grabbing him and never letting go? Like kissing those insanely gorgeous lips—

"Nothing here worth sticking around for, huh?"

She could feel her body pull toward him. She could hear her cells shouting, *You.* "Don't flatter yourself."

"I was flattering Troy."

The cold wind whipped around them. *Troy. He's worth something. Something good out of all this mess.*

James went on. "Anyway, I don't believe you. I think you want to stick around. I think you want me, even if you won't admit it to yourself."

His words hung between them in the frozen air.

"That's because you're a fool, conned by a Gypsy," she lied.

He watched her closely. Finally, he said, "Okay. Two

can play at this game. I need a favor, Gypsy. Pure business transaction."

Amy felt oddly defeated. As if she cared. Which she didn't. "No. I told you. I'm not coming back to Les Fleurs."

"Hear me out."

"No. Forget it, James. You had your chance, and you let it slip away. Get Scottie Jones to do your favor."

He grasped her arm. "I don't believe you want to say no."

"James. I'm done with you—"

His mouth met hers, and his rough kiss lit her on fire as surely as if his lips were match tips. His hands were running through her hair, and it felt like destiny, and their bodies crashed together, and she cursed her stupid coat for getting in the way, but he had her face in his hands, and the look in his eyes betrayed everything they had just said to each other as nothing but nonsense, because they obviously needed each other NOW. She pulled him closer and breathed him in. This man was everything she ever wanted.

A light went on upstairs, and she jumped away from James, fanning the invisible flames.

Just as quickly as the embrace had started, it was over. Had it even happened? Or had she imagined it?

BZZZZZZZ. Someone buzzed the intercom; then Troy appeared at the window, waving like a beauty queen. *Thank you, Troy.* At least one of them still had a brain.

"I better go. I've gotta tell him his mom's coming back." *I better go and take a cold shower and think long and hard about how stupid this man makes me.*

"Come to Les Fleurs tomorrow. One last time. I need to ask you something."

"No." She yanked open the door and bolted inside before either of them could say another word.

She needed to stay very, very far away from that man.

Troy watched Amy let herself in without *really* watching her. He didn't want her to know he was glad she was back, that he hated being alone in the apartment. Stupid TV blocked most of the creepiest noises, but the gaping silence from his mother's room was still a roar inside his skull no matter how high he turned up *South Park*.

He nodded at Amy when she sat down across from him. He didn't have a choice. She blocked the TV.

"Your mom'll be back tomorrow," she said. "I arranged the whole thing."

He stopped trying to lean around her and stared, open-mouthed. She looked smug, like she had booked his mom's flight. Hot anger rose in his gut. First, she lied about knowing his mom. Then, she got cozy with James, two seconds after saying they couldn't trust him. "How's our dear friend James?" he asked. "The one we can't trust?"

"Forget James. He's nothing. Your mom is coming back. Now, I know you're mad at her, but she's been having a hard time. You've gotta be nice to her. In fact, we ought to clean up this joint." She stood and started picking up laundry. "C'mon. It'll be fun."

He sucked in his bottom lip and chewed on it. "Fun like face-sucking with James even though you think he's a jerk?"

"James is none of your business. I'm an adult. You're a kid. It's different. I can control my feelings."

"Yeah, right. Was that what you were doing down there? Controlling?"

She seemed determined to ignore him. She busied herself with gathering a pile of laundry, which she shoved into the liquor cabinet, mashing shut the door. She wiped her hands together as if she'd just finished building the Brooklyn Bridge instead of hiding the dirty laundry. "Your mother's going to need both our help when she gets back."

Troy's stomach doubled over. "She's not pregnant, is she?" He remembered the last time she disappeared. The abortion. They all thought he was an idiot and didn't know.

"Of course not." Now she was gathering empty Coke cans. She looked at the cans in her hands, looked at the already-full trashcan, shrugged, then began building an empty Coke can pyramid on the coffee table.

"So why's she need our help? *Your* help?" He knew how belligerent he sounded, but it pissed him off that Amy, a stranger, knew something he didn't about his own mom. She was such a know-it-all. And telling him he couldn't handle James and she could was such bull. He knew James was just a means to get an education in the kitchen. He wasn't, like, emotionally involved or anything. Like she obviously was.

She balanced a can and stood back to admire her sculpture in progress. "She's hearing voices, Troy. One voice, actually. And I used to hear that voice. So I know all about the spirit that wants your mother to serve her. I can help her break free. I convinced Madame Prizzo to call her back. That's where I was tonight." She adjusted another can.

His body deflated, the resentment inside him escaping like air. He tried to keep the gratefulness out of his voice. *She did bring my mom back.* He should have known that it was that awful Madame Prizzo who had sent her away. He'd have hugged her if he wasn't so pissed at her. "What's the spirit want my mom to do?" He picked up a can and added it reluctantly to Amy's tower.

"It's complicated. It's nothing bad. It's a well-meaning spirit. She'll tell you everything when she gets here." Amy finished another row of cans; the pyramid was five rows high and three rows deep and getting shaky.

Troy added a can. Then Amy. Then Troy. With each can, they held their breath, then exhaled in relief when the whole thing didn't topple over. *If James forgave her for messing up the restaurant, then I can forgive her, too.*

There was just one can left to center on the top.

"You do it," Amy said.

Troy nodded. *I'll see my mom tomorrow*, he thought as he placed the last can. *Maybe, just maybe, the three of us can figure this out.* The last can wobbled but held.

They both stepped back to admire their sculpture.

"Nice." Amy punched his shoulder.

"Yeah. Not bad." He hadn't felt this relaxed since his mom had left.

He looked around the cruddy room, shrugged, then picked up a pair of discarded jeans and began to fold.

*The best kitchen, the best ingredients, and the best
recipes are nothing without inspiration.*
—JAMES LaCHANCE, *The Meal of a Lifetime*

Chapter 18

Roni popped another pill in her mouth. What a night
this was going to be. It was her first day back at Les Fleurs
since the con had begun, and everything felt different—
more sinister, as if everyone had a dark secret like the
one she was harboring. She was even nervous around Stu.
What if Amy had told everyone about the voice? What
if Stu asked her who his One True Love was? She was
so nervous, she kept forgetting his wife's name. Karen?
Carol?

She sank onto a stack of lettuce crates near the door of
the walk-in and tried to breathe. She had come straight to
Les Fleurs without even seeing Troy, and that made her
nervous, too. She should have waited one more day so that
she could see him after school and before work. But she
was so anxious to get this over with, she couldn't wait.

*Amy, I hear the voice; it's coming to me. Your One True
Love's name is . . . Aaron? No. That wasn't it. Axel?*

Her hands were going to shake right off her arms. She wasn't going to be able to pull this off.

"Hi, Roni." James stood at the door to the walk-in, his arms crossed in front of him. "Welcome back."

James was shocked by how uptight and wrung out his waitress seemed. Roni nearly jumped out of her skin when she saw him. Was Amy right? Was James that terrifying to his staff? His server was trembling at just the sight of him. She must think he was going to fire her. "Sorry, didn't mean to startle you." He couldn't take his eyes off her hands. She looked like she had palsy. "You okay?"

Roni put her shaking hands behind her back. "Fine. Sorry for splitting. Sorry—"

"No problem. Your job's waiting for you. You always have a place here." How was she going to wait tables with those hands?

She brought her hands in front of her and clenched them, gripping her right hand with her left, but it didn't help the shaking. "Thanks . . . er . . . I gotta go."

He'd known Roni for years. He'd never seen her like this. The hairs on the back of his neck stood up. *Was she this afraid of Amy?* What if she knew something about Amy that he didn't? Something he should know, before he lost his heart completely. "You know if you ever need anything, you can ask me?"

"Right. Sure."

Poor thing was a mess. He felt terrible. "Hey, have you talked to Troy about Amy Burns?"

Roni turned completely white. "Not yet. I just got back today. Troy was already at school. I came straight here."

James wondered how she knew who Amy was if she

hadn't spoken to Troy. He pushed aside his doubts; they must have talked by phone over the five days she was gone. "You sure you're okay?" She looked like she was going to throw up. It must be Amy she was afraid of, not him. No way was he this scary.

"Fine," she practically whispered. "Where is she?" She looked behind James like a trapped animal suspecting an ambush.

"Why don't you take the night off?" he suggested.

"No. I'm good."

She wasn't even close to good. "You know Amy's been staying with Troy?"

"I know."

Something wasn't right here. "Roni, is there something you want to tell me?"

All at once, a change came over Roni's face. She looked at him like he had just told her the answer to a test she was sure she would fail. Some of her color came back. She stood and came to him. Then, to his surprise, she reached out and touched his arm with a shaking hand. She'd never touched him before, but her touch was as he expected it to be, light and hesitant, like a bird. She closed her eyes.

"Roni? You sure you're okay?"

"Gladys Roman," Roni said. Her hand was shaking a little less now.

"Who?"

"I don't know. It's the name that I hear when I touch you. I think Amy might know what it means. I think that's why she's waiting for me. To help me with these names that come to me. It's awful, James."

Roni looked a lot better now. But what the hell was

she talking about? "I didn't understand a word you just said."

"That's okay, James." She was smiling now, and her hands were vibrating less. "Never mind. Forget it. I just need to talk to this Amy Burns. But, James, thank you for taking care of Troy. And for letting me come back to work. I have to go." And with that, his timid waitress bolted past him and out of the walk-in.

Amy pushed into the darkened dining room of Les Fleurs two hours later. James had called her at Troy's to tell her that Roni had come back and that he had to talk to Amy about something Roni had said. Something that made no sense at all. *Something about a voice.*

Amy had almost not come. But if James had learned something about Roni, she needed to know what it was, and the impossible man wouldn't tell her over the phone. His news could help her get Maddie back. She just had to keep her mind on that.

What if Roni told James that she heard my name when she touched him?

The possibility opened before her, and she slammed it shut like a door. *Do not look into that room. It is forbidden.*

But what if . . . ?

James was sitting at the bar, nursing a Coke.

"A little early to be hitting the hard stuff." Amy looked around, but the room was empty except for James. No Roni in sight. Relief ran through her that she wouldn't have to deal with Roni just yet, and she chided herself for being such a wuss.

Then the relief vanished as she watched James. Something was on his mind; she could see it in his clenched jaw.

She imagined the conversation unfolding: *Amy, Roni told me that she hears your name when she touches me. Why?*

Oh, James, it's because we're meant to be together. Soul mates.

I knew that even before Roni told me. . . .

Amy ducked under the bar and poured herself a cranberry juice. She resisted the urge to add a splash of vodka in deference to the long day ahead, then added the vodka, anyway. A drop more. Oops. Oh, well. Despite leaving Troy's apartment as clean as it had probably ever been, despite the positive vibe she had felt from the boy, she was feeling queasier than ever about Roni's return. After the channeling, she had realized Roni wasn't the one she had to convince of her worthiness; Maddie was. And Maddie was a tougher nut to crack, since she'd known Amy her whole life.

And now James was looking so serious.

James fixed her with his green-and-caramel eyes. "Something odd happened this morning. In the walk-in. Tell me what it means." He told her about Roni touching him and telling him the name Gladys Roman.

At the words *Gladys Roman*, Amy felt like she'd been punched in the stomach. She threw back her drink and poured another shot, this time straight vodka. *How could I have been so wrong about James, thinking he was my soul mate?*

God, she was stupid to hope that he had summoned her to Les Fleurs to tell her that she was his soul mate.

Marry me, Amy. We are destined to be together!
Yes, James. I love you, too!

Ugh!

Was she really that far gone to imagine such a sappy, impossible ending?

Face the facts: James was nothing. Another man in a long string of men who meant nothing. She looked at him closely. So intense and honest and strong and loyal and . . . nothing.

She reached again for the vodka.

He ducked under the bar.

Amy's breath hitched at his abrupt nearness. Didn't angels wear white? Chefs really ought to wear black. The luxurious broadness of his shoulders, the leanness of his waist. This chef really ought to wear nothing at all.

"Tell me what it means, Amy. Who is Gladys Roman?" He backed her against the bar. "Why did you almost fall over when I told you that name? Why do you look so upset now? Like I've just washed you down and wrung you out? What the hell is going on here?"

"It's Gypsy business. You wouldn't understand." Having him so near was bliss. She wanted to fall into him. How could she have been so wrong?

Unless Roni is lying.

But why would she lie? Amy's mind churned through the possibilities. If you were conning someone, you had to want something from them. But Roni already had everything that Amy had to give. Could *Maddie* be conning her? Telling Roni the wrong name? Was a spirit even capable of lying?

James was watching the emotion play over her face, his eyes narrowed with concern. "What do you want from

Roni? Tell me. That poor woman is scared shitless of you."

"She's not scared of me. She's scared of . . . forget it." She had to pull herself together. James wasn't her One True Love; that was good. It meant she could stay near him. Wasn't that what she wanted? After all, he had apologized for being an ass. Now that True Love was out of the picture, they could be buddies again.

Buddies with benefits.

But she couldn't shake the feeling that Roni was lying. *Why?*

"All right. We'll play it your way." He stared at her, and she could see him fighting for control of his frustration. "I need your help." His voice had gone hard.

"Get in line, buddy. Anyway, Roni's your gal. I'm gone from the restaurant biz."

"Roni can't help with the"—he paused—"menu." The slightest hint of a blush rose under his olive skin. "I need a whole new menu to blow Scottie Jones away. Amy, he thinks if we could make a whole menu as good as the new dishes we already created together, we could get a third star." His voice was strained. Like he wasn't sure he wanted to ask her any of this.

Momentary confusion cleared into crystal-clear understanding. *Women inspire his food. He wants to be inspired by me.*

Hot mindless uncommitted sex. That was the favor he wanted?

A pang of hurt shot through her, but she shook it away. This was no time to be getting sentimental. She wasn't his soul mate, which meant that he wasn't hers. Amy had never seen the Fates be cruel enough to do that to anyone.

They could be together—enjoy each other—no strings attached.

And he did say "us" and "we," as if they were in it together. Partners.

This was what she had wanted—to have James and Maddie both. So why did she feel like slapping him across his gorgeous face? Like punching him in the gut so hard he staggered backward, because she felt she was staggering backward now, into an abyss?

How could I have been so wrong about James?

And yet, she could see the next few weeks as if he had laid a map before her, drawn with careful lines. Place to stay. Hot sex with this beautiful, tender man. Access to Roni. It was a win-win situation. What more could she ask for?

A tiny voice in the back of her head whispered, *Love.*

She threw back the vodka and repoured.

"Whoa. Easy there." He took the vodka bottle from her. "Need a few drops tonight for the paying customers."

She grabbed back the bottle.

"Tell me what's going on," he said.

Her vodka sloshed over the side of the glass. "Later." *Never.*

He grabbed the glass before she did and poured it down the drain. Then he fixed her with his gaze. He moved so close, he whispered in her ear, "Okay. Forget Roni and Gladys Roman, whoever the hell she is. I don't give a damn about them. You know we have something together. You think you're using me and I'm using you, but it's more, and we both know it. That's what's got you so rattled."

The way her body responded to him was so unfair.

Why did she feel so drawn to him if he wasn't her One True Love?

Roni is lying. Amy knew it to the core of her being. But why? It didn't make sense. Maybe her instincts were wrong.

"You and me have something, Amy."

"You and me are just a means to an end, James. Let's make that perfectly clear before we take this any further."

"Really?" He didn't look amused. "Is that how it is?"

Not really. But she could figure that out later. "Yes. Look, James, first, I'm a Gypsy. I don't stay put with anyone." *No matter how beautiful and dark and sexy they are.* "Second, you freaked me out when you got all psycho over Scottie Jones. I'm not going there again. I haven't forgiven you. Third . . ."

He waited, arms crossed across his gorgeous chest, the beginning of a smile playing around his burgundy lips.

How could he not be the one?

Third, I need to meet Roni and make sure she's telling the truth, because if she isn't, all bets are off. "Third, there is no third. Now. But I'll think of a third later and let you know. So until then, just hot sex and nothing more."

"You drive a hard bargain." He pulled her close, thrusting his thigh between her legs. "Even if you're lying. I know you care a little bit about me."

The move was so bold and unexpected; her body against his turned her to liquid heat. "This time I'm not lying." She swallowed hard.

"So this is just a roommate arrangement for you?" He pushed his thigh a little closer, spreading her legs, his anger making him even sexier, more dangerous.

She lifted her face to his. *Kiss me.* "Why should I trust you as anything more? You and your restaurant . . ." she murmured, but she was losing herself in the feel of him, the smell of him, the power of him.

He kissed her, hard and yet somehow tenderly. "Be a part of it." His leg pushed harder, pressing her just there, just perfectly. She melted into him.

"You, me, and Les Fleurs? A threesome?" She tried not to gasp.

"Well, if you count in Stu and Dan and—"

She pressed her lips against his to shut him up and felt his smile. And that thigh down below. Oh, that nicely placed thigh. She closed her eyes. She could stay near Roni and get Maddie back and help him out. Naked. And not get involved. Definitely not fall. For. Him. And. His. Thigh.

His hand moved down her back.

He kissed her, deeply, while pressing his leg closer.

Him.

He crushed her against the bar.

Now.

If Gladys showed up, Amy would lock her in the walk-in and never let her out.

She ran her hands through his hair and down his back. The apron strings would need the slightest tug to come undone. *C'mon Captain James, let's you and me put up the full sails and let this baby fly.*

His hand stopped hers just as she was about to release the strings.

"I've got a place in the Bourse, top floor. Go. Take the day off in honor of Roni's return. In honor of our new arrangement. I'll be there as soon as I can." His lips brushed over hers, and the warmth of his skin brushed away the cold. She closed her eyes and inhaled his scent. Such a beautiful man. Such a sexy man. His rough cheek rubbed her smooth one, and she tried to memorize the sensation.

Tonight wouldn't be soon enough. She pulled his hips into her so that his thigh nestled just right.

He murmured, "Later," but his rhythm said, "Now."

She tried to focus her thoughts away from the way his leg moved between hers. She didn't know what the Bourse was, but a building with a name sure sounded good.

Footsteps passed through the dining room, getting faster as they went. Right. Public place. She could wait. James deserved her full attention. The footsteps retreated, and he moved his leg against her, in and out, pressing just so, and she sighed with the ecstasy of it.

"This is crazy," she murmured. Nothing wrong with crazy. Especially when it felt so good. She'd get rational later. Maybe.

They stood together, holding each other. He murmured into her neck, "Nothing's moved like the lobster salad and those scallops since we opened our doors. All artists have muses. Picasso had Françoise Gilot . . ." James seemed to have lost his train of thought somewhere around her left earlobe.

"Popeye had Olive Oyl," she prodded him on.

He bit her ear. "Exactly."

"A muse. I like that." Musedom was responsible. It was serious. It was perfect, really. Almost as perfect as his leg, moving in and out, pressing, probing, promising more good things to come. They could help each other.

How could anything that felt this good be bad?

"But, Amy," he said. "If you tell me you'll do this, you

have to stay. You can't bolt on me in the middle. Do you promise?"

"Yes." She was surprised that she meant it. She didn't want to bolt.

"The whole menu."

"I said yes, James, and I meant it. I won't go."

"Good. Then we're partners."

Roni left the dining room quickly, before James and Amy could see her. She looked at her hands. For the first time since she'd returned, they weren't shaking.

Maybe, just maybe, this was all going to work out after all.

Main Course

Aperitif
Pernod infused with sugar water and absinthe
—JAMES LaCHANCE, *Meal of a Lifetime*,
THE MENU: BEFORE THE MEAL BEGINS

Chapter 19

*I*mmersed up to her neck in James's claw-foot iron tub, it was hard for Amy to remember why she had ever been upset with him. She sank under the scalding water. The imported Belgian soaps were heaven. The French candles, divine. And the Bordeaux the yummiest she'd ever had. The bottle didn't even have a proper label. Just a white sticker with a scribbled note: "For James. Happy Holidays, Jules."

She wondered who Jules was as she emerged from under the water and reached for her wine. Julie, his ex-lover? Julian, a salesman pimping vino for Les Fleurs? Who cared? She was in his apartment now and Jules wasn't, and that was nine-tenths of the cosmic law.

She pulled herself out of his tub and wrapped herself in his enormous terry robe. It smelled like rosemary and lavender. She padded around the apartment while drying her hair with a white, impossibly plush towel that smelled like the robe. Like James.

She took in the expansive room. The place wasn't what she had expected. In the cab on the way over ("The Bourse," she had said to the driver, and he screeched away from the curb without a moment's hesitation), she had imagined a bachelor pad in a sleek glass building, with black leather and chrome and squeaky-clean, thanks to a twice-weekly woman named Lucille.

Then, as she rode up in his semiprivate elevator, she reconsidered. The Bourse had turned out to be an elaborate building—a nineteenth-century, brick-and-terra-cotta palace across from the Liberty Bell with its first six floors converted into an upscale shopping mall, its upper floors businesses and private residences.

So she reimagined his place as a sublime architectural shell with gorgeous moldings, soaring ceilings, and nothing inside but a mattress on the floor and a fifty-thousand-dollar stove in the kitchen.

But when she threw open the heavy, carved, wooden double doors, her heart fell. How could a man this cultured be her soul mate? His place was gorgeous. Classy. *Respectable.*

The apartment was a single huge room, with soaring ceilings and top-to-floor windows set over enormous gilded nap-worthy ledges strewn with pillows. The floors were gleaming hardwood. The ceilings were painted with naked angels, their little wieners jutting out like third eyes. The furniture was a mix of antiques and modern pieces covered with tasseled pillows of every shape and size. Nothing matched, and yet everything fit perfectly. It was the kind of place you'd see photographed in a glossy magazine, with James himself, a perfect mix of sexy and competent, pirate and stockbroker, standing at the stove, surrounded by beautiful smiling people.

Maybe Roni isn't lying. Maybe James is destined for Gladys Roman, who is an architect, no, a professor—no, an art critic from Italy . . .

A cloud of doubt descended on Amy as she opened, then closed, a cookbook written in Italian. Gladys could definitely read Italian, but she wouldn't need to because she could cook up a storm as taught by her illustrious grandmother, most likely an heiress. . . .

Amy wrapped the robe more tightly around herself. *What am I doing here?* When she was with James at the restaurant, it was like a stage set. He put on his chef costume and she put on her server costume, and they played French Restaurant with a show-must-go-on vibe that she relished.

His real self, the cocky, bold, bad-boy self, was under that costume, she had thought. But this was his home, and it was beautiful and classy. It was no act. No stage set. It was for real. He was a cultured, rich, successful man.

Definitely not her soul mate.

He was more stockbroker than pirate, she saw now. With all these books. All these antiques. All this *taste*. What had she expected? Rigging and sails and scurrying rats?

Amy sighed. She would have liked that.

Well, maybe not the rats.

I know nothing about who James is.

She looked around her. The cookbooks alone were intimidating. French. Italian. Chinese. They overflowed the bookshelves, held up tabletops and lamps, and stacked themselves into corners like houseguests. Instead of candlesticks, antique cheese graters lined the mantel.

I'm a muse. I can be his muse even if he's rich and owns lots of books in other languages and has impeccable taste and I'm not his soul mate. There is more to life than love; helping someone I admire and enjoy is worthwhile. And fun.

She moved through the expansive apartment to the king-size bed, which sat rakishly askew behind a Japanese screen. The bed was covered in masculine sheets, whites and browns, just like Les Fleurs. The similarity was vaguely disturbing, as if Stu might show up with a basket of bread.

She sat on the edge of the bed and smoothed the sheets.

"Nice," Oprah said. She sat in the wingback leather chair next to the foot of the bed, sipping James's wine.

"I hate it here. I feel like a bum. He's so cultured. The French posters and the private-stock wine and the pillows with tassels. I thought he was faking the fancy shmancy-French-snob bit, that the real James was bubbling just below the surface. The pirate. The one who'd run away with me. The one who'd—" She stopped and took a deep breath.

Oprah finished her sentence. "The one who'd consider hanging with a Gypsy psychic loner wanderer?"

Amy flinched, then relaxed into the relief of having her feelings voiced so plainly. "I think it's the pillows. What kind of man owns pillows with tassels and then shacks up with me?"

"You've done this sort of thing before."

"It was different before."

"Why? Casual sex isn't exactly a reach for you."

"Yeah, but this feels different. It doesn't feel casual. It feels deeper. Oprah, I think I'm falling for someone else's soul mate."

"He's the first guy you've ever been with who isn't a guitarist in a failing heavy-metal band. The first man you've been with longer than a week, Amy. Sure it's scary."

"It's been six days."

"The first man you've been with for almost a week," Oprah corrected herself.

"I'm not having a relationship with James." Amy shook away the thought. "He's using me, and I'm using him, and he's not my soul mate."

"Roni is lying. You know so. You have to trust your heart."

"I thought she was. Until I saw this place. Now I'm not so sure."

"What's in his eyes? In his kiss?"

Amy fell back on the bed and closed her eyes. How nice would it be to have Maddie and also to live here, in James's robe and bathtub? To make sweet, long love with a beautiful man who cooked like a dream? "I can't love him unless it's even. I don't want him to have all the cards."

"He doesn't," Oprah said. "You're his muse. That means you have something to give him that he doesn't have. Something that he needs."

"Sex?"

"No, dummy. More."

"More? Like what?" Amy opened her eyes, hoping to find the answer in Oprah's shining eyes.

But Oprah was gone.

Good bread is better than the most expensive cut of meat.
—James LaChance, Meal of a Lifetime,
The Menu: Before the Meal

Chapter 20

First seating was over, and the second was hitting the kitchen like a tsunami. The kitchen staff whirled in the steam and heat. Roni lifted two plates off the warmer, and James slid two more into their places before she had turned away.

"Nice to have you back," James said. He noticed that her hands were steady, but she was still pale.

"Nice to be back," she said as she backed into the swinging doors.

It really was great to have Roni back. No one else in his kitchen was polite.

"Fire two Josies. Go soup on four," Burt called.

Keep the mind on the food. If Burt was calling dishes, then he was falling behind. James was working the line on the rotisseur station, handling the sauté. In his kitchen, it was the most complicated spot on the line. He had to make up to twelve different dishes with eight roaring burners and a finishing oven blasting high heat. If he let his mind wander and missed a plate, he could bring the whole kitchen to a screeching halt. You couldn't serve a table of six if one Duck L'orange was missing. The whole process stopped, the food waited, cooled, congealed, curdled. An entire table ruined because he couldn't get his mind off the gorgeous Gypsy who was probably right this moment stealing everything he owned while he slung pork medallions.

Not that he cared much about his stuff. Most of it wasn't even his. Leftovers from the chef who had lived there before and who had split for France at a day's notice—a chance to work the line in Louis Blanche's kitchen. If it had been James's stuff, he'd have thrown every damn book out the window the first day. Every last stinking pillow. He'd sleep, curled up in front of his stove, the memories of another successful night at Les Fleurs lulling him to sleep.

He just hoped Amy had the decency not to touch his knives.

Burt called, "Chef, where's my lamb?"

James put his head down and stared at the eight sauté pans. Twelve more pans stood to the side at the ready, waiting their turns for heat. He never made a mistake.

Except for maybe the woman in my apartment, waiting for me tonight.

He pulled the lamb, perfectly done, from the finishing oven, plated it, garnished it, and slung it into the window. *Perfection.*

Amy awoke with a start.

James stood in the doorway, the door to the hallway still open behind him, staring at her as if she were a ghost.

The cookbook she had been paging through when she fell asleep tumbled to the floor with a thud. She rearranged herself on the leather couch. Had he forgotten she'd be there? "Hi."

"Found the place okay?"

"No problem."

"You like it?"

"It's nice." *Except that I hate it.*

"You hate it."

She tried to cover. "What kind of American has no TV?"

"A guy who would skewer that rat-bastard excuse for a chef Emeril for a loaf of bread. Can't stand watching that man and all his cohorts." James closed the door behind him. "Well, I sort of like Rachael Ray. Except when she tries to cook." He hung his coat in the entry closet, then came into the room and picked up the cookbook. He put the book on the coffee table, picked up the empty wine bottle, and raised his eyebrows at her.

"I was gonna come by and help out tonight, but I started with the wine. When you start with the wine, the rest never quite gets done." Amy stretched. She glanced at the clock. It was two in the morning.

James looked freshly scrubbed. He had changed out of his chef whites and was wearing his jeans and a green long-sleeve T-shirt. Looking at James made Amy hungry. For food, also. He was a curious combination in a man, the food-sex provider in one very lovely package, pleaser of the tongue extraordinaire. . . .

Egad, listen to her. She was drunk. The problem with hanging out with pretend friends like Oprah was that you kind of felt like you were sharing a bottle, when really you were just scarfing it yourself. She stretched out her sleepy muscles again. "I'm starving."

"It's two in the morning." He sat in the armchair across from her, sinking into it as if it were a bed. He closed his eyes. The effect was languid and sexy.

She longed to curl up in his lap. She was, after all, his muse. Didn't muses curl? Now that he was here, with her, her fears melted away. All she wanted was him.

"We were packed. We could've used your hands."

"You were glad I wasn't there so I couldn't spill anything into anyone's lap."

He opened his eyes and smiled. "You do have special psychic Gypsy power, don't you?"

"What have you heard?" she asked, trying to keep the alarm out of her voice that he had triggered with the word *Gypsy.*

He cocked his head at her. "Nothing. Why?"

Good. Roni hadn't spilled her guts about the voice. Amy hoped he wouldn't start asking her about Gladys Roman again.

She got up off the couch, stretched, and kissed him on the forehead as she passed him on her way to the kitchen. Trace aromas of the restaurant rose off his skin, garlic and seared meats. Thank God another chef handled the fish station. She didn't think she could be the muse of a fishy chef.

James followed her into the kitchen. "You're wearing my pajamas," he said.

She looked down at his cozy brown flannels and shrugged. "So? Buy me lingerie if you've got a problem. I'm starving." She went to the cabinets and got out a box of spaghetti. She began reading the instructions on the side of the package.

"My pajamas never looked so good."

She felt him watching her, heat rising inside her.

"Are you reading spaghetti instructions?" he asked.

She turned and leaned against the counter and squinted at the directions. "Does eight to ten minutes mean eight minutes or nine or ten? They make it so confusing."

He shook his head in dismay and took the package from her. He put it back in the cabinet. "Sit." He put a pot of water on to boil, grabbed some garlic off a hanging vine of the stuff, and crushed it slightly with the blade of his knife, just enough to make the peel fall away like clothing.

Me next, please.

She watched him transform the misshapen garlic into paper-thin slivers. How did he do that? He got out a small sauté pan and put it over the heat.

Warmth spread through her, as if by heating the pan, he was also warming her. "I can't remember the last time someone cooked for me," she said, surprising herself with how empty and sad the revelation made her feel.

"Me neither," he said. He pulled a container out of the freezer, then a stick of butter out of the enormous chrome fridge. He picked a few fuzzy green leaves off a plant on the counter. He washed the leaves and began to tear them.

The water was boiling, and he dumped in a hunk of frozen white rocks, not even glancing at the clock or setting a timer. He unwrapped the butter and dropped the entire stick into the sauté pan, an act that shocked her with its recklessness. It wasn't like she was a dieter, but she knew the dangers of an entire stick of butter. *No wonder this guy is excellent in bed. I mean, in the kitchen. He's a madman.*

He salted the pan and watched the butter melt, prodding it with his wooden spoon. It was as if he were God, creating a new universe to his pleasure in the tiny pan. He threw in the garlic, then a handful of the leaves and watched them curl away from the flame, trying to escape the heat. Maybe not God but the devil, she thought. The food smelled like pure sin.

"Pure Sin. If I ever had a restaurant, that's what I'd call it."

He flashed her a devilish smile. "You thinking of opening a restaurant?"

She felt herself blush. "No. I have my own life, thank you very much."

"Maybe you should start thinking about it."

She scowled at him, but he just raised his eyebrows and shrugged.

"So, Roni was talking up a storm tonight," he said.

"What did she say about me?" Amy asked.

He salted the butter/leaf mixture and stirred the pebbles. An earthy, rich aroma rose from the pan, and Amy almost swooned. James turned off the heat under the pan, drained the pebbles, tossed the butter mixture and pebbles into an enormous bowl, and handed it to her. "She said to thank you for looking after Troy."

Amy's mouth fell open. Warmth flooded her; would it all be okay? They'd all be part of a happy family?

"Just kidding."

She deflated, then shoved his shoulder to hide her

disappointment. His impish smile worked its way all the way to her toes, making her feel instantly better.

He turned his attention to the pepper grinder. "She said she's going to rip out your heart and have it for dinner for lying to her son."

Amy scrunched her lips, fighting down her panic. "From what I've picked up about Roni, she couldn't rip off a hangnail."

"Okay, kidding. She didn't say much. Just shrugged and smiled a lot. You know, she's Roni. I was just joking."

"So she didn't say anything about where she'd been?"

"No."

"Forget it. I don't want to talk about her now. I just want to eat." Strangely, it was true. She didn't care about Roni or Maddie or Gladys. Her entire being was focused on the desire to eat those misshapen white things covered in mangled, curled houseplant and glistening fat. She sat at the counter, accepted his offer of a silver fork and a cloth napkin, and dug in.

He crossed his arms and leaned back against the sink, watching her eat as if the food were some sort of magic concoction that he expected would transform her.

She ate a pebble.

But it was no pebble. It had expanded and softened in the water into something remarkable. She closed her eyes and chewed slowly. The leaves were crunchy and salty. The white puffs were rich and dense and melted on her tongue. She opened her eyes.

Transformed. Into a willing slave of this incredible man.

Neither one of them said a word until she had run her finger around the empty bowl, getting the last remnants of butter sauce. She didn't know how to describe what she had eaten. "What were those—clouds?"

"Gnocchi. Potato pasta. Best you can get outside of Verona."

"Who makes them?"

"Me."

"Why isn't this on your menu?"

"They're Italian. Les Fleurs is French. The world would end if I served them. They'd take away my French chef license."

"Would they take your silly hat?"

"I don't wear the silly hat."

"I know. I wish you did, though. I kinda dig the hat."

"Then tomorrow, I wear the hat."

They met each other's eyes, and Amy gulped at the charge she got just looking at him. *I know he's my One True Love.* Her heart thumped a warning.

James broke the spell. "Anyway, this kind of food is too simple. People want truffles and reductions from a two-star joint. This is simple home food."

"This simple home food makes me want to rip off your clothes, even without the hat." She put down the bowl and considered him. His brown eyes fixed on hers. Something inside her shifted. His gaze, his food, his touch. *He is the devil, and his food is his temptation.* As if his eyes and hands and the rest of him weren't enough.

Pure sin.

"That's why they don't serve it in restaurants," he said. "Can't have the customers ripping off the chef's clothes and doing it on the white tablecloths."

"But why not? That's the way a restaurant should be. Since there wouldn't be enough chefs to go around, the patrons would have to get it on with each other. Then if you were hungry, you could stroll around town and look in windows of restaurants and say, 'Oh, look, dear, they're howling at the moon in there. Let's try this place tonight.'"

"Pure sin." He nodded. "But what if it was a business meal with the boss and six guys from the Tokyo office?"

"Oh." She hadn't thought about other people other than lovers who might dine out. That sort of business world was as foreign to her as she was to them. "Well, that could be fun, too." She shot him a wicked smile and crossed the kitchen. He was leaning against the counter, and she pressed herself against him. "You should listen to your muse. Just think of all the customers who might want to give their compliments to the chef."

"They can't; I'm taken." He wrapped his long arms around her, and she let her head rest on his chest, trying not to melt from the beauty of his words. *I'm taken.*

Yes, you are, James. She memorized the feeling of his hard, tall frame. The warmth of his calm embrace combined with the afterglow of the meal and of the wine she had earlier lulled her into a sleepy lightheadedness.

They stood like that, inhaling each other.

She looked up at him. "We have work to do."

He rested his chin on her head and sighed. "We need to redo the whole menu. Start to finish. When Scottie Jones comes back, I want to blow his mind."

"Are we talking about food or sex?"

"Same thing."

She nuzzled into the warmth of his chest. After that gnocchi, she knew what he meant. "So we start with appetizers?"

"Appetizers," he said, nibbling her ear, "are my specialty."

To start: tempt, tease, and always startle.
—JAMES LaCHANCE, *Meal of a Lifetime*,
THE MENU: BEFORE THE MEAL

Chapter 21

$\mathcal{I}$t was an interesting culinary/sexual challenge. How to keep the sex light and small? A bite, nothing more. A tease. A promise of more. That was what an appetizer was, wasn't it? Amy regarded the man who was holding her. "I'll be right back."

He let her go, his gaze trailing after her.

"Sit. On the couch," she commanded.

He did as he was told, a small smile playing around his lips.

God, she dug this man. *Too much*, a part of her warned. She pushed the thought away. She was doing the work of a muse, after all, nothing more. Light and casual. Helping a friend. She looked around the kitchen for inspiration.

Then she saw them.

Ah, James.

This man was a special kind of inspiration all his own. Was he *her* muse? Well, it was possible. When had she ever even *thought* of opening a restaurant? Of doing something besides telling fortunes with Maddie? And she had already found it a name.

She looked at James. And maybe even an executive chef.

She sat next to him on the couch with the pint of strawberries.

A look of bemused curiosity played over his features. "Still hungry?"

"Starving," she said, handing him the berries. "Feed me," she commanded. She leaned back, her head resting in his lap. She licked her lips and waited.

He carefully selected the juiciest berry from the bunch and considered it from all angles. "This is an organic Sparkle from the first California harvest. I have them flown in from—"

"Shut up."

"Right." He let the strawberry descend slowly toward her but stopped so it dangled just above her mouth. She strained up, reaching out with her tongue, but he pulled it away. "What will you do for this berry?" he asked.

She considered. *Just an appetizer.* She unbuttoned the top button of her pajama shirt.

He let the berry descend to her mouth. She licked at it but didn't bite. His eyes lit up as he watched her mouth work the ripe fruit. He pulled it away, then lowered it down and then up again. Her body heated as he teased.

She undid one more button, and he lowered the berry into her mouth. It was juicy and sweet, but she still preferred a man's lips. Well, they'd get to that.

Appetizers.

She carefully bit off the tip of the next berry. Strands of his long black hair had escaped from their bondage, and hung down, tickling her cheek. "Mmm . . ." She rolled the morsel over her tongue. "More, please."

"You have to work for your food." His eyes were black and flashing, and she could feel him coming to life as her head pressed into his lap.

She undid another button, then reached up and slipped off his ponytail tie so that his chin-length black hair fell forward, tickling her face. He grunted and ripped her shirt open, pushing the fabric away, leaving her exposed. He bent down and tasted her nipples.

Her body came to life under the attentions of his tongue. He had slipped his hands under her and lifted her to him. He feasted on her, pulling her closer.

She let her hands trace down his back. Why was this man still wearing clothes? She pulled up his shirt and slipped her hands underneath. He groaned.

But then she remembered: *appetizers.*

She pushed him off her, trying not to wince at the separation. She nodded at the forgotten berries. "I'm just here for the food," she said.

He sighed. "Story of my life." He reluctantly pulled his eyes from her chest and dangled another berry over her mouth.

She closed her eyes, and their game continued. Licking, striving, straining. A drop of stray berry juice ran down her lip, and he stopped it with his thumb, then tasted it himself, then traced his thumb over her lips as if hoping for more.

Amy pulled a berry from the pint and held it up to him. He ate half and she ate the other half. He picked a small berry out of the pint and traced her nipples with the ripe fruit. Then he leaned in and tasted where it had been. The roughness of the berry and the smoothness of his mouth lit her afire.

Appetizers. Must stop.

He put the berries aside and flipped her onto the couch. He climbed on top of her, his body hot against hers. "You are the most remarkable woman," he groaned.

His hardness pressed against her, and her body rose to meet him of its own accord. "My father did always tell me to skip the appetizers to save room for the main course." She ran her hands through his long black hair, then pulled him to her.

"This might be a four-course meal."

His hand began to journey under the waistband of her pajama bottoms, but she stopped him and with a Herculean effort, rolled out from under him, off the couch and onto the floor. *Must not be total lust-driven floozy, but responsible, ethereal muse.* "I'm stuffed," she said. *I'm an idiot,* she thought. *I'm so, so stuck on this man. . . .*

"I'm not," he practically growled. "Come back here."

"Sorry. Appetizer only, James." She stood and rebuttoned her pajama top. It took every ounce of her energy not to dive back into his arms. This muse stuff was hard, disciplined work. Plus, she had never seen him look quite so wild. He might own this place, but here, she had to be the boss.

"You're kidding." His eyes were pure green surrounded by a thin rim of brown. His black hair was loose and hung over his face, throwing it into shadow. His shirt was askew, exposing a strip of trim belly.

Just one more taste?

No. She had to stop. "See you in the morning." She kissed his head. *Ah, this was the power of the muse. Control.*

And despite his anguished groan, she padded off to his bed and climbed in, pretending to be instantly asleep, trying not to let her own desire show.

Salade a la Tres Fleurs
Organic mesclun salad with sliced strawberries
and toasted almonds in a balsamic vinaigrette
—JAMES LaCHANCE, *Meal of a Lifetime*,
THE MENU: SALADS

Chapter 22

The next morning, Amy walked to Roni's apartment, the chilly morning air urging her on, the pit in her stomach urging her to turn back.

Amy took a deep breath. *Just because Roni holds all the cards doesn't mean she* knows *she holds all the cards.*

Think positive thoughts. She could still taste the nutty oatmeal she had eaten an hour ago. James had left it for her that morning with a note: *Heat on LOW for three and a half minutes while stirring CONSTANTLY* counterclockwise. *Do not put in microwave under any circumstances. Sprinkle with berries and syrup. Enjoy. P.S., Come bus and dice at the restaurant tonight. We're booked solid. We need you. —J.*

There was something odd about the note, as if it were written in a woman's hand. She passed a liquor store and stopped. The handwriting on the note was just like the scrawled writing on the wine bottle label in James's apartment. The mysterious Jules, Amy realized, was a woman. And she must be close by to have written the breakfast instructions.

Amy shook her head. She must be imagining things. Why would James get some woman to write her a note on how to cook oatmeal? It didn't make sense.

She waited at the corner for a Septa 44 local to lurch past, spewing another layer of fumes onto the already-gray snow, then walked on through the cold.

Forget the note; the oatmeal was pure James. It hadn't looked like much, but it tasted like maple trees and grandmas. She ate two servings, then licked the bowl. Then the pot. She wondered how much better it would have been if she *had* stirred it counterclockwise like the anal-retentive directions had instructed.

Still, she would have preferred James's warm body to a pot of mush, no matter how delicious. She stopped on the sidewalk, the woman behind her almost colliding with her. *Had their appetizer-foreplay last night inspired oatmeal?* She shook off the horrid thought. She stepped off the curb and made her way down Chestnut Street, bustling amid the people bundled under coats and hats, moving through the slush.

Maybe she shouldn't have left him all hot and bothered like that last night. Maybe he was trying to tell her something.

She pinched her stomach and eyeballed the half-inch of captured flesh. Talk about mush. Maybe that's what made him think "oatmeal." She had put on at least five pounds since she'd been hanging out with James. Who could help it? *An entire stick of butter.* Her mouth watered.

Ah, James.

Who cared about extra weight? More of her to love.

She gulped. Images of James's flashing eyes raced through her mind. And her body. *I inspired more than oatmeal.* She had to stop thinking like a nervous schoolgirl. After all, what did she care? It was just sex. He wasn't her soul mate.

Or was he?

It was time to meet Roni and figure out if this woman was for real.

Roni and Troy's apartment loomed across the street. She stared up at the familiar windows and said a little prayer: *Please, Maddie, see reason.* Then she hopped the soot-black pile of plowed snow that had formed at the curb and crossed the street, her dread building with every step. An angry cabdriver swerved around her, and she gave him the finger.

Amy rang the buzzer to Roni's apartment and waited.

Maybe no one was there. That was fine. She could think another day about how to handle this. Go back for another soak in the tub.

Wait. She had to command Roni not to tell her True Love's name. She had promised James a menu, and finishing her obligation to him meant staying focused: If she found out that he was her One True Love—she still wasn't convinced that Roni was telling the truth about Gladys Roman—Amy would bolt. Plus, she had to also focus on getting Maddie back without being flustered by things that didn't matter, like James. She'd get her soul mate's name as soon as she and James finished their commitment. Or not. It didn't matter. What mattered was that she didn't fall for her True Love, whoever he was. So best not to know.

"Hello?" a small, soft voice came over the intercom. "Who's there?"

Amy felt like a pimpled thirteen-year-old come to pick up a prom date. "Amy Burns. I'm a friend of Troy's."

The door buzzed, but she didn't push through. She rang the intercom again.

"Hello?" Roni asked. Her soft voice was barely audible through the tinny speaker.

"It's still me, listen—"

Roni buzzed the door longer, cutting off any further conversation. Amy waited impatiently until the infernal noise stopped. She rang the intercom again.

"Hello?" Roni was clearly confused. "Push. The. Door." She said the words slowly, as if Amy might not understand English. Or doors.

Amy waited. Roni could only hear her when she pressed the intercom button upstairs. The static crackled, indicating that the line was open.

"Hello?"

"I'm not coming up until you promise me something," Amy said quickly, before Roni could buzz again.

Silence. Then static. Then, softly, "What?"

Amy called into the small speaker, "I can help you. But you can't, *can't, can't* tell me the name you hear when you touch me. Do you understand? Under no circumstances tell me the name or I'm history."

Another moment of static. "You're thirsty?" Roni asked.

"No, history. Oh, damn. Just buzz me up."

Roni obviously hadn't heard a word Amy had said through the shoddy intercom. This was going to be tricky.

Roni buzzed Amy in, and she took the stairs two at a time toward the third floor.

"Aaaah!" she screamed as she came around the second-floor landing.

"Shhh," Troy whispered. "Don't freak out."

Amy gathered herself, embarrassed that she had been so startled by the boy. Then she saw the look on his face. "What's wrong?"

"My mom," he said, slumping to sit on the landing's top step. "Something's really not right."

Amy sat down next to him. This was a Troy she had only seen glimpses of before. He looked utterly beaten.

"You gotta help her," he whispered. "She's like a whole different person. She keeps shaking and then popping these pills." He let his head fall into his hands.

"I will help her," Amy said, meaning it—that is, truly meaning it—for the first time. She inhaled deeply. Troy looked like he might cry, and Amy didn't think she could handle that.

"She's all shook up. She's . . . I'm . . . worried." He turned to her. "Can you really help her get rid of that voice?"

I don't know. Oh, hell, she couldn't let Troy down. Something shifted inside her. *I'm not doing this for me, Maddie. See? I'm doing it for the kid and his mom.* He looked really scared.

Amy felt torn in two. She had no idea if she could get Maddie back, but now, face-to-face with Troy, it seemed to matter more.

He looked so helpless.

She reached up around her neck and unclasped her pendant. "Here, take this. Wear it."

Troy didn't take the necklace. "It's bad luck to give away your jewelry."

"I'm not giving it away. I'm lending it to you."

"Why?"

"Because, it'll keep away evil spirits. If you have this, you can help me help your mom. I can't do this myself." It wasn't really true, but it sounded good. She had to make him believe he had power, to let him know he could help. But most of all, to let him know that she trusted him, so he should trust her.

"Yeah?" He looked doubtful.

"Yeah." She urged the necklace toward him. "It'll give you strength. I promise. Now, c'mon, your mom is going to think I fell down the stairs."

He worked his mouth nervously, then reached out and took the necklace. He weighed the heavy gold in his hand. A twinge of regret rocked her—that pendant was her insurance policy, her life savings, her identity, her good luck. It had been handed down from her great-great-grandmother. There might be two of them like it in the country. Four of them in the world. With craftsmanship and materials like hers, maybe none. The sapphires alone could put the kid through a year at the Culinary Institute.

But right now, she knew it would make him feel better, and that was all that mattered. Anyway, she'd get it back from him. It was just a temporary good-luck charm.

If only her sisters could see her now, they wouldn't recognize her. If only *Maddie* could see her now. *I really care, Maddie. See, I can put other people first. I'm finish-*

ing James's menu no matter what. And I'm helping this family.

Troy cinched the chain around his neck. He didn't smile, but he didn't scowl either, which was progress. "Thanks. But I don't know how this is gonna help."

Me neither. "It will protect you both."

He fingered the gold, and she could see some of his anxiety lifting. She felt her spirits lifting, too.

Roni was peering out of her partially opened door, one dark blinking eye and a stream of long black hair showing in the gap.

A rush of sympathy for her almost knocked Amy back down the stairs. The woman looked truly terrified. No way did she have the balls to be pulling a con.

A flood of memories from when Amy didn't understand the names almost upended her as she entered the small apartment. "I know you're hearing names," Amy said, holding up her hand to silence Roni as she strode into the familiar apartment, Troy right behind her. "But you must not tell me the name you hear when you touch me. Do you understand? I can help you. I know the spirit that's possessing you. But if you tell me the name you hear when you touch me, I'm outta here. I'm history."

Roni was holding an open can of generic diet cola. "So you're not thirsty? I thought you said you were thirsty."

Amy studied the small Gypsy before her and the lousy-looking drink in her hand. The woman looked even smaller than Amy had imagined her. She was tiny, *maybe* five feet small, and delicate as a bird. Amy couldn't help but think of the bird skull at Madame Prizzo's trailer, with its vulnerable, thread-thin bones.

Amy had the urge to feed Roni. When had she ever had the urge to feed anyone?

But Roni looked like she really needed a good meal. Her pin-straight black hair hung to just beyond her shoulders. Her big blinking eyes stared out with such childish innocence from below a fringe of bangs that the woman looked almost younger than Troy.

She had no tits at all.

And her clothes. Black pin-straight pedal pushers, black ballet flats, a pink (pink!) sweater over a pinker (pinker!) shirt. Had she just mugged a boring, goody-goody, teacher's pet twelve-year-old? Her submissive I'm-here-to-serve demeanor wasn't showmanship like Stu's or Dan's when they waited tables. In this woman, it was real. Roni lived to please. She was a server through and through.

Plus, her hands were shaking like mad.

Maddie was definitely loving this.

But where was Maddie? Amy didn't sense her presence in the room at all. Was that because Maddie was contained inside Roni, her presence for Roni alone? A wave of hurt rolled through Amy. Or was it because Roni was lying? Amy watched the woman's hands. Was the shaking Roni's tell, the thing she couldn't help doing when she was lying? Amy filed the possibility away for later.

"You told Madame Prizzo you know about the voice." Roni's small voice broke into Amy's thoughts. She had actually sat down at Amy's feet and was now staring up at her, blinking her huge brown eyes. Troy was standing, arms crossed, by the door, unwilling to come all the way in.

Amy tried to arrange her thoughts. "Okay, first thing, get off the floor."

Roni cocked her head like a sparrow, but she got up and sat opposite Amy. Her hands were still shaking.

"Now, listen very carefully. Now that you have the voice—and the power—you need to be assertive. Got me? Like you know you wield great power and you're not afraid to use it."

To her dismay, Roni took both her hands and held them tightly. "But I am afraid."

Amy yanked her hands free. "You heard a name? Right? Just then? When you touched me?"

"Yes, I heard—"

"La-la-la-la-la!" Amy pressed her palms against her ears. She sang until Roni was forced into confused silence, her hands folded in her lap like a choir girl.

"Do you know what the names mean?"

"Madame de Guize told me they're the names of the dead who need something from me. But I don't know what." Tears filled Roni's eyes. "I don't know how I can help if they're dead. All it says are names, and, Amy, they're not all dead."

"Madame de Guize is a moron." *And a con-woman.* Amy wondered how much Roni had paid her and how much Madame Prizzo got as a cut. A wave of anger washed over her at Madame Prizzo for conning this simple soul. Not that Amy had been above conning the woman until five minutes ago, before meeting Troy on the stairs. It was decided: Roni was too timid to be pulling a con. "Listen, when you touch a person, Maddie speaks the name of that person's One True Love. The one person on this Earth chosen by destiny to be the soul mate of the person you touch. Do you understand?"

Roni blinked. "Maddie?"

Troy made a guttural, coughing noise. "Don't touch me, Mom. Oh, hell. You've already touched me. Is it Andrea Pruis?"

Roni shook her head. "No, Troy, it's someone else."

Amy shot Troy a warning glance. "Don't worry. The voice never gives kids their soul mates' names. I don't know why. Maybe so they don't tease each other." She turned to Roni, who looked a little relieved. "Maddie is the name I call the voice. I don't know her real name, but that's what I made up. She never says a word except for the names, right?" Amy thought back to Madame Prizzo's grungy trailer and all the words Maddie had spoken that night. A haze of doubt clouded her mind. Had Maddie really come? Maybe she had imagined it all. But she had felt the spirit's presence. She was never wrong about things like that.

I don't feel the presence now.

"I call the voice Ms. N.," Roni admitted sheepishly. "*N* for 'Names.' Get it?"

Amy tried not to roll her eyes. Who could make this garbage up? Only Roni could be so nice *and* so unfunny, Amy's least favorite combination in a person.

Roni sat up straight, like a goody-goody in the first row at school. "So, when I touch you and I hear"—Roni paused, alarmed by Amy's frantic arm waving—"I hear a name, it's the name of your One True Love?" Roni looked at her quizzically. "Don't you already know who your One True Love is?"

"See, that's the rub. Maddie won't tell the person who hears the names their own True Love."

To Amy's utter astonishment, tears again rose in Roni's eyes. Her face went pale. "I'll never know the name of my One True Love unless I get Maddie to leave?" The tears spilled over.

Bingo.

Of course this woman wanted True Love above all else—just look at her. Amy had been scheming and conniving over how to get Roni to give up Maddie, but the woman had been through with the spirit before Amy had even begun. This woman didn't want power. She didn't even seem to understand what power was.

If Roni was already won over, all Amy had to do was convince Maddie to come back to where she truly belonged. She was half done already. She really could help this family. "I can help you get rid of the voice," Amy said.

"Oh, thank you!" Roni threw herself into Amy's arms.

Amy felt as if she were holding a child.

After a few moments of awkward back-patting, Roni pulled away. "But you poor thing! You've never heard the name of your One True Love! I could tell you."

Amy lowered her eyes. "It's my fate not to know." A pang of curiosity zipped through her, but she pushed it away.

Roni's eyebrows crested in confusion.

"It's my fate to have Maddie." That pang again, only sharper. Maybe she was hungry.

Roni looked even more confused.

"I used to have Maddie. She used to tell me the names. Since I was five."

"Why did she come to me?"

"Fresh blood."

Roni's eyes widened in horror.

"Joking. Joking." Geez, you had to be careful with this one. "I don't know why she left me and went to you. She doesn't speak except the names, so it's hard to say."

"How did you find me?"

Bribes to some very well-placed Gypsy informants and a wee touch of extortion. "A sense. Maddie and I, I believe, are true soul mates."

Roni threw her arms around Amy again and drew her to her. Amy tried to accept the hug with grace, but uneasiness made her awkward. *I'm not conning her. I'm being up front. I'm helping her. And Troy.*

Amy glanced at Troy. He was fingering the pendant, and his face had lost its earlier pinched look.

"I know exactly what we need to do first," Amy said.

"A séance?" Roni asked, breathless. "I'll call Madame Prizzo! We could do it tonight."

"No. I'm making you both lunch." Amy went to the little kitchen, but the cupboards were bare. Had she really eaten that many crackers while she was staying with Troy? "I'm going shopping, making you lunch, and then we'll talk."

A half hour later, in the kitchen, water boiling and butter melting, Amy felt weightless, unsettled, and happy. Without the necklace, at first she thought that she might float away. But now she was light, free. Plus, she liked the way it looked around Troy's neck. She liked the way giving it to him made her feel proud.

She liked him. And his mother. Well, *like* was a strong word. She could help Roni, anyway, do it for Troy.

The sensation of helping was so odd, she almost couldn't stand it. *Time to go. Time to move on. Don't get close.* Who knew it could feel so good to be so—she struggled to get the word out—*good.* She had to work on trusting people more. She had to stop being so suspicious. Maybe, with Troy and Roni and James, she could stick around a while. Trust them.

Troy was at the table, slicing garlic just like James had, maybe even better. Roni was sipping hot tea. In this apartment, Amy felt useful. It was the way she had felt at James's last night.

I belong. I want to help these people. Roni, Troy, James. I have something to offer.

She felt Maddie's presence in the room. There. She was being paranoid before; that was all. Maddie was here. Maddie was moving toward her, step by step. It was working.

Amy scooped up Troy's garlic pieces and tossed them into the melting butter. "Now, let's talk spirit-voices." She stirred the garlic, trying to flip the pan the same way she had seen James do it, while she told her story.

Troy felt the warmth coming off the necklace Amy had given him. He was dying to inspect the pendant more closely, but he didn't want his mother to notice it and make him give it back.

So he stared at his mom instead. Since she had come back, she'd been different. Shakier. Was this voice really driving her that mad? Was there really a voice? Or were both of these women nuts? And what was with the pills his mom kept popping? Sure, she said they were just herbal, completely natural. But still, the fact that his mother seemed to need them so desperately was not reassuring.

Amy continued to blah blah blah about her past while she cooked. She had even bought fresh sage. How had Amy learned about fresh sage?

As she cooked, she told weepy stories of not understanding the voice. How when she was little she had pretended her teddy bear, not a mysterious voice from the otherworld, was speaking to her. Amy spoke with her eyes and her hands, and even her tits got into the act. You'd think she was on a stage, not here in their filthy kitchen in the gloom of a Philly winter, freezing their asses off, dirty laundry leaking out of the liquor cabinet.

You'd think she wanted them to like her. Like she cared all of a sudden.

And yeah, he kinda liked her show. Liked that she had trusted him with the necklace. Liked the smell of the cooking garlic. His mom never cooked for him.

He shot her a quick glance. Something was up. Something more than she was telling him. She kept looking away from him, not meeting his eyes. Had she heard his True Love's name? God, that would be awful. What if it was someone lame? But Amy had said that kids didn't get True Loves. But his mom sure seemed like she had heard something. He filed the inconsistency away for later.

The warmth from the pendant was turning to heat. It was almost uncomfortable how hot it was becoming. He let his hand cover it, but Amy caught the motion and smiled at him, causing him to pull his hand away. He half-listened to her tell her life story—voices, names, lovers united, lovers destroyed.

Troy let the stories wash over him. The problem with being a Gypsy was that this mumbo-jumbo psychic stuff was in your blood. To laugh it off like he did with his buddies at school was impossible when he was alone with his mother and her friends. The curses, the evil eyes, the possibility of your mother hearing voices that told a person's One True Love—all that mystery was in his life the way other people had their soccer schedules.

He played striker on the weirdo team.

But if Amy could take the voice away with her, things could go back to normal.

Normal*er*.

Amy was going on about breaking up families as she put one bowl of gnocchi in front of him and one in front of his mother. She told them about how she had once read a pair of seventy-year-old brothers who were married to each other's One True Love. Troy couldn't help but let out a laugh at that one, despite the chill that rocked him down to his balls. The brothers almost killed each other. Then one of the wives died of asthma complications caused by the anxiety of the dilemma. The other wife divorced her husband and married the widowed brother.

This voice is fucked up. He snuck a look at his mother, who was eating with gusto. Had she eaten anything since last night? He had heard her barfing in the bathroom earlier this morning.

But Amy's food was pretty good. No, it was really good. She used fresh sage leaves and a whole stick of butter. The gnocchi were store-bought average, but she had done a nice job with them. She wasn't half bad in the kitchen.

Amy regaled them with more stories as they ate. His

mother's eyes were popping out of her head. Why this spirit-voice had to come and bug them was just one more of life's fucked-up mysteries. His mother didn't want psychic power. She was practically trembling, begging Amy to help her get rid of it, whenever she could get a word in edgewise. His poor mother just wanted to get by and wait tables without having to cause tragedies. This voice clearly brought only tragedy.

Well, if anyone could scare away this voice, Amy was the one. He'd never met as fearless a Gypsy as Amy. Well, maybe Madame Prizzo. She was grisly.

Amy winked at him mid–punch line of a story about a born-again woman from Detroit who found out her One True Love was a radical polygamist from Utah named Clive who already had three wives.

His mother smiled, and the relief of her smile let Troy laugh out loud. "Oh, shit, what happened?"

"Oh, that one had a happy ending," Amy said. "After all, what was one more wife? It worked out fine. Best thing that ever happened to that woman. She said she always wanted sisters." She punched his shoulder, and he punched her back. His mother smiled, and for a minute, he thought things might just turn out okay.

That night, Amy and James made love. It was slow and soft and sweet. There were words, and cries, and sighs, and moans. There were caresses and touches and deep, lingering kisses, there, and there, and there, too.

If you had asked Amy how it began (James's kitchen), who made the first move (James), or what that move was (kisses, down the neck, slow and soft), she wouldn't have been able to tell you. In fact, she wouldn't have told you even if she could have separated out the details before her final climax ("James. Oh. God. James."). But she could have told you the look in James's eye when they were done (possessive, demanding, intense; then soft, tender, loving). More likely, though, she would have said something snide like, "He was amazing. Of course, with me as his muse, what else could he be?" But what she had felt had been deeper: a mixture of tenderness and yearning and desire.

And it frightened her.

James, if asked, would have been able to tell you about the taste vision that he got from Amy (figs and foie gras). Warm. Sweet. Rich. A combination that was wrong and shouldn't have worked but yet was perfect. Beyond that, he wouldn't have said a thing, because that was the sort of man he was. But also because, like Amy, he had felt something rare and deep that went beyond the recipe, beyond the body in his bed, beyond the usual hunger of physical desire.

As he lay beside her, sated, images of her filled his head, twirling and settling, then taking flight again. "Ames?"

"Hmmm."

"Why do you draw on the walls?"

"Hmm?"

"The horseshoe with the *A*. There's one in the walk-in, right? And tonight, I spotted one in my bathroom, by the tub, behind the soaps."

She shrugged. "Just a sign that I've been somewhere."

"Not a sign that you're leaving somewhere?"

She kissed his lips. "No."

"I'm going to tattoo it on my skin."

"Yeah?" He felt her smile on her lips. "You could use a few tattoos. I've never slept with such a naked man."

"Do any of yours represent a man?" He traced the snake down her arm.

She kissed him again. "No."

"Do you kiss me when you lie?"

"Yes." She kissed him. "If I did put you on my skin, you'd be a hawk."

"A hawk?"

"A creature of the night. Lone, beautiful, soaring. But ruthless."

"I think I'd make you a chameleon. Always changing to suit your needs. Adaptable. A survivor, no matter what."

"A reptile? Hey, wait. Don't hawks eat lizards?"

"Not this one."

"That's not how I remember it just a few moments ago. I remember—"

"This?" He bent and kissed her.

"Mmm. Yes."

And then they began again.

Foie Gras a la Tres Fleurs
Warm foie gras with black mission figs
—James LaChance, *Meal of a Lifetime*,
The Menu: Appetizers

Chapter 23

The nicest thing about the restaurant business, besides the unreported cash tips, was the family meal. At four o'clock, all the staff, from dishwasher to sous-chef, sat around the dining room's biggest table and ate whatever the kitchen dished out. Usually it was leftovers. But leftovers from a two-star restaurant were something to behold. Today, Manuel had taken leftover roasted duck and some about-to-expire greens—something peppery and sharp that Amy remembered eating once at her sister Cecelia's place—and mixed them up and sauced them with wine and who-knows-what, then dumped the whole mess over pasta.

I could make this for Roni and Troy sometime, she thought, recalling how good it had felt to feed them over the last few days. What didn't feel good was Roni, going on and on about doing a channeling right away. Amy knew she was stalling. But she liked things the way they were. Wished they could stay like this, for a little while longer, anyway.

Man, she was getting soft. In every way. Butter and cream sauce, cream sauce and butter. Poverty had its advantages when it came to dieting. The Gypsy diet: whatever she could steal, beg, or barter.

James wasn't at the table, but he was present in the raucous rock music that blared from the kitchen. He rarely joined this meal. In fact, he rarely ate except for his constant tasting as he cooked. She hadn't seen him eat except for a few choice strawberries. Last night, he fed her bread and cheese and cold meats at midnight, in bed after they had made slow, soft love. But he didn't eat any. Said he was sated by her.

Her skin tingled at the memory.

Things were going so right on every front. She felt good about Troy and his mom. She felt awesome about James. She was at this table like a member of the family. "The family meal." She tried not to like that, but she did. She could wait a little while to get Maddie back, but avoiding Roni and her constant urging to do another channeling was getting harder and harder to defend. And she owed Troy, although he seemed to be less worried, now that he had the pendant and his mother was feeling a little better.

"James blasts Zeppelin when something isn't going right," Stu whispered to Amy, breaking into her thoughts. He was on his second helping of pasta.

"Like what?" She liked Stu more and more as the days passed. He was a man who held his interests solidly in his sights. Amy liked that in a person. Made them trustworthy and predictable, which, strangely, she was starting to appreciate. Plus, he knew absolutely everything about Les Fleurs, since he was in as tight with the kitchen staff as with the floor staff.

"You know, chef stuff. Mealy tomatoes. Stringy quail."

Amy looked around the table. Of course, the news was out that she was shacking up with James; the staff was ecstatic. The buzz had begun around town at the new dishes she and James were creating, causing a rush on tables—and an increase in tips. They were booked even more solid than usual.

The whole staff was looking at her with begging eyes. John-John nodded earnestly.

"You guys planned this intervention," she accused.

"Si," Eduardo said.

"He needs you," Manuel, the sous-chef, said in his lilting accent. "The soup needs you."

Jake, the temporary dishwasher, nodded gravely and crossed himself.

Amy regarded her half-eaten dinner. Then she thought of James, scowling in his kitchen, unable to cook. She thought of his black hair, pulled back, his intense eyes flashing. She thought of making love to him last night in his enormous bed, tender and strong. She thought of Stu's wife and his kid who needed to go to college. Of Manny and Pablo sleeping in the hall until their shifts began, exhausted from working two jobs.

Most of all, she thought of Roni and Troy, needing this job after she and Maddie split.

And then, she thought of James.

James.

That clinched it.

"Anyone touches my dinner, I break their face. Comprendo?" They winced at her lousy Spanish. Whatever, they got the point. "Give me ten minutes. I see one of your nasty faces in the kitchen, and I'll chop off your cojones. Comprende?" This time they didn't wince but nodded earnestly. She must have conjugated the verb right. Her Spanish had improved way more in a few weeks at Les Fleurs than it had in years of school.

They were all grinning now. Except for Roni, who looked from face to face, confused. Thankfully Troy was still in school.

Amy saluted and the entire staff saluted back solemnly and with great feeling.

"Vayas con dios," Raul said, crossing himself.

Why did it feel so good to be part of this crazy team?

James was alone in the kitchen, standing over a steaming pot. He was staring into it, frowning.

"I hear you need to get laid," Amy yelled over the heavy metal blasting from the radio.

He didn't answer. In fact, he had no idea she was there.

She strode to his ancient, sauce-splattered boom box and switched it off.

He didn't seem to notice.

But Amy sure noticed him: his apron tied over his chef whites, his checkerboard pants like battle fatigues, his face dark and troubled. He had a smear of something white on his cheek, and she fought the urge to taste it.

He stared some more into his pot, then tore up a handful of something green and tossed it in. He stirred, the muscles in his exposed forearm tensing and relaxing in rhythm. He hadn't looked at her. He tasted the broth with a wooden spoon and scowled. He added some more of the green stuff.

Over here, big boy! She never had so much trouble getting a man's attention. Especially one she was sleeping with.

He was looking at the pot with such intensity, she wondered if a porno movie was playing in it.

I'm jealous of a pot of soup. Amy couldn't stand it. She studied his mise en place, the prepped food he needed at his fingertips during the busy rush. It was beautifully arranged in front of him, an artist's palette. Amy darted in and grabbed a handful of chopped onions.

James spun around to face her, his eyes wild with alarm.

"I have your onions and I'm prepared to use them," she threatened, eyeing his pot with intention.

He moved between her and the pot like a basketball player on defense. "They're not onions. They're shallots."

Amy bobbed and weaved. She faked left. "Whatever."

"Whatever?" He stopped moving, as if the battle were already lost. "Onions versus shallots are the difference between my food and what people eat at home. Shallots embody the magic of French cooking. They . . ." He was beyond words to describe the glory of the shallots.

Would he ever talk about me that way?

Amy opened her palm to look at what she genuinely thought were onions. James took the opportunity to grab them. After carefully placing the shallots on the counter, he turned back to her. "What do you want?"

You. All of you. "Got your attention, chef-boy?" she

asked as seductively as she could. She ran her hand up his crotch.

"I have a hundred and fifty dinners to serve," he said.

"Not until you serve me."

He inhaled deeply. "Can't. I'm cooking."

"So am I." She looked around the kitchen, trying to think of a way to distract him. She glanced at his steaming pot. Aha. She pulled another soup pot off the shelf and put it on the burner next to his.

He looked half intrigued, half irritated.

Slowly, her eyes never leaving his face, she carefully removed her panties from under her black skirt.

"Underwear? In my kitchen—" he stuttered.

"Underwear?" she challenged. "It's not *underwear*. It's a *La Romance* silk string thong with imported lace." She dropped it into her pot.

"Whatever."

"Whatever? Thongs versus underwear are the difference between awesome sex and the sex people settle for at home."

He realized she was teasing him and relented with half a smile.

C'mon boy. "What else would be yummy? Hmm . . . ?"

James looked back and forth between his soup pot and her untraditional stew.

Amy tried not to roll her eyes. You could lead a chef to a half-naked woman, but how to make him drink? She reached under her shirt and deftly unlatched her bra and extracted it through one of the armholes. "This should add a little zest." She dangled the black lace playfully before she let it fall into the pot.

James took a final look at his soup. "I think yours

needs a dash of this." He moved toward her. He reached his arms around her and undid her hair so it tumbled loose over her shoulders.

He tossed the elastic into her pot.

She smiled in triumph as she shook out her loose hair. "Well, I find those hard to chew, but you're the chef."

For a second, they stared into each other's eyes. *C'mon James, let's set this place on fire. . . .*

He crashed into her before she had finished her thought, pressing her against the counter. He dipped his head to kiss her, igniting every cell in her body. He bit her lips, devoured them. Then pressed his lips against her cheek. He worked downward. "I can't get the broth right," he murmured into her neck.

"Did you stir it counterclockwise?" she asked. She was already losing herself in his divine kisses and bites. He smelled insanely good, like spices and wine. He tasted even better. She threw her head back to give him better access to work his slow, careful way down her neck. His nipping bite-kisses drove her mad, and he knew it. She wondered if the staff would really keep out of the kitchen. She wondered if she cared.

He reached under her long skirts and pulled her to him. He squeezed her with the force of a man undone, his hand on her naked flesh sizzling as if he was branding her.

Nope, she didn't care who watched. She luxuriated in the sensation of his hand on her, working its way from back to front. Ah . . .

"This is crazy," he said. He had kissed his way to her collarbone and settled in for a feast while his hand worked its magic below. Stroking, probing, two fingers sliding inside her to find just exactly the right spot . . .

"God, James." She had no support save his strong arms. Her legs seemed to have turned to jelly. Well, in this place, imported quince jelly with chives . . .

He held her with one strong hand and stirred her with the other until she was delirious with the heat of it. The sensation of his tongue, teeth, lips, fingers, and tongue again on her neck made her crazy with desire. No, she didn't care if the whole kitchen staff came in to observe. Let them learn a thing or two. *Cooking school.* She wanted this man here and now.

He seemed to agree, as he spun her ecstasy-weakened body across the kitchen to a clear counter with the same efficiency he used during the dinner rush. Somehow he had flicked the music back on, and under the mask of the noise, she let out an animal cry she hadn't realized she had been holding.

He pushed her against the counter, her skirts falling around her. He shoved them back with impatience. "God, you're incredible," he moaned as he freed himself from his pants. His apron was already on the floor.

Unable to speak, she let him push her up onto the counter and spread her legs. He plunged into her, filling her completely. *Now that's how to stir it, baby.*

Cockwise.

He rocked into her again and again, his growl barely audible under the music as he held her from behind so she couldn't slip away. She drank in his intensity. *He is good in the kitchen.*

The pressure built inside her in synch with the desire unraveling on his face. Her beautiful man. Dark angel. He reared back as he came inside her full force, and a wave of bliss welled up within her. She closed her eyes and leaned back against the hard counter, enjoying the vibration of her climax. This man could take her anytime, anywhere, and it would be savage and exciting and—

James.

I could love this man.

He gathered her in his arms, biting her lips and kissing her face.

She slid off the counter, letting her skirts fall around her. What she felt from him had been so savage and yet so tender. She almost felt like crying.

Crying? She didn't cry. It was ridiculous. She kicked ass and conned losers and—

—took care of neglected teenagers and healed blocked chefs and cooked for too-skinny Gypsy moms. And worst of all, she didn't just do it for her own purposes; she did it for Troy and James and even Stu. Stupid, wife-loving Stu and his dumb son's college fund. And Manny's cute, crooked smile and lilting accent. And huge John-John with his fiery temper.

What was happening to her? When had she become a team player? When had she committed to these people?

They stood together, unable to separate, gathering their breath. She wondered what he was thinking. Maybe that he felt the same way. Moved by her somehow?

He murmured, "The soup needs saffron. I tasted it just as you came. Fennel and saffron."

For the first time since their menu planning had started, his comment annoyed her. Maybe sex in the kitchen was a bad idea. It made all too clear that sex to him was only about one thing—food. To her surprise, she found herself saying, "Take a day off, James."

"Anywhere you want to go. Whatever you want to do," he said.

She pulled back in shock. Now she really did want to cry. Was she getting through to him? "Really?" *Soup 0, Amy 1?*

"Really." He brushed a lock of hair off her face. "I know you think this is all about Les Fleurs and food and Scottie Jones, but it's not. I feel something more when I'm with you, Amy. It's hard to explain."

"Oh, you just explained it pretty well." She pressed against him. "Let's take off now. Fix the soup. Leave the rest to Manny."

"Okay."

She wanted to whisk him out the back door, before he changed his mind. This was unprecedented, unheard of. James leaving his kitchen in Manuel's hands. He must be really horny. "You wanna go back to your place?"

"No. Let's do something neither of us have done in ages." He pushed another stray hair off her face, and she wondered what kinky thing he had in mind. "Do you know how to ice-skate?"

He didn't just want to go back to his place. It felt like a triumph—a huge breakthrough. No food and no sex. Just them. Amy felt light as a feather. Except she couldn't skate to save her life. "No."

"Me neither. But I've always wanted to try. Let's go." He switched off the music. "Manny!"

Manuel pushed through the swinging doors. He stopped at Amy's soup pot. "Mmm . . . looks good, Chef." Manuel held up Amy's bra on the end of a wooden spoon as the rest of the crew piled in, ready for work. Stu peered into the pot. "Purple," he announced to the kitchen, and held out his hand for his day's winnings.

After all, Amy had already tipped him off.

"You're in charge tonight, Manny," James said quietly to his sous-chef.

Manny looked startled. "Yeah? You sick, hombre?"

"No. Amy and I are going ice-skating."

The whole kitchen stopped. Someone gasped.

"Ice-skating?" Manuel managed to get out.

"Yes."

Manuel looked to Amy and she shrugged, and Manuel grinned. She felt like a million bucks even though she wasn't sure why.

Manuel shook James's hand. "Thanks, Chef. You can count on me. You guys go have fun." He turned to his troops. "Hombres, let's cook!"

Soupe de Tres Fleurs
Oyster stew with fennel and saffron
—James LaChance, *Meal of a Lifetime*,
The Menu: Starters

Chapter 24

James and Amy skated for almost an hour, if skating was what you could call sliding like puppies across the ice, crashing onto their butts, pulling each other down by accident into a soggy heap, their limbs flailing on the slippery surface. Amy hadn't laughed so hard in years.

Now they sat on the hard bleachers of the University of Pennsylvania Class of 1923 rink, watching lovers and friends and families go around and around to the beat of The Jackson Five on the ancient sound system.

"They're pulling this place down," James told Amy.

"Were we that bad?" Amy unlaced her skates and pulled them off her frozen feet.

He smiled and warmed her toes with his hands. "I don't think it's our fault. Well, maybe it's our fault in abstract, since we're one of the millions of people too busy to learn to skate."

"You need parents who care to learn to skate. Parents who'll take you out and rent you skates and break their backs holding you up for a few years."

"Yeah, well, I score zero on all counts, there."

"Me too."

They watched the happy families go round and round.

"They're making way for something more important, I guess," James said.

"A French restaurant?"

"Nah, that's not important."

Amy snuck a glance at him. He seemed to mean it, for the moment, anyway. She sipped hot chocolate they had gotten from the vending machine. James refused to even smell it, saying it was neither truly hot nor truly chocolate. But he hadn't been able to resist her electric-blue cotton candy—which wasn't cotton but was most definitely candy—and his tongue and lips were stained bright, electric blue like hers.

"Are you worried about tonight?" she asked, feeding him a piece of the airy candy. "Manny running the kitchen?"

He ran his hands over her toes. "Nah. It's about time he got a shot at it. Plus, the soup is out of this world." His eyes clouded, and Amy braced herself for the conversation that she'd been dreading. "But I am worried about you. The word on the line says you're avoiding Roni. The boys are all waiting for some kind of fireworks between you two. They're very disappointed so far."

Not as disappointed as Roni was. The poor woman was desperate for a showdown—the channeling—and Amy didn't blame her. But so much could go wrong. Amy could find out Maddie wanted nothing to do with her. Or, she could discover that Roni lied about Gladys Roman and that James was her soul mate, and she'd have to leave him despite her promise to James, because she still needed Maddie back.

She'd rather keep things as is. James, his beautiful stained blue lips, his long eyelashes cast down as he rubbed her toes warm with his rough, kitchen-scarred hands. She and Troy and Roni—friends. Cooking together. Sharing Gypsy stories.

"They are right, Amy. It's kinda strange that you waited for her for days, and now you avoid her like the plague." James was watching her, waiting. He shook off the morsel of cotton candy she offered.

Amy turned away from him, grateful for the distraction of the skaters rushing past. A woman twirled gracefully on the center ice as amateurs floundered around her. For years, Amy had felt like the chosen one, the one who could skate circles around mere mortals. Lately, she felt like she was mostly on her butt, unable to even stay upright. She watched a woman fall, pulling her boyfriend down with her. *Falling isn't all bad if you do it together.*

James took her hand. "And Stu told me that the boys believe you're really a psychic."

"I told you I was." *Was* being the key word.

James pressed his lips together. "They say that Roni has a spirit-voice that used to belong to you. What does that mean? And why didn't you tell me?"

Amy shrugged, trying to hide the dread that was shooting through her like black tendrils, circling her heart. Of course James would know everything. There weren't any secrets in a restaurant. "It's Gypsy business. You wouldn't understand."

He shook his head and crossed his arms. "Amy, I know that look on your face. You're searching for the exits. Don't. Stay, trust me. Tell me what's going on."

Amy let out a breath she hadn't realized she'd been holding. "Do you believe in psychics?" She studied his face.

"I believe in lovers telling each other what's happening in their lives."

Lovers. The word caressed her, filling her with longing. She stuffed a piece of cotton candy into her mouth to stifle the emotion. He wasn't her soul mate. Unless . . . But *why would Roni lie? What did she want?* "We're not lovers, James. We're business partners. Menu planners. Muse and . . ." *Musee?* "Man."

"I want more." His voice had gone deep with emotion. "I want in, Amy."

"You don't believe in psychics and voices. You won't believe what I say. So why bother?"

He leaned back along the bleachers, long and languid. "Forget what I believe. We're not leaving this rink until you level with me about what you believe. I have your shoes, ma'am." He dangled the key to the locker where they'd stashed their stuff.

Despite his silly threat, he was serious about wanting to know, and it terrified her. "I believe that we have nothing in common besides sex," she blurted. *Push him away, then run.*

His eyes flashed as if she had slapped him. He considered her for a long time before he spoke. "When we make love, I get visions. They're not voices, more like flavors. Fully formed dishes enter my head, and I know exactly how to make them and how they taste. It's as if I've eaten them before. In another life, maybe. It's like a psychic voice." He was watching her closely. "So if my spirit gives me recipes, what does your voice give you?"

Amy stalled while she watched the attendants clear the rink of skaters. The Zamboni came out of its cave, waiting for its turn to wipe the ice clean.

"Does the voice tell you something awful? How to make British pub food, maybe?" he asked.

She rolled her eyes at him. A family came off the ice and sat nearby. A wave of longing rose in Amy.

"Recipes for liver hash?"

Amy took a deep breath. Funny, gorgeous, man. She was lost. Sunk. Gone. She watched the parents dote on their two children, whose snowsuits were soaked through from falling.

She was turning into Stu.

"Blood sausage and beans?" James asked.

"God. Stop. Not that bad. She tells me the names of peoples' soul mates." As soon as the words were out of her mouth, she was sorry. She held her breath. *You still with me, James?* She wished Maddie gave her something as mundane as bean recipes. She watched her words register as a shadow over James's face as he processed what she had said.

His voice came out guarded, his eyes on hers. "Who's your soul mate?"

"Oh, relax. It's certainly not *you*."

The green specks in his eyes flashed, then faded to brown. "How do you know?"

"I don't know. The voice never told me my True Love's name. I have no idea who he is, and I don't ever want to know. But Roni told you your soul mate is named Gladys Roman."

He cocked an eyebrow. "Me and Gladys, huh? Lets you off the hook." His voice was flat and hard.

"My soul mate could be anyone. He might be a she. He might be a five-hundred-pound shut-in who needs a crane to lift him through a hole in the roof. He might be a wife-beater."

"He might be a French chef," James said matter-of-factly. "Roni and that spirit might be full of shit."

"You think this whole thing is ridiculous." A shiver went down her spine, and she shook it away. "But it's not, James. I've seen the power of Maddie and her names. You have to find this Gladys Roman woman and you'll see."

He thought for a while, watching the Zamboni make lazy circles like a hawk. "Why didn't the voice tell you who your soul mate was?"

"Some screwed-up spirit rule. The one who has the voice doesn't get to know the name of her One True Love."

"But Roni could tell you?"

Here we go. She braced herself for his scorn. "I forbade Roni to tell me."

"Why?"

"If I fall in love with my soul mate, I can't have the voice back. And I'd rather have it back than have my One True Love."

His eyes scanned hers, but she couldn't read them. "So you agreed to stay and help me with the menu only after

you knew I wasn't your soul mate. So you could still get
your power back. If Roni had heard my name in the walk-
in, you'd have split?"

Amy rushed to defend herself. "If I told you that you
could have your One True Love but that you'd never have
another recipe enter your mind, fully formed, as if in a vision, what would you choose? The power to create amazing food or True Love? Think of that third star, James.
If you had to choose your stars or me, what would you
choose?"

"The stars." He didn't hesitate, and her body relaxed
into his answer. *So there.* But then her body tensed again.
The stars? What about me?

He fixed her with his hard brown eyes. "Because I
don't trust you, Amy. If I chose you, you might split, and
I'd be left with nothing. Give me a reason to trust you.
That's all I'd need. Then the rest could go to hell."

They walked silently to James's silver Audi. Everything
had changed; she could see it in his eyes. She had hurt
him. *I'm with you because you're nothing.* Of course he'd
take it that way—wouldn't she if she were in his shoes?
She shouldn't have told him so much. She shouldn't have
told him anything.

He got into the driver's seat and she slid in beside him.
He started the powerful engine and eased the car into the
traffic. "So you think Roni will give you the voice back?
That's why you're hanging around here?"

Amy stared at the city passing by. He was angry, and
she didn't blame him. It was a lot of information to take
in, especially for someone who obviously didn't believe
in the spirit world and psychic power. She knew that his

talk about recipes was just a metaphor to him, a way to explain his own power and its mystery. He didn't really believe that a spirit gave him his recipes.

Well, the man might as well know the whole truth. He'd find out anyway through the restaurant grapevine. "Roni doesn't want the power. She begged me to take it back when I told her she couldn't have One True Love and the voice. But it's not hers to give. We have to convince the spirit to come back to me. We're going to try a channeling. Soon."

"And when you get the voice back, you leave?"

"I'll help you finish the menu," she said. "If that's what you're worried about. Hell, we're almost done, right?"

"Yep. Almost done. No further business here with some second-rate guy who poses no threat of True Love." He stared at the red light swinging on its tethers as if it were the saddest thing he'd ever seen.

James gunned the Audi's engine at the first flash of green, shooting past the crawling buses. So, she was using him to get to Roni. She not only didn't love him, but she also didn't believe she ever could love him because of some whacked-out Gypsy prophecy.

So, he'd let her go. It was nuts, and he didn't need any part of a woman who couldn't stay put. But something was bothering him. Something about the whole situation didn't seem right. Something about the way Roni had acted in the walk-in. "I want to be at the channeling," he said.

Amy shook her head. "It's Gypsy business." She stared out the window, her arms crossed.

He pulled the car to the curb, slamming it into park

and turning to her. "Amy, I let you into my restaurant, my home, my life. You owe me. I deserve to see this power that you trust when you don't trust anything else in this world—not your own feelings, not experience, not even me. So don't even bother saying no, because you can't stop me. I'm coming, whether you like it or not."

Always pause before the main course. Drink a glass of wine. Relax. Get ready for the revelations yet to come.
—JAMES LACHANCE, *Meal of a Lifetime,*
THE MENU: BETWEEN COURSES

Chapter 25

"What's he doing here?" Madame Prizzo asked, scowling at James. She was wearing her white Chanel suit and a diamond bracelet around her wrist. If it weren't for the fact that they were in her filthy, skull-filled trailer, she could have been a customer at Les Fleurs.

"James is okay," Troy supplied.

James knew there was a reason he liked that kid. He flashed him the three-finger salute, and Troy returned it discreetly. It was the day after he had skated with Amy, and he had held firm on his need to come.

"He's gadje. If he's here, the voice won't come," Madame Prizzo insisted. She checked her BlackBerry irritably. "I rushed here from the club. I don't like when people waste my time."

"Aunt Alex, it'll be fine," Roni implored. Poor kid was at the end of her rope. Her hands were shaking again. "We have to work this out. Now. Please?"

Troy slumped in the chair, a study in teenage detachment, the black cat purring on his lap.

Madame Prizzo harrumphed and sat herself at the card table. "Okay, but I'm not putting on a show for him." She closed her eyes, and Roni sighed with relief.

James whispered in Amy's ear, "Shouldn't we all hold hands or something? Turn down the lights at least?" They were next to each other on the tattered couch. The early afternoon sun streamed in through the filthy windows. It was the second day in a row he'd left Manny in charge of the kitchen, and he didn't care.

I don't care.

Amy was taking him over.

"Shh!" Madame Prizzo scolded.

Amy patted his hand. "Don't believe what you see on TV." She had picked up a nail file, or maybe it was the bone of a small animal, and started in on her left thumb. Despite her attempt at calm, James could tell she was nervous.

Madame Prizzo began to rock.

Amy and Roni sat up straighter. Roni leaned forward. James looked from face to face, confused.

"She's here," Amy whispered to James. "I can feel her."

They all stared at Madame Prizzo. Even Troy glanced up from the cat, his eyes passing over the old Gypsy, then darting away as if he couldn't care less.

"Shouldn't someone say something?" James whispered after what seemed like a whole minute had gone by.

Amy raised her hands over her head. "Oh, speak to us, great spirit from the beyond!" she boomed.

Troy chuckled.

"Amy, you'll ruin it," Roni scolded. "Be serious."

Amy shrugged. "Just messing around. Sorry."

Troy continued stroking the cat. He must have gotten fur in his eyes, because he shook his head, rubbing his eyes irritably. He sat forward, wincing as if in pain. Maybe the kid was allergic to cats.

Madame Prizzo's eyes rolled back in her head. In a flat, soft voice she said, "Prove to me your worth."

"Is that her or the spirit-voice?" James whispered.

Amy ignored him. "Maddie, I've been proving myself. I've been taking care of Troy. And Roni. Plus, I've been *working*. At a job."

James nodded. "She has. I'm her boss. Two jobs, really."

Amy kicked him and whispered, "I don't think my *work* as menu planner counts in the 'good' category."

"Prove you're worthy," Madame Prizzo said louder.

"How? What do you want me to do? Does the kid need money? Is that what I need to help him with?" Amy asked. She whispered to James, "I feel Maddie's presence. The spirit is here."

"The boy," Madame Prizzo said. "He needs your help."

All eyes went to Troy, who still had his head in his hands.

Amy jumped up. "Yeah. I got that. But how? Because I have been taking care of him, Maddie. What else do I need to do?"

"You have not," Troy said, not looking up. "I take care of myself." He looked like he was suffering a migraine. The cat jumped off his lap and marched away, tail swishing, ears upright, flicking in annoyance.

"Are you okay?" James asked Troy.

Madame Prizzo shuddered. Then opened her eyes. "Well? Did she come?"

James looked puzzled. "That's it?"

"Did you want the smoke machine and light show?" Amy asked.

"I think I would have liked a few special effects," he admitted. He was having a hard time understanding what these people thought had just happened. An old lady told Amy to take care of Troy? Why had they thought it was a spirit? Why couldn't Roni tell everyone what the spirit wanted if she was the one it possessed?

Roni hugged herself gleefully. "Maddie will leave me. She'll go back to you! She basically said as much. We just have to figure out how you're gonna help Troy. Since you've already helped him by staying with him and taking care of him, Maddie must want something more. Oh, this is great. I'm so happy! We can make this work, Amy. We have a chance of getting the voice to leave me! To go back to you. She all but said it, didn't she? She'll go back to you."

Troy scowled. He shook his head as if he was also coming out of a trance. "I don't need help."

Madame Prizzo was already half out the door, her cell phone to her ear and a lit cigarette dangling from her lips. "I've got a lunch date. Good luck. And someone feed Louie on their way out."

An hour later, they were all back at Les Fleurs, except for Louie, even though James was reluctant to leave him behind. The cat would be better off with the alley cats than with that odd old Gypsy.

Troy had finagled the rest of the day off school, claiming his head was killing him. Of course, once the boy was back in the restaurant, he was begging to get into the prep kitchen. James let him dice with Denny.

Unfortunately, Manuel had managed everything so well, *again*, while James was gone that James felt at loose ends. Two hours to service, and he wasn't even needed.

Which gave him time to talk to Amy about that crazy channeling. She had hardly said a word the whole way back, but she kept grinning, practically exploding with excitement. James loved to see her so happy, and yet, he wanted to tell her that he thought the whole thing was a load of crap. He had to choose his words carefully.

"Ames, you wanna learn how to take stock in the walk-in?" James figured he could get her alone.

She gave him a knowing smile. "Sure, James. Show me how to take stock." She could pack the most innocent phrase with the most sexual intent.

He shook off the effect she had on him. "No. I mean really take stock. C'mon. I'll show you where the clipboard is."

They went down to the walk-in together. As soon as they were inside, she threw her arms around him. "James. Kiss me. I'm so happy I could dance!"

He ducked out of her arms. "I want to talk about that channeling." He searched his mind for gentle words. "It was a load of crap," he blurted. Oh, well. Careful was for floor staff, not chefs. "I have a bad feeling about Madame Weirdo. I don't think she was telling the truth."

Amy took the clipboard from him. "Don't ruin my mood, James. I'm too happy to let you rain on my parade. I've been searching for months for Maddie, and now I'm so close I can taste it. I know you're annoyed she says we're not soul mates. But we can still be lovers. True Love is way overrated, believe me."

"I'm annoyed you listen to a spirit-voice instead of your own feelings." He didn't understand how she could be so cold about this.

She ignored him and studied the clipboard. "So I go down this list? Check off what's here in this column, how much of it in this one? What's to learn?"

"Forget the stock. I don't think that lady was telling the truth," he said.

Amy lowered the clipboard. "Maddie was there. I could feel her."

"Okay. But all the same. I think that lady's conning you. She tells you to help the boy. What does that mean?"

"I knew I shouldn't have taken you. It's impossible for an outsider to understand. It felt fake to you, but that's because you couldn't feel the spirit's presence and I could." She looked down her list. "So I check off the artichokes here, then write in"—she counted—"twenty-two." She scribbled on the pad.

"Why do you trust that woman?"

"She's my people, James. We con outsiders but not each other. It's like a code. Why isn't this lettuce unpacked? Do I count it?"

"Sometimes there's an overdelivery. Count what's in the pans first, then the crates. Anything there's too much of, we'll make a special with." He was pacing, taking boxes off the shelves, looking into them, putting them back. He couldn't get through to her.

She counted the lettuce containers on the shelves, then went to the crates. "Sorry, James, but I am who I am. You couldn't possibly understand that. You and your uptight restaurant and your fancy life are all solid and real, but my world is murkier. More mysterious. You can't count up spirit visits and check them off on lists."

"Fancy and uptight? Is that what you think of me?"

Her back was to him, and she didn't speak.

"I'm not an uptight snob, Amy. My life was privileged in some ways, but in others it sucked."

She had stopped moving. He couldn't see her face.

"I'm not the snob you think I am," he insisted.

Nothing.

"Ames? You okay?" He touched her shoulder and she flinched.

She pointed at the crate.

"What?" He looked at the lettuce. "Was there a bug?" He pried open the crate and took out a head of lettuce. "It's good stuff. Flown in from New Zealand. See the deepness of the green . . ." He looked at her face, which had gone completely white. "Ames?"

She was still pointing at the crate. "Read what it says." Her voice was low.

His stomach sank. She thought he was an uptight snob. Well, this should change her mind. He took a deep breath. He had never told anyone this before. "I can't."

Her eyes didn't stray from the words on the crate. "What do you mean you can't?"

"I'm dyslexic." His heart was beating hard. Why was he telling her this? His deepest secret. If his staff found out, he'd lose face in his kitchen forever.

She turned to him, distracted. "Dis what?"

"I have difficulty processing written letters and words." A pain jabbed through him, as sharp as it was when he was seven years old and his teacher had sat his mother down and explained the situation to her. *Don't let's ever tell your father,* she had said. And James, even at that age, understood. *My father doesn't accept weakness. He runs from it without looking back.* "Remember when we were cutting carrots way back when down in the prep kitchen? I told you I don't blame people for what they can't control. That's what I can't control. My secret."

Amy opened her mouth as if to speak, but then closed it again.

James realized that she had no idea what he was talking about. He could still back out. Not tell her.

But he wanted to tell her, because he wanted to know if she'd stay. This felt like a test to him, making his heart hammer even faster. "I can hardly read," he explained. "If I concentrate, go real slow, I can get it. But it gives me headaches to even try. I got through school only because people owed my dad favors, and our household help did most of my work." Now that the words were flowing, they wouldn't stop. "I might not believe in broken-down old Gypsies pretending to hear spirits, but I'm not a snob. I can't ever be a snob. No one knows like I do what it's like to have a huge gap in your abilities that you can't control."

"Can you write?" Amy asked, her voice the softest he'd ever heard it.

"Sure. It just looks like a five-year-old's scribble. The woman who lives across the hall, Jules, writes notes and stuff for me if I ask her to. She thinks I have eye trouble."

Amy stared at him. Then at the crate. Then back at him. The look on her face was a mixture of horror and joy.

*   *   *

Amy stood mute, staring at James, then at the crate. Then back at James. This was too much to take in at once.

Okay, deep breath. Les Fleurs had no sign. Practically no menu. No order tickets fluttering over the chefs' stations like in a normal kitchen. And those breakfast instructions James had left her, they weren't written by him but by a kindhearted neighbor.

He was a lousy reader! Dis-whatever-he-had-called-it. She hadn't heard anything so joyously excellent since she'd heard the first rumor of Roni's existence weeks ago.

But then there was the news on the crate. Which she'd sort of known all along but had been ignoring.

Okay, she'd get her head around that next. Amazingly, it seemed less important than the news James was telling her now. "What about all those books in your apartment?" she asked him.

He shrugged. "None of them are mine. The chef who lived there before me split for a gig in Paris. I'm just staying in his place till he gets back. Knowing Paris, he may never come back."

Oh, joy! Oh, happiness! He had no home. He was a Gypsy wanderer just like her. She had to contain her elation.

Which was easy. She looked again at the words on the crate. *Shit.* She had known and yet not known. But now she knew. Her stomach tied itself into a knot.

Okay, focus on the good news: This accomplished, rich, beautiful, intelligent man had a flaw the size of the Grand Canyon. She let days of frustration at feeling like a first-class idiot around him pour into the gap and disappear. Then she looked back to the crate. "So you can't read that?"

"Well, sure, if I really focused. But what I do instead is compensate. I know that says *romaine,* because I can see the leaves inside, and I can get the *R.* They call that *contextual reading.* Us dyslexics figure stuff out pretty well. You'd be amazed. I get the *N* and the *Z,* so I know it's New Zealand Romaine without giving myself a headache. But the rest of the letters are twisted; they're swimming, moving. If I really concentrated, I could work them out. But it would be hard—too hard to do before needing to cook for five hours. It would suck me dry."

"How do you get through life?"

"When I was a kid, I'd convince our cook to read my schoolwork to me in return for doing his prep work. Our chauffeur loved history. He'd write my reports. Multiple-choice tests are easy to pass, if you know the tricks. Plus I had a tutor, who was basically a reader. It was easier than you'd imagine. Now I control my world. I have an accountant to handle everything bookish. Staff to do the rest." He nodded at her clipboard. "Like take stock."

Happiness alternated with terror inside her. "The tassels?"

"Tassels?"

She looked back at the crate. This was so good and so bad at the same time. She felt pulled in two. "The tasseled pillows? They're not yours either?"

"Hell no. I hate those things."

That was it. The happiness won out, bursting through every pore. She threw her whole weight into James, almost tackling him.

"Whoa, hey!" he protested.

She knocked him hard in the chest with the clipboard. "That is so great!"

"It's great that I barely graduated high school?" She had him backed up against the shelves.

"Yes!" She shoved him again. "Me too!"

"Why is that great for either one of us?" He braced her shoulders to stop her attack.

"Oh, James! It's great because I knew a fancy guy like you could never love a woman like—" She stopped, realizing her slip.

The world fell still around them.

His grip on her shoulders lessened.

Amy cursed her big mouth. Now he was going to think she wanted him to love her. Gah.

And that stupid crate. She tried to keep her eyes off it.

He stared at her, long and hard. "I can't believe you thought I'd buy pillows with tassels," he said, pulling her into him.

"I can't believe you thought I'd give a shit about something dumb like reading." Her face rose toward him of its own accord. *Forget the crate. Pretend you never saw it. Let this go on forever. Just like this.*

"If I knew my illiteracy would make you this happy, I'd have told you right away."

"As far as pickup lines go, that would be an original. 'Hey, good-looking, I can't read words, but I can sure read in your eyes that you're gonna love me.'"

Oops. There went that love *word again.* She looked to the crate. She felt dizzy.

The distance between them vibrated. "Hey, gorgeous, I can read in your eyes that you're gonna love me."

He pulled her against him, and she melted into him and

thought, *This is it, the end of my life as I know it, and it feels divine.*

She looked to the crate. It read, "Romaine lettuce. Gladysville, New Zealand." *Gladysville. Gladys. Romaine. Roman. Gladys Roman. Roni was lying about James's soul mate.* She had made up that name right here in the walk-in, staring at those crates just the way Amy was staring at them now.

If she lied about the name, she may have lied about more. Amy had to talk to Roni and find out what was going on. Because if James was Amy's soul mate, she had to choose—him or Maddie.

She looked at James, long and lean, his brown eyes watching her with—dare she say it?—love.

She had to talk to Roni. Now.

*When considering a main course, the simplest dish on
the menu will always be the best.*
—James LaChance, *Meal of a Lifetime*,
The Menu: Between Courses

Chapter 26

James was called back to the kitchen for a lamb emergency, leaving Amy in the walk-in with the clipboard and the lettuce crates. As soon as he was gone, she realized with full force the bind she was in. She felt betrayed. Gypsies didn't con other Gypsies.

People betray other people. Mothers betray daughters. Fathers betray sons. Happens all the time, stupid.

James could betray her.

It could happen. She'd have nothing.

When he was in front of her, holding her, she was sure of him. *I had wanted him over Maddie.*

But when he was gone, all her emptiness and doubt rushed in.

Amy kicked the middle crate. Hard. The crash of the crates toppling onto the concrete floor echoed around the walk-in, but no one came. Amy sank to the floor, hugging her knees, her back against the shelves.

*   *   *

"*Choose love,*" Oprah said.

"*That's easy for you to say.*" Amy reached for a head of lettuce that had fallen from the broken crate. She peeled back a leaf. *He loves me.* Then another. *He loves me not.* Amy felt light. Everything had changed. All her doubts about James being too cultured and settled for her evaporated.

But Roni lied. James might still be Amy's One True Love.

He loves me. He loves me not. The darker outer leaves were gone from the head, exposing the more delicate leaves below. "*Have I already lost Maddie forever by loving James, Oprah?*"

Oprah shrugged. "*I don't know what goes on in your crazy Gypsy spirit world, honey.*"

"*Maddie was at the channeling. She was, Oprah. I felt her there. So why would she promise to come back if I've already blown it? See, that's why I think I haven't blown it yet.*" Amy had peeled back enough leaves to expose the heart of the lettuce. The leaves were tender now, such a light green that they were translucent. *He loves me. He loves me not.* Discarded leaves lay around her as if they'd fallen from a tree. "*It could be that James is not my One True Love. Or, it could be the way it is in the stories, that I have to say the words* I love you *to him to lose Maddie forever.*"

"*Or you could ask James to teach you to cook,*" Oprah said.

Amy looked incredulous. "*Cook? How can you talk about cooking at a time like this? I'm trying to get my life figured out here. This is pivotal, Oprah.*" Sheesh, that woman always had food on her mind.

Amy thought back to the stories her father and grand-mother had told her about the Gypsy legends surrounding Maddie. In all those stories, you actually had to say the words I love you *before everything was lost. Like a fairy tale.*

But life was no fairy tale.

Or was it? Maddie was such a wuss, Amy wouldn't be surprised if she lived her life by fairy-tale-land rules.

"I'm talking about cooking," Oprah said, talking loudly to penetrate Amy's racing thoughts, "because you could use it to build a life without Maddie."

"Oprah, I suck at everything I've tried in this place. My carrot dice still gets trashed after I leave. They think I don't notice."

"You haven't tried." Oprah's lips were drawn tight.

He loves me. He loves me not. Amy had a stub of tiny, frilled lettuce leaves the size of her thumb left. The heart, it was called. Stupid hearts. If Amy left right now, this second, before she said those magic words I love you *to James, she could go to Baltimore, hit up her sister Cecelia for Troy's cash, get Maddie back, and never see James again. Or, better yet, she could go to New York or L.A. or wherever her other sister Jasmine and her famous, movie-star husband, Josh Toby, were right now. Josh would give Troy the cash to go to France or to chef school or wherever the kid had to go to fulfill his dreams. And she'd get Maddie back.*

If I left right now. Before I commit to loving James.

He loves me. He loves me not. A tiny knot of leaves were left, folded over each other as if they were asleep.

"You're still just guessing about everything," Oprah

reminded her. "Isn't it about time you found out if James is your One True Love for sure?"

Down at the corner of the walk-in was her mark, the upside-down horseshoe with the A inside that she had drawn when she was originally going to leave.

She should have split then.

"Oprah, I don't need Maddie or Roni to tell me; I knew the minute I laid eyes on that man that he was my One True Love. But you're right. I'll find out for sure. And if he's my soul mate, I'm out of here."

She pulled off the last leaf: he loves me.

I think I love him, too.

She ate the stupid last leaf, kicked the rest of the scattered leaves under the shelves, then went upstairs to find Roni. It was time to find out if James was her One True Love once and for all.

"Do you think she bought it?" Roni asked Madame Prizzo. Roni had snuck out through the back alley door and now sat in Madame Prizzo's Mercedes, which was idling in the handicapped spot. The heat radiating through the car's seats lulled Roni into a sleepy trance. She was always so sleepy.

Madame Prizzo said, "Yes. I'm sure she did. But I didn't like that James character being there one bit."

"Did the voice really show this time? Or was that you?"

Madame Prizzo shook her head. "I felt a presence in the room, but it didn't enter me. That disturbs me. It's the second time it's come. I made the rest up about Amy having to help Troy. But you already knew that."

Roni sank back into the leather seat. In just a few days,

this con would be over and she'd have her own Mercedes, her own heated seats.

Wait. That wasn't the point of all this.

The point was Troy. Troy would have his tuition and trip to France, and her baby would have a future.

If there was anything left over, she'd get the car. She ran her hands down the lush seats. Her hands weren't shaking at all anymore, and she had taken only two pills that morning, down from her usual three. "I still think we should just take the necklace and run."

"No. Too dangerous. We have to con her without ever letting her know she's been conned. That's the difference between common crooks and us. I have no intention of giving up my place at the club to go on the run from some bimbo Rom and her knife-wielding boyfriend."

"But won't she know she's being conned when the voice doesn't come back?"

"No, honey. Not if we play it right. After all, that woman knows deep down inside that she's too selfish and self-centered to truly win Maddie back. Anyway, what can we do? It won't be our fault. We're just bystanders, remember? We can't control the voice, can we? She'll just have to keep giving more and more until you tell her that—what do you know—the voice has left you, too."

Special a la Tres Fleurs
Roasted rack of lamb with bean quenelle
—JAMES LaCHANCE, *Meal of a Lifetime*,
THE MENU: ENTREES

Chapter 27

Troy and James didn't look at each other as they chopped shallots in the basement prep kitchen. Asking the boy to help him chop was a ruse to get him alone, away from his mother. He wanted to know what Troy thought of Madame Weirdo and the channeling.

"You want another five pounds, J?" Troy asked, pushing the shallots into a pile on the edge of his board.

James glanced at Troy's shallots. Thin enough to melt with the first blast of heat. The kid was good, but he should be out on the playground, having fun. Or at least doing homework. James shuddered at the memories. "How's school?"

"What are you, my dad? It sucks. It's boring shit. What do you think?"

"That it's boring shit. I wish I could have said that to my dad when I was a kid. *How's school?* A disaster. How was your day, Pops?"

"So why didn't you? If I had a dad, I'd tell him what was what."

No, you wouldn't, James thought. *You'd do anything in your power to make him love you, and you'd be devastated when you failed.* He fought back the pain stabbing through his gut. "You wanna make the stock tonight?"

Troy stopped chopping. "No shit?"

James put down his knife. "Definitely no shit. Shit would ruin the flavor of the broth."

"Veal, chicken, or beef?" Troy asked.

"Start with chicken, then you won't cost me so much when you screw it up." He looked at Troy, who was so excited his eyes were shining. He'd talk to the kid about his mother and Amy later. Why kill his buzz? After all, this was between him and Amy. He shouldn't involve the kid. "I'll be back in an hour to check on it."

"No prob, boss." Troy had already pulled down the stockpot and set it under the faucet. "You can count on me."

Troy squeezed his eyes shut, trying to concentrate on the stock.

Damn, he hadn't been able to keep his head on straight ever since that channeling.

Chicken parts, bones, celery, onions, carrots, leeks, fresh parsley, and thyme. He searched the walk-in for the ingredients, stacking the containers in his arms.

It was the damn pendant around his neck. The one Amy had given him.

He went back to the prep kitchen and dumped the containers on the counter. He checked his water, then started adding chicken bones and pieces to the pot.

He wished he could take the pendant off and toss it in the pot, too. That would get that baby boiling. Sometimes he half expected to see the circle of the pendant branded into his flesh. After they had left Madame Disgusto's trailer, he actually checked. The thing had practically been on fire.

He studded the peeled onions with clove and added them whole.

He should rip the necklace off. After all, he hadn't agreed to wear it.

But since he had been wearing it, luck had come his way. Scary good luck. Like Andrea Pruis winking at him in third-period bio. And his mom being so happy about meeting Amy. And now, not only getting into James's prep kitchen, but also getting to make the stock.

He cleaned the celery stalks and dumped them into the boiling water.

Of course, it probably had nothing to do with the necklace.

He scrubbed the carrots, then put them in, one by one, letting them slide below the surface like divers.

A flash of heat from the pendant scorched him.

He should rip off this crazy necklace and pawn it. He wondered if it would get him through the culinary institute. He had tried to leave it in his drawer at home, but it had felt so wrong, as if it were calling to him, that he had slung it back onto his neck. His chain-link collar. He was starting to wonder if Amy had cast some sort of spell on the thing.

It was definitely, somehow, getting into his head.

He stirred the stock clockwise, adding the herbs.

A hand gripped his shoulder. He glanced out of the corner of his eyes. James. "Should've known you wouldn't trust me with the stock," Troy muttered.

James leaned in close and inhaled, his hand still on Troy's shoulder. "Just checking. Nice start. Too much thyme."

Troy smirked at him. Any dishwasher could take it this far.

James looked over the array of ingredients. "Clean the leek at least three times. And remember, don't add salt until the end."

He put his hand on James's arm to push him away. "Back off. I need room to create here, Chef."

But then he heard it clear as day.

A voice.

A woman's voice.

In his head.

"Amy Abigail Lester Burns," it said.

"You okay?" James took a step back. "You look like you just saw a ghost."

Troy's hand flew to the pendant. *One True Love. Hearing names. When you touch someone, you hear the name of their One True Love.*

Troy stared at James, his blood cold with dismay. *Amy is James's One True Love. I touched him and I heard her name.*

I have the voice. I have the power.

James asked, "You sure you're okay? You look pale. Kinda sick."

Troy stirred the liquid in the pot. What was it again? Right, chicken stock. *Focus.* "Get lost. I'm fine." He hoped his voice wasn't too shaky. He hoped he wouldn't throw up. This was wrong. It was bad. It was everything he never wanted. He was a kid—what did he care about True Love? He had a good ten years of True Lust still ahead of him.

Worse, what did he care about the spirit world? He hated all his mother's Gypsy mumbo jumbo. And yet, he knew without having to be told that the voice was a calling—a destiny that needed to be fulfilled and respected. And how could you fulfill a spiritual destiny when what you really wanted to do was cook? Really cook. The kind of cooking that took all your time and dedication.

If my destiny is to have this voice, maybe I'm not meant to cook. Troy bit his lip hard, fighting back anger. Why couldn't his mother just keep the voice? Why'd it have to come to him? He had plans.

James's eyes narrowed. "If the stock's too much responsibility, I understand. I didn't mean to spook you. I can get Denny down here to help."

Too much responsibility. That was what this voice was. He understood why his mother hated it. Troy felt weak with dismay.

Well at least she didn't have it now, which should make her happy. But why did he feel so nervous and sick, like he thought she'd be mad as hell?

The terror gripping him was making him dizzy. He wished there was somewhere to sit down. But a chef never sat. Chairs were for the customers, he'd heard James tell a second-rate garde manger one night after a hellish night on the line just before he fired him.

Amy and James.

Who cared about those two? That was the least of his problems.

James was watching him closely. "I'm nervous leaving

you here, Troy. You look like you're ready to do something awful."

"Like add salt?" His voice came out weak and shaky.

Manuel called down the stairs. "Chef! The sauces are done. *Ahora.*"

James looked uneasily at Troy. "I gotta check the sauces. I'm sending Denny down." James withdrew with a last look back. "Don't demo the place before he gets here." He disappeared up the basement stairs.

As soon as James was gone, Troy leaned his elbows on the counter, dropping his head to its cool surface so he could breathe. He squeezed his eyes shut and counted to ten. Easy. Work to do. The stock, concentrate on the stock.

He picked up his spoon angrily and stirred the stock, clockwise, unable to smell or taste or even see. Anger at his mother—he felt like this was her fault, for not being strong enough to keep the voice herself—clouded all his senses with bitter, smoky hatred. *I wish I had a normal family.*

Normal. He'd never be normal again.

He smashed a head of garlic against the counter, and its cloves flew across the kitchen.

I'm one of them. I have a power. A stupid Gypsy power.

What now? Was he really expected to go forth and spread True Love throughout the land?

James was Amy's One True Love.

Why did *that* bother him, too? After all, what did he care about who James shacked up with?

But Troy knew the answer to that as clearly as he knew it was a stupid, baby-ass wish: He had hoped that somehow, James and his mom would get together. Which would—*stupid, stupid, stupid-ass baby*—make James his dad.

Oh, who gave a flying fuck? *What about me? What about my dream of being a chef?* He could imagine it now: The Love Café. Folks would line up around the block to have dinner and learn the name of their soul mate. Only no one would give a shit about the food; all they'd care about was the name.

He needed air. He'd take a quick pace in the alley. Kick in a few walls. Tear the town down.

He ripped off his apron, then stopped.

This was his life. He was making the decisions. Not some stupid spirit. If he didn't want her, he'd just get rid of her. Amy would know how to do that.

Amy. She was strong, unlike his mother. He could count on her.

He took a deep breath, then retied his apron and ripped off the necklace instead, breaking the clasp with a snap. He thrust it into the nearest drawer and slammed it shut.

Troy felt like dumping the entire pot of water on the floor.

He felt like tearing out all his hair.

He felt like disappearing and never coming back.

Troy was glad James was gone. He'd freak if he could see Troy's tears disappearing into the steaming pot. All that salt, added way too soon.

He had to find Amy.

Amy charged down the basement stairs just as Troy charged up them. They almost collided.

"Where's your mom?" Amy demanded. "I've been looking for her everywhere."

"Amy. Oh, thank God. We have to talk." His eyes were wild, darting around, as if he were being chased.

"Your mother lied to me, Troy. We need to *all* talk. You weren't in on this, were you?" Amy was rigid with hope that Troy hadn't known about his mother's lie.

"I am now." Troy sat on the stairs.

Amy's heart sank with him.

"Amy, I have the voice."

"That's funny; I thought you just said that you had the voice." She must really be losing it if she was hearing things.

"I do. It came to me. Just now. Downstairs. And you're James's One True Love."

That stopped Amy cold. She sank onto the stair beside him. "What? Wait. You? How?" She wanted to back up the stairs, start this conversation all over again. Or better yet, go back up the stairs and run.

"Just now. In the prep kitchen." He reached out and touched her. "Oh. Hell. I never knew James's middle name was Daniel."

Amy's eyes grew wide. "Are you screwing with me, Troy? Because I don't think I can handle any more lies today." *James was her One True Love.* She had known it all along, and yet to hear it spoken still knocked the air out of her. *Unless Troy's lying now, too.* The look on his face was too confused and pained to be an act—the boy wore his heart on his sleeve. But Troy with the voice? Why? What had happened?

James. She wanted to run to him and from him in equal measure.

"Amy, I think you gave me the voice. By giving me the pendant. It's been like a spell, getting all hot, and I've been feeling so weird. What am I going to do? I don't want it, and now you can't take it back. Right? 'Cause you love James? So I'm stuck with it?" He bit his lower lip.

Denny pushed past with a tray of raw meat, giving Amy time to think. As Denny brushed Troy's leg, the boy squeezed his eyes shut hard, as if trying to block the voice.

Had she given it to him with the pendant? Did Maddie see that as a changing of the guard? Had Maddie been waiting for her to *choose* her successor?

Or had Maddie led her here because Troy was destined to be her successor? Was that the connection to James? They all were meant to meet?

And did any of that matter? She had to keep her focus: *Don't trust Troy.* Don't trust anyone. He and his mother might be in on this together. She had felt Maddie at the channeling, which meant that maybe the channeling was real and that she still had a shot to help Troy and get Maddie back. After service tonight, she'd call Jasmine; if she and Josh were in New York, she'd go right there and beg for money for Troy.

Or was it all a lie? Was it all over, and now she was a waitress/buser/nobody for the rest of her life?

Maddie gone forever? Like her mother?

Stu appeared at the top of the stairs. "Showtime, boys and girls. First tables are filling. Quit yapping and start smiling!"

Amy looked to Troy. "Okay. The show must go on. After service, we'll all sit down and talk."

Dan yelled down the stairs, "Yo, let's move it. Full house."

Troy pushed back his hair. "Okay. I'll try. But I feel really weird. Everyone I touch, I hear her voice. It's creepy. I don't like it. This is gonna be a long night."

For me, too, Amy thought. *The first one of the rest of my life.*

Tarte aux Noix de Pecan
Pecan tarte with crème anglaise and French vanilla ice cream
—James LaChance, *Meal of a Lifetime*,
The Menu: Dessert

Chapter 28

Roni felt a strange vibe from her son, as if he was avoiding her. She didn't blame him; she had been feeling so physically ill lately, she could hardly bear to look at herself in the mirror. He was probably disgusted with her. He was so strong and independent, she often felt like the child around him. Finally, during the lull between first and second service, she got a minute alone with Troy at the barista station.

He met her eyes with his alarmingly intense ones. "Mom, are you okay?"

"Just tired. Why?" Roni was always exhausted. She remembered the constant, overwhelming fatigue of the first trimester with Troy. At least her hands weren't shaking. But she had taken maybe three—well, she had lost count—pills to get there, and she felt woozy. It was so hard to keep track, especially with her mind spinning like this. They were just herbs. That website had assured her they would be fine, "but everything in moderation!"

"Mom, when you brushed that guy's shoulder at table five, did you hear the voice?"

"Of course I did," Roni said irritably. What was Troy going on about? She poured herself some water from a pitcher and drank quickly so no one would see her transgression.

"Really? Are you sure?"

"Troy, what are you getting at? Shoot, table seven needs bread."

He grabbed his mother's arm to stop her from leaving with the basket. "Mom, stop. Remember when you said that Andrea wasn't my One True Love? But Amy said I didn't have a One True Love, that I was too young. You didn't know that, did you? Why didn't you know that?"

"Troy. This is not okay on the floor." Her eyes flashed to Elliot, who was smiling at a party of recent arrivals.

"Mom, I have the voice," Troy whispered.

Roni stared at her son. "What?"

"Just now. In the walk-in. It came to me. Mom, James and Amy are each other's One True Loves. Did you know that? You must have known that, if you had the voice. And—"

Roni felt the blood drain from her body. "Did you tell her?" She could hardly find her voice. A pain started in her stomach, sharp and jagged.

"Yes, of course I told her—"

"No!" Roni cried, much too loudly. The soft murmur of the dining room stopped. All eyes fell on the two of them. Amy, who was across the room, stared the hardest. But Roni didn't care. She hit Troy on the shoulder with her too-small hands. "Stupid! I don't believe you! You're lying!" She pushed Troy in the chest, her tiny weight having no effect. "You're ruining everything!"

"Mom?" Troy looked dumbfounded by her anger. He glanced around the room, which was totally silent now. It was as if two actors had abandoned the script and tossed aside their costumes in the middle of the stage. The play was over. Amy and Elliot rushed over.

"Take it into the kitchen," Elliot hissed.

"Troy?" Amy grabbed his arm.

Roni turned and strode to the kitchen, one hand on her stomach, Troy and Amy on her heels.

James looked up as the three Gypsies burst into his kitchen: Roni white and shaking harder than ever, Troy white as a ghost and sweating, and Amy watching them both like they were two fighting cats she was afraid to touch but badly wanted to control. "After second service, tear each other's heads off. But now, back to work!" James commanded.

Without hesitating, Troy pushed for the alley door, leaving a trail of cursing runners and line cooks behind him. James stared in amazement at the awful breach of kitchen etiquette. Troy knew better than to push through a busy kitchen like that. Something must be really wrong. James looked to Amy, who looked grim and wouldn't meet his eyes.

Roni followed Troy, elbowing everyone in her wake, a transformation so remarkable that no one even cursed her, but just stared after her in shock.

"I don't believe you have the voice," Roni cried, her voice icy and booming. James had never heard anything but near-whispers from the tiny woman. Apparently, no one else had either, as they had all turned to stone, the kitchen at a complete standstill. "You're lying. Amy, he's lying!"

Troy's hand was on the handle of the door to the alley, his knuckles white from his death grip. He didn't turn to face his mother. Every eye watched the boy's back as if he might spin around and come out shooting.

"Prove it," Roni challenged, coming up behind him. She sounded desperate, a woman who was on the verge of losing everything.

Roni's bitter tone must have been too much for Troy. He turned around so slowly, Raul crossed himself. An eerie vibe filled the kitchen like smoke as mother and son faced off.

Stu crashed into the kitchen, stopping just inside the swinging doors when he saw the showdown. Dan pushed through a moment later, bumping into Stu. It took Dan a moment to adjust to the wrongness of the silent kitchen, his server's aloofness transforming into mute alarm.

"What's on?" James called to his servers. "Orders. Now!" But his call was met by utter silence.

"Okay, I'll prove it," Troy said so calmly James's skin went icy. James stood in mute horror as the boy started down the line, touching each person in turn. "Lucille Cartwright," he said to Denny. "She's your One True Love. Your soul mate, buddy."

"The spirit-voice!" Eduardo said, crossing himself. "The boy has the Gypsy power to foretell True Love!"

"My high school girlfriend!" Denny cried. "How did you know? That is some weird shit."

"Ralph Vishnu," he said to John-John.

John-John went red as Troy named his "roommate." Snickers rose from two of the runners, then abruptly stopped as John-John raised his enormous knife and glared at them.

James stood aghast at his stove. He should stop Troy, but he felt powerless to move. The looks of recognition, shock, and then happiness on the faces of his crew as Troy told them the names of their One True Loves were too astonishing. It was clear most of them had heard the names before, remembered their owners fondly.

How could he come up with all these names if there wasn't some truth to the voice?

Troy worked his way down the line. When he got to James, he stopped.

"Chef? You want to know?" he asked as if the sight of James made him remember where he was for the first time.

James looked at the boy. Then he looked across the room to Amy. She met his eyes, and the look she gave him was half fear, half hope.

He felt about the same. "Yes," James said. "Tell me."

Troy closed his eyes and put his hand on James's shoulder. "Amy Abigail Lester Burns."

James swallowed hard. He looked at Amy, even though he knew his face must look like everyone else's: full of joy and wonder. She held his gaze, shrugged, and smiled, as if to say, "So do you believe in spirits now, Chef?"

When Troy had made his way down the line, the kitchen was so silent, they could hear the low murmur of the diners on the floor.

Stu and Dan still stood frozen in the doorway.

Troy took Dan by the arm. "Julianna Smith," he told

Dan, who exclaimed, "Hey, I've slept with her! Twice!" He paused. "If doing it drunk counts."

Stu flinched away from the boy, taking a step backward.

"No!" Amy yelled to Troy. "Don't!"

But it was too late. Troy touched his shoulder. "Daphne Herrellos," he said.

Stu grimaced and a weight settled over the kitchen like a blanket. Stu's wife's name was Carol. Was their happy marriage over? Was the pull of True Love too great to overcome, even for a family man like Stu?

Troy backed away from Stu, realizing what he had done. He murmured, "Sorry," to Stu and then to Amy, and then to his mother, then to the kitchen in general, and finally, to James.

James stared at his stove. He didn't feel like cooking anymore. Looked like no one did. But it was his job to keep this show going, even if the place was on fire. Which in a way, it was. He was about to speak, when a blur out of the corner of his eye stopped him.

Roni had slumped to the floor with a dull thud. James was the first to her side. "Someone call an ambulance," he yelled. "Dan, go and see if there's a doctor in the house. Now. Move it, dammit. She doesn't look good."

"She's pregnant," Stu said, kneeling at her side.

They all stared in shock.

"No," Troy said.

"How do you know?" Amy asked.

"I've been suspicious for days—she showed all the signs. So last week I asked her."

"Why didn't you tell me?" Troy demanded.

"Because some things are private," Stu shot back.

Troy turned red.

No one said another word until the EMTs arrived.

Amy had rushed with Troy and his mother in the ambulance to Jefferson Hospital, just a few short blocks away.

Now, an hour later, everything was calm. Bad, but calm. Amy hesitated outside the door to Roni's room. Roni would be fine, the doctors said, but she had lost the baby.

Poor Troy. First the voice and now this. Amy took a deep breath and entered the room, trying to look confident. Roni was asleep in the narrow bed, Troy in the chair by her side, paging through a book. Mercifully, the other bed in the room was empty.

Wordlessly, Troy handed her the book.

"The nurse told me she's doing great, Troy." Amy tried to sound upbeat. *Great for having lost a baby.* Amy glanced absentmindedly at the book. *The Art of the Con.* She had read that way back when, in her early days. "What's this? You planning to give up cooking to take your new power on the road?"

"I found it in her purse," Troy said, his voice flat. "Open it."

Amy didn't want to open it. She wished she could tell Troy she would help him by taking the voice back, but she wasn't sure she could anymore. She wasn't sure of anything anymore. Maddie going to Troy from Roni had confused her. What was Maddie up to? What did she want from Amy? If only there were a rulebook somewhere so Amy could know exactly what was required of her, instead of having to guess all the time. Did Maddie go to Troy because she knew that Troy would tell the truth about Amy's soul mate? Watching James's face as he heard her name made something inside of her solidify. *He was happy.* And even better, he wasn't surprised. He had known. She felt whole for the first time since Maddie had left her. Her usual urge to flee evaporated like smoke.

But now, in this sterile, cold hospital, when she had some time to digest it all, she wasn't sure.

Amy sucked in her cheeks. "Troy, nothing that happened in that kitchen was your fault. She was taking some kind of herbal pill to calm her nerves, the doctor said. She didn't know not to take too many. She messed up, Troy. Not you. None of us knew."

"The book. Look at it," Troy said, as if he hadn't heard her. He was gray with sorrow. "Page forty-two."

Amy glanced at Roni, asleep in the bed. The nurse had given her something to help her sleep after the tragic night. Amy sighed and opened the book to the page he had indicated. Passages were underlined, and Roni had scribbled notes in the margins in her spidery, barely there hand. Amy tried to concentrate on the type. Highlighted in bright yellow and then underlined in ballpoint three times were the words *You can only make a person do what they want to do already.* Roni had scribbled, *Leave T. alone w/ A. so they can bond? 2 wks too long?* in the margin.

Amy lowered the book and looked at Troy. Her heart began to thump uncomfortably.

"Amy, she never even had the voice," Troy said. "Look at page twelve."

Amy looked. Sure enough, scrawled in the margin over an underlined passage about finding opportunities by observing the troubles of others were the words *Oprah episode w/ A.B.? Pretend to have True Love voice? Find A.B.? How?*

Amy looked at the sleeping form in the bed. She waited to feel anger rise within her, but instead she felt even more sadness. "Well, she did a good job. I never guessed she didn't have the voice." Amy tried to sound calm, but she was starting to come apart at the seams. It was worse than she thought. The whole thing was a lie. The last few weeks were nothing but lies. Amy felt sick. Maybe she could take the empty bed next to Roni and sleep for a week, trying to sort out what was going on.

Troy handed Amy a piece of white paper, crinkled and folded. "It was stuck in the book."

Amy read it all the way to *Step four: fake channeling— pretend Maddie says she'll come back to A. if she helps Troy w/ $$$.*

Amy felt dizzy. So the channeling was a lie. Both of them? "I swear I felt Maddie at those channelings."

"I think she was there," Troy said. "She was there for me, though. I sensed her, too. I felt her enter me."

Amy crumpled up the paper and threw it in the trash. She should have known. Roni's shaking hands were such an obvious tell, and she had seen them and ignored them because she wanted so badly to have found Maddie. She felt incredibly sad for Troy and for his mother, despite the failed con. And sad for herself, too. The last channeling was a lie; Maddie had chosen Troy. It was over. "Come and sleep at James's tonight. He called a few minutes ago. He wants you there."

"No. I'm staying here. The hospital people said it was okay since there's an empty bed."

She couldn't force the boy to come. "Okay. But I'll be

back tomorrow morning as soon as I can. Troy, I'm sorry. It'll all be okay."

"Yeah, right," said the kid, looking at his sleeping mother.

Too bad he wasn't dumb.

Digestif
Bas Armagnac, aged thirty years
—James LaChance, *Meal of a Lifetime*,
The Menu: After the Meal

Chapter 29

Somehow, James and his remaining staff had stumbled through the rest of the night at Les Fleurs, Stu locking the doors at eleven on the dot, ignoring the angry couple on the other side, their breath freezing against the glass, hollering that they just wanted a drink at the bar.

The cooks who had stayed through second service left one by one as the last order was fired and ferried out of the kitchen by a delighted Dan or a morose Stu. No one hovered to joke and drink and decompress like they usually did.

When Amy got back from the hospital to see the last of them go, she had the sinking feeling that she wasn't going to see some of the cookies ever again. Once you knew the name of your soul mate, it was impossible to ignore it. Almost always, the name rang a bell from the past, awoke old, buried passions. Confirmed what you already knew, deep down, but had ignored for years. Life, as most people suspected, wasn't completely random. True Love usually struck early and locally, but it was rare that a person believed they had reached the limits of love so early. People wanted to believe their whole lives were ahead of them, because, of course, once you found your True Love, that was as good as it would ever get. It was human nature to hope for more, no matter how good it was.

Amy swiped a slice of peach pie from the dessert cart and sank into a chair at the back table closest to the kitchen. It hadn't been bused, like most of the restaurant, which was usually spotless and ready for the next night's service by now. She glanced around the room at all the tables still covered in used dishes and half-empty wineglasses. Just three diners remained, lingering over chocolate tortes and handmade pistachio ices, oblivious to the drama that had taken place earlier in the kitchen.

Stu was slumped over a drink at an unbused table for two. Amy wondered if he recognized his True Love's name. From the looks of the man, he did. His table was littered with the detritus of a couple's multi-course, satisfying meal as if it were the remains of life as Stu had known it.

He didn't look ready to talk.

Amy sampled the pie, closed her eyes, and focused on her own situation for the first time that night. *James.* She might still have a shot at getting Maddie back if she left now. But where would she go? What would she do? She didn't want to leave, but staying with James meant she had James and nothing else. Was that enough?

"Hey." James sat down across from her. He was disheveled but loose, like a runner who'd come in from a workout. He was still in his chef whites, which were stained and spotted with evidence of the hard night's work. He sat back in his chair, watching her closely.

"Hey," she replied. She stuffed another bite of pie into her mouth.

"They told me Roni lost her baby. Poor, poor kid."

"Yeah. They say she'll be okay, though. Physically speaking, anyway. She was taking some kind of pills to calm her nerves. She didn't know. So stupid." Amy picked at the pie. "And speaking of stupid, James, she was totally conning me. She never had the voice."

"Oh. Hell. I'm sorry. You came here for nothing." His eyes searched hers.

"I know you still don't believe in the voice," Amy said. "But—"

"Actually, after tonight, I do believe. That was a pretty awesome display. Even if it did wipe out my staff." He leaned forward, his voice grave. "John-John was outed pretty harshly. He just called to quit. My guess is he'll leave town. Manuel, Raul, and Pablo already hit me up for plane fare so they could go back to their native villages to reunite with their soul mates. Dan was out of here so fast it made my head spin. Roni and Troy, well, who knows? Look at this place—it's a mess." He raised his arms to take in all the unbused tables. His eyes rested on Stu, and his hands fell. He shook his head sadly.

Amy looked to Stu. "He'll be happier in the end."

"Yeah? I hope so. He sure doesn't look happy now."

"No one is at first." She snuck a look at James. Did he really believe? "Are you?"

"That depends," he said carefully. "Are you leaving?"

"I was," Amy admitted. "But I'm thinking now, I might hang around. I mean, if you don't mind."

"Mind? Amy"—James took her hand, his green-brown eyes flashing, his gaze intense—"you have to really want this. I don't want to be your consolation prize. I don't want you to regret choosing me when what you really wanted was that voice."

"I want you, James."

"I need you to be sure. Totally sure. I don't want you to decide now. I want you to really think it through. Because I want you." He hesitated. "I love you. But you have to think about what you're giving up to be with me. Don't make any decisions tonight. I'm shutting the place for a week so I can restaff. Water damage, I'm telling everyone. Let's let this all sift out and see where it falls."

Amy helped James clean up the restaurant with Charlie, the night porter who mercifully wasn't in the kitchen when Troy changed everyone's life.

When the last table was bused, she sat down with Stu, who still hadn't moved. He was staring into an empty water glass.

"You okay?" she asked.

"I know the woman Troy named. My soul mate? God, that was the weirdest thing I've ever experienced."

"Yeah. People usually do recognize the names." He was staring so intently into the water glass that Amy looked into it to see if there was anything there. It was empty.

"I loved her—but from afar. We went to grade school together. I never dared even speak to her. God, I'm such a putz."

"We all make mistakes in our lives. That's why the voice lets a lucky few people know how to fix their mistakes." Amy paused. "But only if they want to."

Stu shook his head. "You know what, though. I've been thinking this through all night. I don't want to. I'm not going after her. She might have been my One True Love as destined by fate, but Carol is my One True Love as decided by me. Isn't that worth something?"

"It's worth a lot. You don't have to do anything you don't want to do." This was why Amy never told good people the names of their soul mates if she could help it. It was information for the desperate, for people in need of transformation.

For her?

"Carol is my rock. I couldn't leave her. Ever. I love her. She's not second best. What we have isn't second best."

Amy smiled at Stu. "True Love is what's destined. We don't have to accept our destinies. We can change them."

"Yeah? I won't get struck by lightning?"

"You might. But if you do, who do you want at your side? Carol?"

"I better get going. Carol's waiting. She'll worry. Even if I am her second-rate love."

"Any love isn't bad," Amy said. "Most people would kill for their second-best love. Or their third. Number one is so overrated."

"You got that right," Stu said, pushing out of his seat. He patted Amy on the shoulder. "Guys like me, we do fine without the medals and the stars and the excitement." He looked around at the empty restaurant. "Good luck with James. You two really were meant to be together. I'm happy for you both." He stopped and looked at her. "So don't you blow it!"

*　　　*　　　*

Amy went out into the alley to get some air. She felt melancholy and wanted to talk to Oprah. She was sad for Troy and for Roni and even for herself. To never hear Maddie's voice again felt like losing something precious. Was James right that she would end up resenting him? She thought back to the first day she had set foot in Les Fleurs. She had acted cocky and confident and sexual, when really she felt lost and scared. But then she thought she was on to something, thought she had figured out how to get where she wanted to go.

Now, she just felt lost. If she stayed with James, what would happen to her for the rest of her life? Would she wait tables? Bus in his restaurant? Was love enough, or was she like Stu and needed something different?

"Hey. Don't you have a job or something?" James opened the door to the alley.

"Nah. Some chef dude pays me, but he's a sucker 'cause I sleep with him."

James stepped into the alley, glistening with sweat like an athlete just off the field. "Whole place is closed up for the week. I'm actually looking forward to a vacation. Haven't had one in years."

"You're gonna die of pneumonia," she said.

"Does that mean you care?"

Yes. She imagined nursing him, toweling his forehead, feeding him chicken soup. The scene was strangely appealing.

What if she chose James? Lived with him and nursed him if he fell ill. Joined his crew. Learned to stir counterclockwise. Staring at him, the faint stirrings of the possibility of the alternative life that Oprah had been pushing her toward seemed possible.

He slid his back down the wall so that he was sitting next to her on the empty crates. He knocked his knee into hers.

She let her head fall to his shoulder. Sitting with him made her feel better. The warmth of him was comforting. "Think the menu's done?"

"A menu's never done." He reached out and brushed a stray piece of hair off her face. "But we're ready for Scottie, if that's what you mean. Every dish is perfected except that braised duck. We did awesome, Ames. We're ready to knock him dead. Once I can restaff, that is."

"Do you think . . . ?" Amy's voice caught in her throat. What was she doing?

James turned to her, his eyes light and curious.

She gulped. God, this was dumb. But she couldn't form the words.

"What's wrong? More bad news?"

She sucked in the frigid air. "Do you think I could ever be any good at this restaurant thing? Maybe in the kitchen," she blurted. Her eyes darted to his, then closed tightly. "Forget it."

He didn't say anything. She didn't dare look at him. Instead, she put her elbows on her knees and let her head fall into her hands. She hoped her cascading hair hid her face. *Could this be any more humiliating?*

He still didn't say anything. What could he say, after all? *Look, I enjoy getting naked with you, and you're doing fine with your one table and busing with Troy and chopping with Denny, but I can't let you touch anything important in my restaurant just 'cause we're good in bed and are soul mates.*

Why didn't the jerk say something?

She dared a glance at him, and the insufferable man was smiling.

She hid her face back in the cradle of her arms. "Forget it."

"You wanna learn to cook? Really cook?"

"No. I said forget it." But she didn't want to forget it, despite the hot red blush she could feel creeping up her face.

More silence.

Another snuck glance.

Another unbearable shit-eating grin.

She kicked him hard in the shin. What had she been thinking? He wasn't going to let her cook.

James put his face next to hers, startling her. His cheek warmed hers; his condensed breath mingled with hers. "You could cook. I mean, not just chop or sling salads. I mean really cook. I wasn't laughing at you. I was happy. I've been waiting for you to tell me that you want to do this. With me. I've been thinking about it for a while. Almost since the beginning."

She raised her head and met his gaze. His brown-green eyes had never looked so sincere. "Since before we slept together?"

"Since the minute I laid eyes on you, I knew you had the balls for my kitchen."

"You think I could be a chef? You're not just teasing me?"

"Nah. I didn't say chef. I said a cook. A lineman. Woman. A line *stud*. You'd be great. If there was ever a woman who could take the heat of a professional kitchen, it's you."

Amy let the distinction settle over her. *A cook.* It was

better than being a chef. Chef was intellectual. Uptight. *French*. But a cook had balls. Had *fun*.

"You gotta start from the bottom," James said. "Work like a dog. There's not a single thing that's easy about a professional kitchen. It's shit work with shittier hours in the most god-awful shit conditions. The hardest job in the world." He paused. "The best job in the world."

She considered what he was offering her, imagined the chaos of his kitchen—the shouting, the cursing, the mosh-pit steam bath. It was sweaty and hard and . . . *possible*? The small animal of hope that had stirred earlier raised its head again. Not bussing or waiting tables but cooking real food. Real fire. *With James.*

"The kitchen is the last place in America where sexual harassment is still the rule," James went on. "A woman in a kitchen is a dangerous thing. You've got to give it and take it and swing it over your head like a cowboy. You've got to get burned and slashed and then get slashes on your burns and burns on your slashes and love it so much you come back for more. My boys will rib you extra hard, because they'll know you're sleeping with me. And you'll deserve it, because in the beginning, you'll suck. You'll screw up. And every screwup will ruin some server's night on the floor and four cookies' nights on the line and cost me hundreds of dollars—"

"The idiots I can handle. It's the food . . ."

James smiled. "Oh, the food's the easy part. Anyone can learn the food. Professional cooking isn't about food. It's about having cojones. Oh, and it's also about speaking Spanish, but you're getting good at that."

"Why are you doing this?"

"Because I know you can do it. I knew the instant I

saw you. Cook with me, Amy. It'll be even more fun than sex."

"God, you're a sicko."

He grinned. "Exactly. We all are. C'mon. Join the family. Well, what's left of it."

They made love that night so softly it was like starting anew.

The next day, James disappeared at the crack of dawn, reappearing with bagels and a brown package just after ten. He tried to pull Amy out of bed.

"Can't we finish perfecting the braised duck before we eat?" Amy asked. They had been working on the duck last night by making love in the shower to test if it needed more salt. Braising, as James had explained, is the careful, steady application of hot liquid to flesh.

Indeed.

"Nope. I got you a present. Come into the kitchen and open it." His eyes were shining.

The package James had put on the kitchen table between them was wrapped in brown butcher paper.

"What are we celebrating? The destruction of your staff? The closing of Les Fleurs?"

"Temporary closing. We're celebrating the prophecy. And your new career. And the menu. That was it, partner. We got the final entrée last night—braised duck. I figured out the sauce. We did it, Amy. You and me."

"And to celebrate, you got me pork chops?" She turned the brown package over.

"Open it."

Amy tore through the string and paper to reveal three gleaming silver knives.

"They're Japanese," James explained. "The best."

Amy was speechless. She picked up the biggest knife and weighed it in her hand. It was solid and satisfying. Like James.

"I want you to take the idea of cooking for me seriously." James pushed the knives aside and drew her into his arms. He leaned in and kissed her, warm and soft, his lips brushing hers. "Amy?" James was staring at her intently.

"Hmm?" She rested her head against his chest.

"Will you promise to stick around? Will you really stay? Because I don't want to waste time training someone who's just gonna split on me." He rested his chin on the top of her head.

"I'll stay." She knew he wasn't talking about just the kitchen. And neither was she. She took a deep breath. This was it, now or never. *Good-bye, Maddie. I'll miss you.*

I love you, James.

She couldn't say it.

She braced herself. *James, I love you.* The words wouldn't come out.

He wrapped her in his arms. "Are you okay?"

If she said the words out loud, she could never get Maddie back. So she was going to say them. She was going to commit.

Except that she couldn't get the words out. *Roni was lying and Madame Prizzo was lying. It was all a great big con, and now I have no power, will never have psychic power ever again.* The urge to flee pulled at her. Why would she want to learn to work in a hot, brutal kitchen? She'd be beholden to James, and then he'd leave her, too, one day. Just like Maddie and Amy's mother and then she'd be back to square one with nothing.

He held her tighter. "What's wrong?"

She pulled away from him. "I can't do this, James. I just can't. It's not enough. I don't want to be trained. I don't want to play second fiddle. I just can't. I need things to be even. I'm sorry. I thought I could do this. But I can't." She handed him the knives. "I know I suck. But I can't help it. It's the one thing I can't help, you know? I have to go."

Dessert

Sometimes you just don't feel like eating. Even chocolate.
Well, maybe still chocolate.
—AMY BURNS

Chapter 30

Amy plodded toward the train station, the wet slush bleeding through her boots, soaking her feet. But she didn't care. The stinging numbness at least felt like something, as opposed to the gap of nothingness that laid before her.

No Maddie.

No power.

No James.

Eventually James would understand why she had to leave. Why she couldn't play second fiddle and be happy.

She plowed through the red lights, daring the lumbering buses and screeching, cursing SUV drivers to hit her. It felt good to give them the finger back, to yell about nothing but who went first. But now, over the river, in front of the grand train station, she was forced to yield to the traffic racing off the expressway.

And to acknowledge that her feet were taking her exactly where she needed to go: home to Baltimore to start her life over again.

She stared up at Thirtieth Street Station, its white pillars majestic, its American flags flapping. The huge station seemed to offer hope. She just had to get on a train and get out of this city, to leave it behind as if it were all a bad dream.

She pushed through the station's revolving door into the teeming station. Around her, people hurried, bustled, and ran. These people were all going somewhere. Damn them.

"Amy Burns?"

Oh, great. Just what she needed. It was Bob, the Baltimore land developer she had scammed ages ago who had made a scene at Les Fleurs. "Get lost. I've got nothing to give you. Your money's gone. So just forget it."

He stared at her, an odd expression on his face. He looked . . . peaceful. "I don't want your money," he said.

Amy looked at him closely. He wore a name tag: *Robert Stutz, Food and Shelter.* "Bob? What are you doing?"

"I found her, Amy. I found Susan Lord. After I left the restaurant that day, I couldn't sleep for a week. So I looked her up, and she was right here in Philly. We're getting married."

Amy blinked at him.

"I gave up my business so I could volunteer. I'm at the station now five days a week looking for homeless folks who need a hand."

"I'm not homeless," Amy reminded him.

He took her by the elbow and steered her to a narrow bench. "Oh, but I think you are. We're all homeless until we find our One True Love. Amy, you helped me. It took years, but you showed me that True Love was all that mattered."

"Well, not *all* that mattered." She tried to look around him to the train schedule flipping through arrivals and departures on the huge board in the center of the concourse.

"Oh, you're such a kidder. I still had that note you left me when you scammed me years back. After I left the restaurant that night, I reread it. And I realized that my life was all about me—and that was a horrible way to be."

"Well. Sometimes. But other times, you have to think of yourself first." The next train to Baltimore was leaving in four minutes on track six. She still needed a ticket.

"No. Not once you find your One True Love. Amy, I had no idea what a total loser I was until I found Susan."

"Not a total loser. You were rich and powerful—"

"I was an idiot." A homeless man moved past them, reeking of everything vile Amy could imagine. "Excuse me," Bob said. "Duty calls. Amy, thank you. Without you, I'd go through my entire life being a self-centered loser who thought money and power were all that mattered. Thank God you found me!"

Bob jumped up and chased after the homeless man.

What a boob.

The loudspeaker called for her train, boarding, first call.

I am not a self-centered loser.

She watched Bob take the homeless man's bag and escort him like royalty across the station floor, and a thought hit her that numbed her whole body: *I have never, ever in my life had a real friend.*

Tears started to come, a tsunami of emotion. *I thought all these people at Les Fleurs were my friends, but they were conning me. I thought James was my friend, but . . .*

But what? He hadn't conned her.

But still I'm furious at him for taking away the best thing in my life, even if I know it's not his fault.

Bob and the man disappeared into the crowd. Bob had even lost a little weight.

The last call for the 11:03 to Baltimore sounded.

She didn't move.

The final call sounded. She jumped up, suddenly sure of what needed to be done. She raced down the escalator to track six and snuck through the doors of the train just before they closed, avoiding the conductor taking tickets at the other end of the car.

She watched the empty, dark platform as the train began to pull away.

"I can't believe I'm here," James said, picking up a bird skeleton. It was the second night after he had closed the restaurant; unable to stop thinking about the old Gypsy, Madame Prizzo, he had come to visit her. Roni was out of the hospital, feeling fine physically but too depressed to get off the couch. She had called him to her couch-side yesterday and confessed everything. Most of it was sad and depressing, especially because he would have given Troy whatever he needed if she had only asked.

But what stuck in James's mind most of all was what Roni had told him about Madame Prizzo: that before she had been in on the con, she had summoned the voice from the beyond. Despite his lingering skepticism, it was too much to resist. Now that Amy was gone and the restaurant was closed, there didn't seem to be much to lose.

Madame Prizzo shrugged. "Oh, you'd be surprised who ends up here." The old woman was wearing a stylish black knit skirt and black wrap top. She looked like she was going somewhere swank. Like Les Fleurs. Not that he had any idea how he'd open the place again for anyone stylish and swank. He had gotten six messages on his cell phone in the last two days, including John-John, telling him about his new job over at the Fondy; Raul saying he was going to Ecuador to find someone named Esperita; and Denny asking for James to front him four hundred bucks for a flight to Nebraska.

Which he did.

Madame Prizzo was staring at him, and he shook himself into the present. What had they been talking about? Right, she was bragging about her clients.

She held up a Philadelphia Eagles jersey and flashed the signature on the back. James vaguely recognized the number of the quarterback, a nice guy who used to come in after Sunday-night home games. He'd leave huge tips and diners breathless, although the scribbled name on the shirt was gibberish to James, and he didn't have the energy to decode it. "Don't bet against them this weekend." She moved around the trailer, holding up objects with a smile: a giant key with a long ribbon ("Ever meet the mayor? Key to the city") and a firefighter's cap ("He's still with us; enough said").

James wondered what Madame Prizzo thought her

memorabilia proved. That people were suckers, no matter what their background? And now he was here, just like the rest of them.

"You'll like this one." She held up a wooden spoon that was signed down the handle. Luckily, Madame Prizzo was proud enough to read out loud: "To Madame Prizzo, much thanks, Frederico."

"Frederico Pena?" He was the executive chef of the best Spanish fusion in town. James didn't even try to keep the surprise and awe out of his voice.

"You don't think he came up with that braised rabbit and tortilla soup without a little help from the other side, do you?" Madame Prizzo smiled proudly.

She sat back down and regarded him carefully through a haze of cigarette smoke. "So, what are you doing here?" She squashed the cigarette that had been hanging from her lips and lit another. "I just came from seeing Roni. Very sad." Madame Prizzo faltered for a moment, but recovered. "She told me about Amy finding out about our scam. Her scam, really. I just came in at the end. I hope you don't have any ideas about being a hero and bringing me to justice." She inhaled deeply, enjoying the smoke like fine wine.

"Justice? Hell no. I'm in the restaurant business."

Madame Prizzo took a long, hard drag. She expelled the smoke through her nose. James wondered how she ever tasted any of her food. You could serve a smoker like this cardboard, and she wouldn't know.

"I want to know if you know any way for Amy to get that voice back and stay with me."

She looked at her cigarette as if maybe it was speaking to her. Heck, maybe it was. He looked around the creepy trailer. Why was he even listening to this old woman? Just because she said the first channeling was real, how could he be sure? After all, Madame Prizzo had been conning Amy; what would stop her from conning him? But the power of what Troy had done was still with James. It was impossible not to hope for just a little more magic.

She sucked on the cigarette. "You know that if Amy stayed with you, she'd resent you forever for taking away the one power she ever had. Oh, don't look so surprised. I've met Amy, remember? You don't have to be psychic to know how she thinks. You're the consolation prize, sweetie, and you're wondering if there's a way to fix that, because you love her and want her to be happy. It's very sweet, James. But the answer is no. It's you or her power. There's no way around it. I'm sorry if she didn't choose you."

The black cat jumped into Madame Prizzo's lap, and she stroked it thoughtfully. "But let me give you a word of free advice. You should stop worrying about how to make Amy happy and start thinking about yourself." She took a long drag over the cat's head like she was inhaling oxygen. "There's something you need to know. The real reason you're here."

James's blood ran cold. What was she talking about?

"You didn't come here to find out about Amy. You want to know about you."

"That's not true."

"Everyone always wants to know about themselves, James. You're not any different." She stroked the cat, who closed his eyes, in bliss. "James, your father is dying."

"Dying?" He hadn't talked to his father in years. "What do you mean? How do you know?"

"I deal in the land of the dead, James. It's my specialty. I'd say he's got about a week. And guess what—he doesn't even know it yet. So forget about making Amy happy, because you're about to get blindsided by a fate all your own."

When all else fails, eat.
—Amy Burns

Chapter 31

Amy had banged on the kitchen door to no avail. She had come straight from Baltimore to Les Fleurs, hoping to find James. It had taken her eight days to get everything she needed. All that time, she had called him over and over, leaving message after message. But he had never called back.

Well, she didn't blame him. She had run off just the way she had promised not to.

She was dying to see him. To explain what she had understood on that train platform and why she had to leave. But where was he?

Les Fleurs should have been reopened by now. James surely could have restaffed in the time she'd been gone. Instead, she opened the alley door with the key hidden behind the bricks. The alley cats whined and circled, as if they hadn't been fed in days.

A jolt of fear ran through her. What was going on?

James hadn't been here for that long? Had something happened to him?

She slipped into the empty restaurant, holding the crying cats at bay. Once inside, it was silent except for her footsteps echoing off the chrome surfaces. She made her way into the dining room. A stack of mail had been pushed through the mail slot and had piled onto the wooden floor like a mountain.

James hadn't even checked in.

The hairs on the back of Amy's neck stood up. She reached for her cell phone, ready to call the apartment, when the restaurant phone began to ring. Amy answered it, hoping it would be James, even if that didn't make a lick of sense. "Les Fleurs."

"Yes. Reservation for three tonight."

"Sorry. We're still closed. Water damage," Amy said, quoting the sign that hung on the front door. She looked around the pristine restaurant as she hung up the phone. How long did James intend for this ruse to go on?

She called the apartment but didn't leave a message on the machine that picked up. She called James's cell phone and left what must have been the hundredth message. "James. It's Amy. I'm sorry. We have to talk. Call me."

The restaurant phone rang again.

She ignored it for ten rings until the person hung up.

Amy went back to the kitchen, but before she left, she remembered the cats outside. She went downstairs to see what she could find for them. She knew where James kept his secret stash of cat food and decided to bring the whole five-pound bag upstairs. Someone, at least, would eat at Les Fleurs tonight.

On her way out, the phone rang again. On a whim, Amy picked it up. "Les Fleurs."

"Scottie Jones here. I'd like a reservation for one tonight."

Amy sucked in her breath. "Mr. Jones?"

"Yes. I told James LaChance I'd tell him when I'm coming. Well. I'm coming tonight. Is there a problem?"

"Problem? Well, we're closed tonight."

"Closed? But I'm only in town for one night. If he wants to be in the book with a shot at his third star, tell him to open. I have deadlines, you know. I'll be there at seven." The line clicked dead.

Amy looked around at the completely empty restaurant. Why had she picked up that call? She tried James on his cell again and left a desperate message. "James! I've done something bad. Crazy. Just. I couldn't help it. It was an accident. Scottie Jones is coming tonight. I couldn't— oh, hell, just call me!"

She could hear the cats crying outside.

She called Roni. Troy answered the phone. "Troy? Where's James?"

"Amy? Where'd you go? James took off. And so did my mom. Amy, she stole the necklace and split to go after her One True Love."

"She left you alone again?"

"I refused to go with her. Amy, I'm afraid she pawned your necklace."

Amy thought of Davey and his pawnshop. "Don't worry about that. I'll get it back no problem. Oh, Troy. I'm so sorry. I shouldn't have left. Where is James?"

"Boston. His dad is sick—dying, even, I think. Madame Prizzo told him, and he took off, just like that. Are you in town? Amy, we have to talk! The voice is driving me nuts. I haven't left the apartment in, like, a week."

Amy winced. She should have never left. She had underestimated how much these goofballs needed her. "Troy, forget the voice. You need to get in here, now."

"Where?"

"Les Fleurs. It's an emergency. I'll explain when you get here."

Her apprehension growing, Amy consulted the sauce-stained list of phone numbers scribbled haphazardly directly onto the wall by the men's bathroom. "Denny, I need you at Les Fleurs. Now," she yelled at the sleepy prep cook.

"I'm leaving this morning for my soul mate, hon," Denny reported, his happiness cutting through his sleepiness. "I already told James days ago. He lent me the cash for the flight. My high school sweetheart—my soul mate!—is picking me up at the airport. She just got divorced, Amy. She's got a kid. But I don't mind a kid. I can't believe that Troy could come up with her name like that. Out of the blue. It was like he kicked me in the nuts to get out there and change my life, and it was like she was waiting for me—"

"Call her and tell her you're not coming."

"What? Why?" Amy heard Denny's feet hit the floor.

"Because James needs you here. Now. He needs us all here. You owe him this, Denny. We all do. So keep it in your pants one more day and get your sorry butt down here."

* * *

By noon, Amy had contacted everyone she could find, and the kitchen was hopping. The staff who were still in town had filed in one by one and gotten right to work, no questions asked. Manuel got on his cell, and within the hour, a whole troupe of Ecuadorians, most of whom Amy had never seen, pulled up in an unmarked white van. Manuel took charge, getting them hoofing around the kitchen like soldiers. They obviously knew a thing or two about kitchens. Then he started in on the vendors, demanding special orders *ahora*. "James's dad is lying in a hospital dying, and you're telling me you can't get me globe artichokes?" he shouted at Jenny from Baldor, who showed up at the back door half an hour later with everything Manuel needed, plus some choice berries in an unmarked carton that were supposed to go to Le Bec Fin.

"Who's the tiny dude on garde manger?" Amy didn't recognize him, and yet he looked somehow familiar.

"Marti Cornell," Manuel said, naming the executive chef who arguably had single-handedly created the Philadelphia restaurant scene. Manuel smiled. "He's probably just here to steal Jamesey's recipes, but he's a whiz on the sauces, so I'll take him."

"Doesn't James despise him?" Amy asked.

"Well, yeah. These dudes hate each other, but there's a code, and they pull in when a boat's going down."

By the time Troy got there, it looked like everything might go okay.

"What's the deal?" Troy asked.

"Scottie Jones. Seven o'clock. Go talk to Manuel. He's in charge. He said he needs someone on sauté."

"Sauté? No way, that's James's spot."

Amy shrugged. "Not tonight it's not. I still haven't

heard back from James. Now move, Troy. This isn't messing around."

"But after, we talk," Troy demanded.

"After, we'll talk."

Amy's cell rang and her heart froze as she looked at the number. "James? Where are you?"

"I'm at the airport. In Boston. My plane leaves in ten minutes. I got your message. What's going on?"

"James . . ." Where to begin?

"Shoot—they called my plane. I'll be there in two hours. Don't worry. Tell everyone I'll be there."

"James—" But the phone was already dead.

By one o'clock, John-John, who had heard through the restaurant grapevine that James's father was dying and that Scottie Jones was on his way, strode into James's kitchen in his La Fondue hat, trailed by three of their best servers. He stuffed the hat into the garbage, cursing it roundly, and was back at his grill, threatening to kill anyone who had any problem at all with his boyfriend, Ralph. The stock was simmering, the meat cut and prepped, the mise en place in place.

"We have a problem," Elliot confided to Amy as quietly as he could as the kitchen bustled around them. "The place is gonna be too empty. We canceled all the reservations last week, and everyone thinks we're closed. Scottie Jones won't like it. It'll feel dead, no matter how good the food is."

"Let's give away free food," Amy suggested. "That'll fill the seats."

Elliot shook his head. "We've got to fill the seats with

quality people. Scottie Jones has to think this place is happening. Freebies won't bring in the right people. We're dead in the water, no matter how good the food is."

Amy pulled out her cell. "I have an idea. Leave this one to me."

By the time Josh Toby, movie star and *People* magazine's sexiest man alive, appeared at five after five, the press was already waiting at the door. Four local news crews, plus a crew from *Entertainment Tonight* and *Insider Today,* battled against the paparazzi that always followed Josh everywhere. It didn't hurt that Josh's publicist, Mo, had alerted them and the Philadelphia arm of Josh's fan club, which had come out in force.

Josh stood outside Les Fleurs, signing autographs and answering questions while he talked about the amazing new menu that he'd flown down from New York City on his private plane to try.

Jasmine Burns, his wife and Amy's little sister, left him outside and came in to embrace Amy. "So, where is this man you told us about?" She looked around the space.

"I wish I knew. He should have been here hours ago. Thanks so much for coming, Jas. This means so much to me."

"Josh gets the credit. He said he wouldn't miss meeting the man who stole Amy Burns's heart for anything. Plus, he thinks he owes you eternal gratitude." Jasmine blushed thoroughly. The debt she referred to was Amy's prophecy that Jasmine was Josh's One True Love.

Amy was pleased that Jasmine was still as bashful as ever, despite the constant media glare.

"I read in the tabloids that you're pregnant," Amy said.

Jasmine blushed again. "Yeah, but it's not triplets like the *Inside Dirt* said."

"Hot damn!" Amy engulfed her smaller sister in a bear hug, then backed off. "Oh, hey, sorry, little guy." She patted Jasmine's stomach.

"Girl."

"Hey, that's good news. The world couldn't handle another man as good-looking as Josh." Amy looked around at the seats, which were quickly being filled by early diners, some of Philadelphia's hippest, hottest faces, who had all been tipped off by Mo that they could eat near Josh Toby tonight and that the press would definitely be there. Amy grinned. "I can't believe you guys made it in time for us to be on the evening news. Elliot told me we're almost fully booked."

"Well, I guarantee that every woman who shows up tonight will be dressed to the nines in hopes of catching Josh's eye."

"Oh, you poor thing," Amy said, not the least bit sorry for her sister, who had snagged the most famous movie star in the world, with a little help from the spirit world, of course.

"I can't wait to eat," Jasmine said. "Is it as good as the hype?"

"Honey, I inspired the chef. It's even better."

Stu, looking as happy as ever, was describing the menu to the first diners. Every item was new, created either in James's bed or in his shower or on his kitchen floor in the middle of the night. As Amy listened to Stu describe each dish, she thought about how she and James had gone through the names of all the Pussycats and moved on to Ginger and Mary Ann from *Gilligan's Island,* and Daphne and Velma from *Scooby-Doo.* They even named a fig-mascarpone-thyme-honey dessert Amy. Out in public at last, as if everyone didn't already know.

She had played a part in all this. She had been such an idiot to leave. She prayed that James would give her another chance.

She prayed that he would make it back in time. His plane had taxied down the runway, then turned back for mechanical difficulties. Still, he should have been there by now.

"Scottie Jones is in the house!" Stu called into the kitchen, stopping the line as surely as if he had slammed on the brakes.

"Shit." John-John wiped his forehead with the back of his hand. "We still haven't heard from James?"

"Snow in Boston," Amy reported. She had just gotten off her cell. "His plane never took off."

"Shit," John-John said again.

Troy looked at his stove as if it had transformed into a jet plane on an icy runway and he had to get it into the air.

"Joey just seated him at table three," Stu reported. "So let's not screw this thing up. One dish at a time. Do it for James."

Scottie started with a Josie, and from there, everything was a blur. Dan and Stu raced in and out of the kitchen, ferrying out everything the kitchen offered up. By the second course, the mood had changed. Stu and Dan were smiling, dancing in and out of the kitchen as they urged on the cooks. "Scottie's in heaven! He cracked half a smile! Onward, men! Onward! And nonmen, too . . ."

"Watch it!" John-John waved a ten-pound frying pan.

"Geez. I meant Amy!" Stu called as he disappeared onto the floor.

After the scallops, Stu body-hugged Troy from behind. "He licked the sauce off his plate with his finger. I saw him. With his finger! That little putz! Doesn't he know he's in a three-star joint?" Stu did a little jig.

"Now that I'm at the helm, maybe it's four-star," Troy said. He smiled through the profusion of obscenity that rained down on him, flashing them all his cocky three-finger salute.

By dessert—a tasting menu carried out by a grinning Dan—everyone collapsed, silent, exhausted, and spent.

"Someone should tell James," Troy said finally.

Everyone looked at Amy.

Her feet hurt so badly, she was ready to dunk them into the boiling sauce pots for relief. She tossed Troy her cell phone. "You try. You're the hero."

Troy punched in the numbers and put the phone to his ear. "Actually," he said to Amy, "you're the hero. But I'll make the call."

Always stay hungry.
—AMY BURNS

Chapter 32

Josh Toby and Jasmine went back to New York. Most of
the staff went on an inebriated celebration bar-crawl after
Scottie Jones left with assurances that all went spectacu-
larly. Amy, unsure where to go, sat alone in the empty
dining room. She wasn't sure if the doorman at James's
would let her in, and she dreaded being turned away.

Troy sat down across from her. "That was awesome."

"I wish James had been here."

"Yeah, me, too."

She looked at the boy. "So you're alone again?"

"Yeah."

"It's like the first time we met." Amy smiled sadly.

"Not really. So much has happened, you know."

"I know."

"You wanna stay with me?" Troy asked. He had lost
his sheepish I-don't-care facade. "I'd really like it if you
did. I don't know how long my mom will be gone. She

was really pissed at me at first, and then I told her the name of her One True Love, and she talked to him and they hit it off."

"Both of you come and stay with me."

Amy whipped around. It was James, his travel bag still on his shoulder.

Amy stood, her heart racing. "James."

"Can't a person get a bite to eat in this joint?" He echoed the first words that she had ever said to him.

"I'll go help Charlie clean up," Troy said as he stood. Such a good, smart kid. "In fact, I'm gonna get Charlie to take me home."

James tossed him his keys. "Tell Charlie to take you to my place."

Troy's eyes lit up. "Yeah, Chef? Really? Okay. We're out of here. You kids have fun." He hurried out of the room, raising his three-finger salute. James tousled his hair as he passed.

James didn't move toward Amy. "My father died three days ago. A massive heart attack."

"I'm so sorry, James."

"Yeah. Well. I got to see him before he died. I got to cook for him. I made him our entire menu—the one we created. He ate it alone, at his huge dining room table, while I watched. And it occurred to me that I'd never seen anything sadder in my life than this man who had no one because he'd lived his life like an idiot. Running around the world making money and nothing else. He was rambling on and on about the food, like that was what mattered. I hadn't seen him in years, Amy, and he was talking about opening a restaurant chain called 'LaChance' and marketing my sauces. He took three cell phone calls during the soup alone. Next day, he went to play golf with two business associates and died right there on the course. Neither one of those guys came to the funeral."

Amy watched him, unsure what to say.

"I don't want to live like him, Amy. I don't want to eat the best meal of my life alone."

"I don't either, James."

He let his bag fall from his shoulder. He left it and crossed the room to her. "Then why did you leave?"

"I got scared. It was a habit. I couldn't help it. But, James"—she felt her breath hitch—"I came back."

He didn't look impressed. "I got your messages."

"It went great, James. Scottie Jones—"

"Honestly, Amy, I don't give a rat's ass about Scottie Jones. I want to know what you intend to do. I won't be your consolation prize." He raised his arms to take in the room. "I won't let Les Fleurs be your prison. What are you doing here, Amy? Why'd you come back?"

She came forward and held out something to him. It was an envelope. She was more beautiful than ever, and yet, tiredness claimed him. Arranging the funeral and seeing it through had been a special kind of hell. The seven hours stuck at Logan International hadn't helped.

"Open it," Amy urged.

He couldn't think of any reason not to except, of course, that he was way too tired to be able to read it. He slid his thumb under the seal and pulled out the paper inside. His eyes went wide with confusion. Even this exhausted, he could decode a long row of zeros on a check when he saw them.

"It's from my sister Cecelia. A loan. But I think it's enough to get me in, right?"

"In?" *Into my heart?* He sincerely doubted she meant that. He was so tired and so sad from dealing with his father's funeral and estate. He was a very, very rich man now, as his father's only heir, and he couldn't have cared less about Scottie Jones or Amy's check.

"Into a new place. I think it's about time Les Fleurs had some real competition. It would be ours, together. I was thinking we'd call it Pure Sin."

He carefully tucked the three-hundred-thousand-dollar check back into the envelope and held it out to her. "I don't need your money."

"Yes, you do. Because without it, I won't feel equal. And I have to feel equal. I need something of my own. It's my way. I can't change, James. I wish I was okay with us being lopsided, but I'm not. If I'm going to give up Maddie forever for you, I need this."

Was she saying she wanted back in with him? He watched her carefully, unsure of how to proceed. This was a woman who left him and could do it again at the drop of a hat. And yet, all he had wanted for the past week was for her to come back so that he could change his life and not turn out like his father.

"James, please?"

Then he saw it, in the way she gulped, the sheen on her forehead, her pursed lips. She was nervous, too. She did come back. "Lopsided? Amy, we weren't lopsided."

"So we'll own Pure Sin together, and then it'll be part mine and part yours and then"—she inhaled and looked right at him—"then we can be equals and be together. James. I want us to be together. And I know it's fucked up, but I can't change. This is the only way I can do it. I realized when I ran into that stupid Bob. I'm not gonna be the type to get all nice and kind. I'm just gonna keep on being me, and if you want to love me, you're gonna have to deal with that."

"What if I say no?" He could feel his chest expand and contract in slow motion.

"Then I'll open next door and kick your sorry ass."

He sucked in his cheeks, trying not to smile. "Really? I'd like to see you try."

"My place will be fun. Gnocchi with a stick of butter and mixed houseplants. Oatmeal stirred clockwise. None of that truffle bullshit. Just real food. And real people. Oh, and music. I like music. You won't stand a chance in your fluffy Frenchie place. No matter how many stars you get from that jerk Scottie."

He stared at her, not sure whether to kick her out or take her into his arms.

They watched each other for a long moment. In the pristine perfection of Les Fleurs, she still looked like a mirage. Just the way she had looked the first time he'd seen her. Only that time, she had seemed so supremely alone. And he saw now, after watching his father die, how alone he had been, too. If he turned her away just because she was an impossible nutcase, he'd have no one. It was the one thing she couldn't help. He had to forgive her. She was, after all, his soul mate.

"So, are you okay?" she asked. Her voice was quieter now.

"Yeah. I'm over it," he said. "My father was a dick his whole life. It was more like coming to terms with the fact that a stranger died."

"I'm sorry."

"A stranger who left me a boatload of money."

"Give it to Troy," she suggested.

"I intend to," he said.

"Roni left him for her One True Love."

"Yeah, Manuel called and told me. She probably felt too ashamed to ever show her face here again."

"James, I want us to take Troy in."

"Well, of course, stupid. How could we not? You know how much help we'll need running two first-class restaurants?" He was feeling very much like kissing her. In fact, he was feeling very much like doing more than that.

"Only thing is," she said, "if we opened a new place, we'd need to do a whole new menu."

"Yeah. That would be a problem."

She moved in close to him. "I get my inspiration from beautiful men," she said. Her lips quivered around the corners, and he didn't think he could last another minute without tasting them.

He wrapped her in his arms. "Beautiful men, huh? Think you could settle for me?"

"Does that mean you're accepting my apology?"

"I didn't hear you apologize," he pointed out, pulling her closer.

She leaned into him. "James. I'm sorry."

"Didn't hear you."

"I'm sorry. I was a ninny. I need you. Let's do this. Together. Please?"

"You were a fool for leaving me?"

"Yes."

"You're never going to leave me again."

"Yes. Well, I'll try. I mean, probably, I will. But I'll always come crawling back."

"You're going to come home with me and let me make soft, slow love to you?" His lips brushed hers.

"Yes. Well, after Troy's asleep."

"And you're gonna let me tear up that stupid check." He said it into her hair, then bit her ear.

She pulled back. "No way. Didn't you understand a word I just said?"

He smiled, maybe for the first time in days. "That's my Amy. I just had to make sure you were the right woman, not some Gypsy imposter."

"Oh, I'm the right woman, all right. And don't you ever forget it."

They never did make it back to James's place. By the time they got to the deserted kitchen, he pushed her against the chrome counter and kissed her full and hard. "Amy," he murmured. "Don't ever change."

"Hell no," she said. Or, rather, she said "hell" and then it sounded more like "hello" as their lips crashed together again. *Hello.*

He pressed his hardness against her, and the thought of what it could do to her made her think of, well, what it could do to her, and the thought was so delicious that she sighed.

"Madame." He scooped her up into his arms.

"Put me down!"

But he didn't. He carried her across the kitchen, banging into pots and counters and cursing them.

"Where are we going?"

He made for the back stairs.

"Ouch! You brute."

He maneuvered her down the stairs, grunting. "Damn, you're heavier than a side of beef."

"If you're trying to be romantic, you're failing desperately," she said. But then she shut up because he kicked in the door to the walk-in.

"Amy, will you marry me?" he asked, standing on the threshold.

"What?" The walk-in was like a chapel, white and clean.

"Not 'what?' Yes. I'm about to carry you over the threshold into my temple, so you'd better agree to marry me. Because let's be honest—I can't trust you not to leave unless I get a major legal commitment."

"I can't—"

"I'm not taking on a business partner who's gonna scram again. We need to be married. In every way. True love. Forever and all that."

She didn't know what to say. She was so shocked, so stunned.

"You're heavy, lady."

"I've been eating too much French food."

"This is only the beginning. Decide. Now. Say yes."

"Yes."

He dropped her. "Really?"

"Yes."

"You'll marry me?"

"What, do I have to spell it out for you?"

"Is that a dyslexic joke? Because if it is, it isn't funny."

"James." She pulled him into the walk-in. "No one carries anyone in this relationship. C'mon." She pushed him to the floor, collapsing on top of him.

He smiled. "Right. Sorry. Forgot. I'm going to have to get used to that."

She pressed her full length against him, feeling his hardness against her stomach. "Guess I'm gonna have to get used to *that*."

"You better believe it." He rolled her over, then suspended himself above her on straight arms, dipping low to let their noses touch. "I love you, Amy. But if you ever leave me again, I'll kill you."

"Got it." She took a deep breath. This was it, now or never. "James, I love you."

She waited to feel the emptiness and sadness of Maddie being gone forever. But it didn't come.

In fact, she felt fantastic.

He let his weight settle on her, and she felt so good and protected and warm.

And when they were done, she told him about the nachos that he had just inspired for Pure Sin, with artisan organic tortilla chips and pomegranate seeds in a passion-fruit salsa.

Epilogue

$\mathcal{A}$my and Troy climbed out of the cab. The early spring breeze was colder here in Chicago than in Philadelphia, but it still felt good after their three-hour plane ride and endless cab ride.

The enormous gate towered above them, blocking access to a winding driveway.

"Are you sure this is the place?" Troy asked.

"Yep. I've been here before, it might surprise you to know." Amy buzzed the intercom on the gate. They waited, staring into the camera that rotated with a whir, taking in the scene. The cabdriver waved.

A few minutes later, a golf cart appeared. The driver, a young man in a baseball cap, studied them, then opened the gate with a clicker he held in his hand. The gate sprang open. "Five minutes," he said to Troy and Amy.

They clamored inside the little cart, which then zipped out of sight of the bored cabdriver, up the driveway.

When they reached the house, Troy gasped. "Holy shit. She sure is rich."

"Yeah, well you're not doing so shabby yourself, young man." James had put his father's inheritance in a trust for Troy for when he reached age *and* finished culinary school. The kid had been living with them for three months, and he already felt like family. He'd gotten used to the voice, although he wasn't sure what he was going to do about it yet. But Amy insisted that he learn to cook. Because one day, Maddie would leave him, and he had better be ready for it with a life of his own. She wasn't going to let him make the mistakes she made.

Oprah appeared at her front door, staring down at them. She didn't smile. Didn't even move.

The driver stopped the cart and turned off the engine with a key. "Go on," he said.

Troy looked a little shaky, but Amy was sure she was more nervous as they climbed the imposing marble stairs to Oprah's front door. She touched the hawk she had had tattooed on her wrist for luck. James had an upside-down horseshoe on his wrist, and Amy imagined him touching it as he started to prepare for the night.

Oprah nodded. "Amy Burns. If you're here to flog you and your new cheffie's book, forget it. I'm on a diet." She was referring to James and Amy's first cookbook, *The Meal of a Lifetime,* which would come out next year. James could hardly read it, of course, but, then, he didn't need to. He could just kiss Amy, and the recipes would come to him. Never failed. Stupid jerk got to have his muse and eat it, too.

"Amy LaChance now," Amy said to Oprah. "And, no,

the book will do fine without you. I'm here to introduce you to someone."

Oprah looked confused. And a little thin. Amy would have to remember to send her something from Pure Sin when she got back. Maybe gnocchi in butter sauce. Oprah shook her head. "Amy Burns is not here to sell herself? I can't believe that."

"Believe it. This is the new Amy Burns. And this is Troy. He can tell you, well, you know, what I couldn't. If you want to know."

Troy nodded politely at Oprah, but he couldn't stop staring impolitely. She had that effect on people.

"Oh. Well, isn't that interesting?" Oprah hesitated for a split second, and then held out her hand. "Okay, lay it on me."

Troy took her hand in his. Then he closed his eyes. He listened for a few moments. Amy watched, a little jealous, a little awed. But not too jealous. She had made the right choice. She wouldn't give James up for anything. Even a shot at Oprah.

Troy leaned forward and whispered a name in Oprah's ear. She nodded, then shook his hand. "Thank you." She turned to Amy. "Now that was more like it. He's a good boy. Good luck." And then she shut the door before Amy could ask her about coming on the show with her and James's book.

As she and Troy made their way back to the waiting golf cart, Amy felt like skipping; she felt so light and free.

So she did skip. Back to the cart, then the cab, then the plane, then into her husband's waiting arms and their new no-star restaurant.

Pure Sin.

Dear Reader,

Still hungry for more?

Romance novels are like chocolate—no matter how much you get, you always need more. Or is that just me? If you missed the beginning of this feast, don't worry. Nothing wrong with eating dessert first!

First Course
Make Me a Match, the first book in the One True Love trilogy, is the story of Amy's oldest sister, Cecelia. Doctor Cecelia Burns has it all—gorgeous fiancé, great job, promising future—until Amy shows up to tell her that her One True Love as destined by Fate is dying. If Cecelia wants to save her only chance at True Love, she's got to ditch her perfect life and find this stranger. Fast.

Main Course
Sexiest Man Alive, is the second book in the trilogy. It tells the story of Amy's youngest sister, Jasmine. Jasmine Burns's One True Love as des-

tined by Fate is named Josh Toby. Of course, he might not be THE Josh Toby, the biggest movie star of the decade. After all, a shy girl like her could never be loved by a movie star like him? Could she?

Dessert

Luscious, rich, full of flavor, *Hungry for More* is the last book in the Burns sisters' saga, when Amy finally gets to find her own One True Love. The best for last? You'll have to read all three and let me know what you think!

For more treats, snacks, and nibbles, visit me at www.DianaHolquist.com. You can read an excerpt of my next book, enter my contest, or just say hello. I love to hear from readers, so please stop by.

THE DISH

Where authors give you the inside scoop!

From the desk of Amanda Scott

Dear Reader,

An incident during the Lake Tahoe fire of June 2007 proved to me once again that ideas come to a writer from unexpected sources of every imaginable kind.

BORDER LASS (on sale now) was outlined and its teaser chapter written when I decided, because of the way that first chapter brings together the hero and the heroine—Sir Garth Napier (a Scottish knight) and Lady Amalie Murray—that I should add a brief prologue to show readers why Sir Garth acts as he does.

I was sitting on the porch at the cabin where I spend much of each summer, on a lake a thousand feet above Tahoe, trying to decide how I wanted to structure such a prologue, when I looked up to see a yellow-white cloud of smoke billowing above the granite peak that shoots up another thousand feet directly across the lake.

To anyone in a forest, such a sight is terrifying, but with a medium-sized lake and a tall granite mountain to protect me, I felt fairly safe staying put.

The incident that awoke my imagination occurred a few days later when an irate man accosted a firefighter and his wife in a Tahoe supermarket. The firefighter's T-shirt identified him as a member of the South Lake Tahoe Fire Department.

The community had signs out everywhere, thanking the firefighters for all they had done and were doing to save the many, many houses they were able to save. As a result, most folks the firefighters met were friendly and grateful. Many called them heroic.

The man in the supermarket loudly began berating the firefighter about the department's "failure" to bring in "the bombers" (planes dropping retardant) sooner. The firefighter, although exhausted, tried to explain that such planes have to be called in from other areas and asked sympathetically if the man had lost his home.

Admitting that his house was not in danger, the man continued his tirade until the firefighter walked away to avoid losing his temper, only to look back minutes later and see the same irate man approach his wife again in the checkout line and begin poking her in the chest as he shouted at her. Fortunately, a large candy rack stood between the firefighter and the other two, and the store's security people quickly removed the antagonist from the premises, so no blood was spilled.

When I heard about the incident, my always busy gray cells began to turn the incident into a more violent confrontation in fourteenth-century Scotland. Soon I was recalling other firefighter anecdotes I'd heard that likewise suited my hero's character and were irresistibly easy to translate into plausible knightly actions.

My brief comparison of today's firefighters with knights of old gave me a fresh perspective on both. I hope you enjoy the result when you read BORDER LASS.

Until then, *Suas Alba!*

Amanda Scott

http://home.att.net/~amandascott

♥ ♥ ♥ ♥ ♥ ♥ ♥ ♥ ♥ ♥ ♥ ♥ ♥ ♥

From the desks of Rita Herron and Diana Holquist

Dear Reader,

Something remarkable happened this month that is too interesting to be a coincidence. In the Deep South, outside Atlanta, Georgia, Rita Herron wrote INSATIABLE DESIRE (on sale now), the first book in her new trilogy *The Demonborn*. Meanwhile, in the deep North, outside of Philadelphia, Pennsylvania, Diana Holquist wrote HUNGRY FOR MORE (also on sale now), the last book in her *One True Love* trilogy. These books couldn't be more different; the authors have never met; and yet, each book is about a being with almost the exact same remarkable talent.

Almost.

The authors discuss:

Diana Holquist: Rita, I can't believe that in your book INSATIABLE DESIRE, the God of Fear touches people, then knows their greatest fear and uses that fear to kill them. In my book HUNGRY FOR MORE, the heroine, Amy, touches people and then knows the name of their soul mate, their greatest love. And guess what—the soul mate almost always turns out to embody the person's greatest fear in some way. Of course, in HUNGRY FOR MORE, no one's trying to kill anyone. . . .

Rita Herron: Yeah, killing demons probably wouldn't work so well in romantic comedy. But seriously, the idea that what people fear most is the very thing they have to face to make them whole is such a visceral, primal theme. It works across genres, from my dark paranormal to your romantic comedy.

Diana Holquist: Which is what makes this month so fascinating: two very different authors treating the same theme. And we really couldn't be more different. HUNGRY FOR MORE is a sexy romantic comedy about a Gypsy con-woman who falls for a sexy chef.

Rita Herron: And INSATIABLE DESIRE is a dark paranormal thriller about a medium who falls for a sexy FBI agent. Only he is part demon, part human, and must battle his inner dark side while fighting demonic crimes.

Diana Holquist: Even the titles of the books are similar. HUNGRY FOR MORE. INSATIABLE DESIRE. Er, do your characters' insatiable desires have to do with sex? Because in HUNGRY FOR MORE, they're not just talking about food . . .

Rita Herron: Hmm . . . maybe there's another similarity between our books. My hero's insatiable desires are definitely for sex, lots of it. In fact, he needs a woman daily to keep his dark side at bay, and only his soul mate's love can keep him balanced.

Diana Holquist: I love that! It's just like in HUNGRY FOR MORE. Well, the soul-mate-balance part, not the dark-side-at-bay stuff.

Rita Herron: In INSATIABLE DESIRE, the hero also possesses a dark hunger for blood, which enables him to get into the minds of killers and to track them down. And evil has definitely risen from the underworld to test him. . . .

Diana Holquist: OK, so I don't have the blood-lust or evil-from-the-underworld stuff, either. HUNGRY FOR MORE is about really, really yummy food, though. A dark hunger for truffles, maybe—it's about the inner workings of restaurants. Also, it's about how food and sex are linked in mysterious, funny ways.

Rita Herron: Which is why I can't wait to pick up HUNGRY FOR MORE. It sounds really fun.

Diana Holquist: And INSATIABLE DESIRE sounds exciting, scary, and very sexy! I can't wait to read it to see how you treat this material. So let's stop writing and get reading! Enjoy, everyone! Two very different books with a lot in common. Happy reading!

Yours,

Diana Holquist

www.dianaholquist.com

Rita Herron

www.ritaherron.com

Want to know more about romances at Grand Central Publishing and Forever? Get the scoop online!

GRAND CENTRAL PUBLISHING'S ROMANCE HOMEPAGE

Visit us at www.hachettebookgroupusa.com/romance for all the latest news, reviews, and chapter excerpts!

NEW AND UPCOMING TITLES

Each month we feature our new titles and reader favorites.

CONTESTS AND GIVEAWAYS

We give away galleys, autographed copies, and all kinds of fun stuff.

AUTHOR INFO

You'll find bios, articles, and links to personal websites for all your favorite authors—and so much more!

THE BUZZ

Sign up for our monthly romance newsletter, and be the first to read all about it!